*Gripping Novels of
Intrigue and Suspense*

SIGNET DOUBLE MYSTERIES:

THE BRAZEN

and

THE STRIPPER

SIGNET Mysteries You'll Enjoy

☐ **SIGNET DOUBLE MYSTERY—TEN DAYS' WONDER by Ellery Queen and THE KING IS DEAD by Ellery Queen.**
(#E9488—$2.25)*

☐ **THE DUTCH SHOE MYSTERY by Ellery Queen.**
(#E8578—$1.75)*

☐ **THE FRENCH POWDER MYSTERY by Ellery Queen.**
(#E8577—$1.75)*

☐ **THE GREEK COFFIN MYSTERY by Ellery Queen.**
(#E8579—$1.75)*

☐ **THE ROMAN HAT MYSTERY by Ellery Queen.**
(#E8470—$1.75)*

☐ **THE EGYPTIAN CROSS MYSTERY by Ellery Queen.**
(#E8663—$1.75)*

☐ **SIGNET DOUBLE MYSTERY—THE DRAGON'S TEETH by Ellery Queen and CALAMITY TOWN by Ellery Queen.**
(#AE1310—$2.50)

☐ **SIGNET DOUBLE MYSTERY—THERE WAS AN OLD WOMAN by Ellery Queen and THE ORIGIN OF EVIL by Ellery Queen.**
(#J9306—$1.95)*

☐ **SIGNET DOUBLE MYSTERY—THE LOVER by Carter Brown and THE BOMBSHELL by Carter Brown.** (#E9121—$1.75)*

☐ **SIGNET DOUBLE MYSTERY—SEX CLINIC by Carter Brown and W.H.O.R.E. by Carter Brown.** (#E8354—$1.75)*

☐ **SIGNET DOUBLE MYSTERY—THE BRAZEN by Carter Brown and THE STRIPPER by Carter Brown.** (#J9575—$1.95)

☐ **SIGNET DOUBLE MYSTERY—WALK SOFTLY, WITCH by Carter Brown and THE WAYWARD WAHINE by Carter Brown.**
(#E9418—$1.75)

*Price slightly higher in Canada

Buy them at your local bookstore or use this convenient coupon for ordering.
THE NEW AMERICAN LIBRARY, INC.,
P.O. Box 999, Bergenfield, New Jersey 07621
Please send me the books I have checked above. I am enclosing $_____
(please add $1.00 to this order to cover postage and handling). Send check or money order—no cash or C.O.D.'s. Prices and numbers are subject to change without notice.

Name_____

Address_____

City _____ State _____ Zip Code _____
Allow 4-6 weeks for delivery.
This offer is subject to withdrawal without notice.

THE BRAZEN

and

THE STRIPPER

by
Carter Brown

A SIGNET BOOK
NEW AMERICAN LIBRARY
TIMES MIRROR

association with Horwitz Grahame Books

PUBLISHER'S NOTE

These novels are works of fiction. Names, characters, places, and incidents are either the product of the author's imagination or are used fictitiously, and any resemblance to actual persons, living or dead, events, or locales is entirely coincidental.

The Brazen Copyright 1960, 1980 by Horwitz Publications, a division of Horwitz Grahame Books Pty Ltd. (Hong Kong Branch), Hong Kong B.C.C.

The Stripper © Copyright 1961, 1980 by Horwitz Publications, a division of Horwitz Grahame Books Pty Ltd. (Hong Kong Branch), Hong Kong B.C.C.

All rights reserved. Reproduction in part or in whole in any language expressly forbidden in any part of the world without the written consent of Horwitz Grahame Publications. For information address Horwitz Grahame Books Pty Ltd. Cammeray Centre, 506 Miller Street, P.O. Box 306, Cammeray 2062, Australia.

Published by arrangement with Alan G. Yates. Originally appeared in paperback as separate volumes published by The New American Library, Inc.

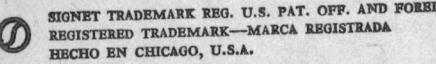

SIGNET TRADEMARK REG. U.S. PAT. OFF. AND FOREIGN COUNTRIES
REGISTERED TRADEMARK—MARCA REGISTRADA
HECHO EN CHICAGO, U.S.A.

SIGNET, SIGNET CLASSICS, MENTOR, PLUME, MERIDIAN, AND NAL BOOKS *are published by The New American Library, Inc., 1633 Broadway, New York, New York 10019*

FIRST PRINTING (Double Carter Brown Edition), JANUARY, 1981

4 5 6 7 8 9

PRINTED IN THE UNITED STATES OF AMERICA

THE BRAZEN

Chapter One

I WAS JUST SITTING there in the bar minding my own business, when this guy dropped dead at my feet.

Sitting on the next stool in line was a misty-eyed female with blonde hair, who looked like a potential investment of the short-term kind that always interests me. Who needs long-term growth? A generous yield would suit me fine.

Right then she was watching the body on the floor with a curiosity that grew more intense with each passing second.

"What's with that guy?" she asked finally, when it had gotten unbearable. "Drunk?"

"Dead," I said apologetically. "I think."

The misty look was rapidly replaced by the glassy look, and I just missed catching her as she slid gently off the stool. A couple of seconds later she was stretched out on the floor alongside the corpse and it made for an embarrassing situation.

The bartender glared over the counter at both of them, then shifted focus to scowl at me.

"If those two lushes are friends of yours," he said in a cold, brittle voice, "I'll thank you to get them the hell out of here fast!"

"I don't figure it was your liquor that got to them—potent as it may be," I told him confidentially. "The lady just fainted—I saw it happen. My guess is the guy dropped dead about ten seconds back."

"Dead?" His eyebrows lifted violently, seeking sanctuary in his nonexistent hairline. "You're kidding?"

"If you know a good funeral parlor, here's your chance to make a fast twenty bucks," I said. "You don't believe me, take a look for yourself."

He came around the bar quickly and knelt down beside the body while he felt for heartbeats. When he came up onto his feet again his face was chalk-white, matching the bald dome of his head.

"You're right," he croaked, "the guy is dead! I'd better go call a cop."

"You don't need to holler real loud," I said morosely. "I'm still a cop even if it is my night off." I showed him my shield. "Lieutenant Wheeler, county sheriff's office."

"Then you'll take care of it, Lieutenant?" he asked hopefully.

"I guess so," I said without any enthusiasm. "I'd rather take care of the girl, but with cops—like morticians—corpses come first. You'd better have somebody do something for her—and move that body into a private room." I looked at the interested faces of the small crowd that had gathered. "Right now he's screwing up your business."

"Right away," the bartender said, nodding vigorous agreement. "I got a small room in back of the bar." He groped under the bar counter and lifted the phone out for me.

I called the Sheriff's office and found Sergeant Polnik on duty. After I'd used a lot of one-syllable words very slowly, he got the picture. I told him to send the doctor

THE BRAZEN

and the meat wagon, and maybe he'd better call the Sheriff at his home and tell him what had happened. By the time I'd finished, the bartender was hovering at my elbow.

"She's O.K., Lieutenant," he said. "I put her in a cab and sent her home."

"I never saw a potential investment depreciate so fast," I said bitterly. "You just can't trust the market any more."

"Huh?" He looked at me blankly.

"I was talking in code," I explained. "Us cops do it all the time."

"Yeah?" He sounded impressed.

"What about the stiff?"

"Through that door." He pointed the way. "Anything else I can do for you?"

"Make me another Scotch on the rocks, with a little soda," I told him. "Chivas Regal, huh? Looks like it could be a long night."

Inside the small back room was a couch with the body laid out on it. I took a close look at the dead man while I lit a cigarette—a neatly dressed guy in his middle-forties. The kind of John Doe face you wouldn't remember even if he sat up in your soup and yodeled.

I lifted the wallet from his inside coat pocket and checked the contents. Around two hundred in cash, a driver's license—the kind of things you expect to find. There were two different varieties of calling cards. The first one read: Wallace J. Miller, Berkeley & Wallace, Attorneys-at-law. The second: Mr. & Mrs. Wallace J. Miller, followed by a Cone Hill address.

The bartender arrived with my fresh drink, closing the door behind him carefully, all tippytoe, like he was making a social call on a working mortician. I flipped one of the calling cards between my fingers while I tasted the Scotch.

"You ever see this guy before?" I asked.

"No." He shook his head positively.

"Did you see him come in?"

"The first time I saw the guy, he was draped all over the floor with that broad beside him," the bartender grunted. "I figured the two of 'em were stoned."

"O.K.," I said despairingly. "Thanks for the drink, anyway."

"Sure," he said. "Two dollars."

Maybe five minutes later, Polnik arrived, closely followed by Doc Murphy.

"That's the stiff, huh, Lieutenant?" Polnik said intelligently, pointing at the corpse on the couch.

"That's the stiff," I agreed, "even if it does look like your Aunt Fanny!"

"I never had an Aunt Fanny, Lieutenant," Polnik blinked at me slowly. "So I don't even know if it looks like her or not."

Murphy went over to the couch and stared down for a few seconds, then snorted suddenly. "I'm disappointed in you, Al! This is just an ordinary, no-account cadaver—what happened to all the glamor?

"I goofed," I said. "Like it happened on my free night and I wasn't prepared."

"How did it happen?"

"He walked in off the street and never made it to the counter—just keeled over and hit the floor instead."

"Coronary, most likely," Murphy grunted. "We'll know for sure after the autopsy. Who was he, anyway?"

"A lawyer—name of Miller."

"Kind of funny when you think about it," the Doc mused. "Maybe right now he's arguing his most important case ever for the defense."

"Why, Doc!" I said admiringly. "Philosophy yet—and all this time I had you figured for a plain, old-fashioned butcher."

"The trouble with coronary occlusions is they never happen to the right people!" he said in a brooding voice. "Was he married, do you know?"

"Sure he was married," I said. "How else would he get a coronary?"

THE BRAZEN

"You going to tell the bad news to his wife—or leave that to the Sergeant?"

"I guess I'll go tell her," I said. "I got curiosity—and my free night's shot to hell and gone now."

"You wouldn't catch me volunteering to break the news!" Murphy shook his head decisively. "Give me an autopsy any time."

"Make this a good one, Doc," I said. "You know—like different from all the others?"

For a change of scenery I looked at Polnik whose homey, repulsive face was set in a deep frown of concentration.

"What's with you?" I asked impatiently.

"I got me an Aunt Marsha on my mother's side, Lieutenant," he volunteered, "but she don't look like this stiff at all—he don't even have a mustache!"

"I wouldn't let it keep you awake nights," I said hastily. "You can get back to the office. There's nothing else to do here."

"Whatever you say, Lieutenant," he said, nodding happily. "I guess there ain't any females in this one, huh?"

"*Quién sabe?*" I said airly. After a two weeks vacation in Tijuana all I'd gotten out of the two hundred bucks I lost at the bullfights was those two words in Spanish—and I wanted to get my money back.

"Sounds kind of classy," Polnik said respectfully. "Some foreign broad, huh? A countess, maybe?"

"When I find out I'll let you know," I promised him.

After the door closed behind him, I lit another smoke and became conscious of Doc Murphy's cold stare.

"I want to know more about that dirty crack of yours a while back," he said. "Something about me making it a good autopsy, not like the others? Ignoring the slur on my professional talents I'd like to know just what's cooking in that fermented mess of leftovers you jokingly call your brain?"

"It was a meeting," I said. "He called me this morning—got my home number from the office when he found

I wasn't there. Told me he had some vital information he couldn't give over the phone, but he'd meet me someplace instead. This bar—and the time of eight—was strictly his idea. Then he winds up dead on arrival."

"A heart seizure doesn't worry about coincidence, Al."

"And maybe truth is stranger than fiction—like the girl said on her wedding night," I agreed. "But I never was crazy about coincidence, and that coronary has all the earmarks of one."

"It figures," Murphy said cheerfully. "He took one look at you and dropped dead—who wouldn't?"

I was still trying to figure an answer to that when I walked out through the bar to where I'd left my car parked against the crub. Thirty minutes easy driving brought me into the driveway of the Cone Hill house, and I got out of the car slowly, still trying hard to come up with an original line of dialogue to soften the impact when I had to tell the wife she was now a widow. Like Murphy said, I should have gotten smart and sent Polnik—that's what sergeants are for.

A butler opened the door a few seconds after I'd pressed the buzzer. He gave me a fish-eyed stare but it didn't throw me any—he was expected. To the people who can afford to live on Cone Hill, butlers are like television sets are to most other people—sometimes you even get tired of just looking at them, but they're a necessary status symbol around the house.

"I'd like to see Mrs. Miller," I told him.

"I'm sorry, sir!" His voice was starched to match his shirt. "Mrs. Miller has retired for the night."

"You're kidding?" I checked my watch and saw it was only a quarter after nine. "Who won?"

"I beg your pardon?"

"If she retired this early, she must have thrown in the towel," I persisted logically.

"Good night, sir!"

He started to close the door, so I put my hand against

THE BRAZEN 7

it and pushed it open again. For a moment there it was a real contest—then I cheated and told him who I was.

"You should have mentioned it before, Sergeant!" He looked at me reproachfully as he opened the door wide.

"It's important I see Mrs. Miller," I said, "and it's Lieutenant."

"Please come in, Lieutenant," he said coldly, having a bad time resisting the impulse to tell me to wipe my feet first.

I followed him along the wide hallway into the library. All Cone Hill houses have libraries; they buy them along with the air-conditioning plant and kidney-shaped swimming pool. While I waited for the widow to show, I looked along the shelves at the book titles. Either the Millers had been foundation members of the Bird Brain Book Club, or more likely the books had been bought by the interior decorator to harmonize with the color scheme. I meet so many people who do damn stupid things with their money, instead of giving it to me.

"You wished to see me, Lieutenant?" A cool voice jerked me back to reality.

I turned around and got my first look at Mrs. Wallace J. Miller. Her glistening midnight-black hair was pulled straight back across her head and tied in a careless knot at the nape of her neck. Its color made a vivid contrast to the pearly, almost luminous whiteness of her skin. Her dark eyes were serene and completely impersonal as she waited for me to answer. I was having a little trouble there and it was all her fault.

She wore a loosely belted pink robe that was open far enough for me to appreciate the smooth milky rise of her firm breasts. Beneath the robe, her legs were long and slender. How the late Wallace J. Miller had managed to go out nights and leave her alone, I'd never know.

"I'm afraid I've got some bad news for you, Mrs. Miller," I said limply. "Maybe you'd better sit down."

"I don't think that's necessary," she said crisply.

"It concerns your husband." I could feel the small,

clammy beads of sweat gathering on my forehead. "He's
... had an accident."

"An automobile accident?" She still sounded like she was passing the time of day.

"Not exactly," I floundered miserably. "More like a sudden heart attack—a coronary occlusion."

"When did it happen?" Her face remained devoid of any expression—no tears, no nothing.

"About an hour back, in a downtown bar," I said. "He walked in, then it hit him. . . ."

"He's dead, of course?"

"I'm sorry."

"You'll want me to identify his body," she said evenly. "Please excuse me, Lieutenant, while I go and get dressed."

"There's no hurry," I mumbled.

"No hurry?" For a moment her dark eyes reflected the question, then understanding showed in them. "Oh—I see. There's to be an autopsy?"

"Just a routine in any case like this."

"Then I'll take my time about getting dressed," she said, smiling faintly. "And when a woman says that, it's fair warning, Lieutenant. You'd better sit down."

"Thanks," I told her. "You've made it a lot easier than I figured it would be—that takes courage."

"Or a lack of personal interest in my late husband?" For a moment malicious humor showed in her eyes. "But I wouldn't want to embarrass you, Lieutenant. Excuse me."

She turned and walked out of the room, leaving me standing there with my mouth hanging open. In my time I'd seen some women get hysterical over their pet poodles being run down on the highway. This was the first purely cold-blooded reaction I'd seen to sudden news of widowhood. Maybe she was an alcoholic and had iced vermouth running through her veins instead of the conventional red corpuscles.

Chapter Two

"I HEAR you had a date with a corpse last night, Lieutenant," Annabelle Jackson said sweetly as I came into the office around nine the next morning. "It must have been a pleasant change."

"Reminded me so much of you, sweetheart," I said in a wistful voice. "The same fast reactions—the same passion and fire."

"I guess you think that's clever," she said frigidly. "One of these days that's *all* you'll have left—clever remarks. Maybe that day won't be too far off, Al Wheeler, so I guess you should start taking things a little easy." Her smile returned, even more sickly sweet. "A corpse is a good enough start. It doesn't take so much out of you."

I thought of a suitable retort, then decided against it. I remembered the old tag about he who fights and runs away was a fool to start a losing battle in the first place. Two seconds later I was inside the Sheriff's office with the door shut, making a protective barrier between me and the pride of Virginia.

"I figure he's corpse-prone," Sheriff Lavers said in a reflective voice. "You get lots of people who're accident-prone, don't you? With Wheeler it's corpses—if there's a potential cadaver within a two mile radius of him, it'll finish up dying right at his feet!"

Doc Murphy shuddered violently. "What a dreadful way to die!"

I gave them my dignified look. "Any time I get prone it's got nothing to do with cadavers," I assured them. "And before you ask the next question, the answer is it's none of your damned business!"

Lavers took the cigar out of his mouth and looked at it blandly, like he was waiting to hear it give out with the latest gold prices.

"Tell me how it happened with the corpse, Wheeler?" he asked in a too-smooth voice. "I want to hear every detail."

"Nothing to it," I shrugged. "He walked into the bar and just dropped dead."

"Like that?"

"Dead," I repeated tersely. "*D-E-A-D*— as in *stiff!*"

Lavers rammed the cigar back into his face, then looked at Murphy with an almost smug expression. "You hear that, Doctor?"

"Were you watching his face when it happened, Al?" Murphy asked carefully. "Did you notice anything peculiar? Did he show any sudden pain?"

I thought about it a moment before I answered. "Not that I remember. He stopped suddenly like he'd been hit by a bullet, but his facial expression didn't change any. More like he'd been quick-frozen, no emotion at all." I stared at them both suspiciously. "Since when did we all get so hot about a coronary occlusion?"

Lavers shook his head slowly. "It wasn't heart failure, Wheeler—it was murder."

"I was there, remember?" I said patiently. "Nobody fired a gun or pulled a knife—no nothing! So what killed him—a private joke?"

THE BRAZEN

Murphy studied the fingernails of his right hand with elaborate care. "You ever heard of a poison called curare?"

"Sure," I said. "Every kid that ever read a comic book has heard of..."

Then it hit me and I sank into the nearest chair, burying my face in my hands. "Oh, no!" I muttered hoarsely. "You're not going to give me that poison dart routine—little brown men in sarongs darting in and out of the traffic on the freeway?"

The Sheriff winced visibly. "Don't say it like that!" he snarled. "I can see the newspaper headlines saying it exactly the same way."

"You mean it's for real?" I lifted my head and looked at him wildly.

"Ask Murphy! It was his idea in the first place."

"I triple-checked," the doc said aggressively. "It was curare that killed Miller all right—there was a scratch on the back of his left hand where the poison entered his blood stream."

"Well, it shouldn't be too tough." I smiled wanly. "We know what the suspect looks like already."

"We do?" Lavers asked hopefully.

"Sure—a little brown guy around five feet nothing, wearing a sarong and a bone through his nose. When last seen, was carrying a blowpipe..."

"Shut up!" Lavers growled.

"It's not only the little brown men who use curare," Doc Murphy said mildly, "it's used in modern medicine—tubocurarine for example. But nobody could accidentally scratch their hand on something containing pure curare—so it must have been deliberate."

"Maybe he was a suicide," I suggested eagerly.

Lavers shriveled me with a glance. "You've been a cop long enough to know how people kill themselves, Wheeler! They just don't do it this way. Would he poison himself just two minutes before he walked into that bar to meet you?"

"I guess you're right, Sheriff," I admitted.

"Maybe he scratched himself on Wheeler's personality." Murphy grinned evilly. "That's enough to poison anybody!"

"Maybe you did it for a switch from that do-it-yourself project robbing graves every Friday midnight," I said coldly.

"Cut the clowning," Lavers said irritably. "We'll get plenty of that from everyone else. It's your case, Wheeler, and you'd better get started on it as of now!"

"Yes, sir," I said listlessly, then hauled myself out of the chair.

"You can have Sergeant Polnik to help," he said with a generous grin.

"Who wants Polnik?"

"I don't," he said smugly. "So you got him."

Somewhere around ten-thirty, I read the sign on the door which spelled out, BERKELEY AND MILLER, ATTORNEYS-AT-LAW, then walked inside. The office was modern, with lots of potted plants, glass, and sleek blond furniture, in which the receptionist looked right in place. She had red hair, and wore a white blouse and dark skirt, which emphasized rather than concealed the generous curves of her body.

Her eyes were a candid, interested gray as she looked me over appraisingly.

"Good morning," she said in a pleasant voice. "May I help you?"

"You sure can," I said earnestly. "The nights are so long and empty. It gets worse all the time."

"I can understand that." Her voice was still pleasant. "Whom did you wish to see?"

"Mr. Berkeley."

"Have you an appointment?"

"No," I confessed sadly. "All I've got is a car and some expensive sound equipment."

"I can understand that, too." She smiled, showing even,

THE BRAZEN

white teeth. "You're much too preoccupied with your sex life to worry about making appointments—is that it?"

"Well, you can't blame a man for trying," I said fervently. "And another thing I've got is very good taste." I straightened and put on my official face. "Would you mind telling Berkeley I want to see him. Lieutenant Wheeler—from the sheriff's office."

"You surprise me, Lieutenant," she said casually, as she flicked a switch on the intercom beside her. She spoke into it for a few moments, then looked up at me. "Mr. Berkeley will see you right away, Lieutenant. The second door to your left. What kind of sound equipment?"

"Like I said—expensive. I'll give you a detailed breakdown on the way out."

"I can hardly wait," she said frostily as I walked toward the second door on the left.

Berkeley got up from behind his desk to greet me as I came into his office. A small, fragile-looking guy, a little too well-dressed in a dark suit. He didn't look like the West Coast at all—most of the guys I know button their shirts at the neck only if it looks like its going to be a formal occasion.

He shook hands with me like I was a client, worried until I was sitting comfortably in a moulded chair, then retreated behind his desk again. His eyes, like shiny black buttons sewn into the shrewd face, watched me attentively.

"How can I help you, Lieutenant?" He spoke quickly with the unconscious impatience of the guy who's always got four other things on his mind and maybe not even one of them is a woman.

"I want some information about your partner, Wallace Miller," I told him. "Anyhting at all would be a help."

"A tragedy!" He shook his head rapidly. "Wally was a brilliant lawyer, brilliant!" He closed his eyes for a moment against the painful realization that even a brilliant lawyer like Wally could lose the verdict because of a lousy trick like death.

"His wife called me last night after she'd identified his body," he continued at a fast clip. "Wally always seemed like such a healthy guy, and yet he went like that!" He shuddered as he snapped his fingers, "It makes me nervous, Lieutenant."

If he wanted a wake it was his privilege, but I hadn't stopped by for the whisky and clam chowder.

"It wasn't a coronary occlusion, not according to the autopsy report," I told him. "Your partner didn't die a natural death at all, he was murdered."

"Murdered?" His face twitched painfully. "I can't believe it!"

"He was poisoned—but keep that fact to yourself for a while."

"It's fantastic!" he muttered. "Who would ever want to kill Wally?"

"That's my question," I said irritably. "How about you, Berkeley? Maybe you wanted his share of the partnership along with your own?"

"That's absurd!" He got the facial muscles under control again, and his unblinking eyes were shrewd and watchful.

"So who does get paid off by Wallace's death?"

"I am one of the witnesses to Wally's will," Berkeley said in a tight voice. "Which proves I don't benefit for a start. His estate is divided equally between his wife and another woman. Maybe you know already, but Wally was an orphan—no family at all other than his wife."

"Who's the other woman?"

"Rita Keighley."

"How much is the estate worth—approximately?"

Berkeley shrugged his shoulders. "Around two hundred thousand, before taxes."

"Not bad," I said. "Who is this Rita Keighley, anyway?"

"Some lady Wally must have felt a deep affection for?" he suggested, smiling nervously. "He was my business partner, but his private life was his own—you understand, Lieutenant?"

"What about the partnership? What happens now?"

"We had an agreement worked out during the first month we were together," he said. "If one partner died, we'd value his share on a simple formula—the last five years' profit. The surviving partner has first option to buy, and if he refuses, then the share is offered on the open market."

"Are you buying?" I asked him.

"Naturally."

I lit a cigarette and asked him if he had Rita Keighley's address, then waited while he dug into a filing cabinet and finally came up with it.

"Was Miller handling any special assignment either right now or in recent months, which could have given anybody a motive to kill him?"

Berkeley smiled faintly. "That's a 'What do the people do in New York?' type question, Lieutenant! Offhand, I'd say no."

"What kind of legal work do you handle here?"

"Criminal work mostly, we spend—that is, we did spend a lot of time in courtrooms. We specialize in this type of practice."

"Was Miller handling one of those special cases right now?"

"It just so happens he was," Berkeley said reluctantly.

"Like what?"

He straightened the deskpad in front of him maybe a quarter-inch. Wally was to represent a witness in that congressional committee gambling investigation."

"Who's the guy he was going to represent?"

"A man named Shafer—Pete Shafer."

"I don't think I ever heard of him," I said thoughtfully.

Berkeley shrugged again, and the nervous tic in his face came back suddenly. "I don't think he's a big wheel in the gambling hierarchy!" He giggled suddenly at his own pun. "His boss is paying all the expenses."

"Who's that?"

"John Quirk—he's one of the biggest manufacturers of slot machines in the country."

"Sometimes it frightens me—all the people I never even heard of," I said soberly. "The obvious inference is this Shafer guy knows too much about his boss and Quirk wants to make sure he doesn't spill it to the committee?"

"I wouldn't know," Berkeley said blandly. "It was Wally's affair—not mine."

"But it'll be yours as from now?"

"Along with a lot of other work!" He sighed gently. "I guess I'll have to look for a new partner."

"Where would I find Shafer—and his boss?"

"Mr. Quirk is renting a house out on Cone Hill, I believe," he said. "And where you find Quirk, you find Shafer, I understand, Lieutenant."

"Thanks," I told him. "Just for the record—where were you last night around eight?"

"I was home."

"Which is?"

"Cone Hill."

"Who else was with you?"

"No one I'm afraid—I'm a bachelor, Lieutenant. I do employ a cook and a valet but it was their free night so I was quite alone." He smiled gently. "If it's an alibi you want, I'm afraid I just don't have one!"

"If you had a watertight alibi, I'd be real worried," I said.

He shook hands with me again as I got up to leave, leaning forward across the desk that was bigger than he was.

"Call on me any time at all, Lieutenant," he said briskly. "I have a personal interest in seeing that Wally's murderer is brought to justice."

It was the kind of statement they don't even use in the worse TV shows any more, and I didn't bother to answer.

The red-haired receptionist smiled vaguely when I reached her desk again, like she was sure she had seen me

THE BRAZEN

someplace but couldn't remember where or when, and what the hell anyway.

"I'm the guy who never takes no for an answer—remember?"

"Mind you, don't trip on your way out, Lieutenant," she said warningly. "Your ego's spread all over the floor."

"We could have dinner, listen to some music—on my expensive sound equipment. Maybe we could think of something else to do."

She studied me thoughtfully for a long time, then said, "I'll give you the answer in one word."

"Like no?" I asked sadly.

"Like yes," she smiled suddenly. "I haven't had a date with a real gone screwball like you in two weeks now. Make it tomorrow night and you can pick me up around eight." She gave me her address and precise instructions on how to find her apartment.

"That's great," I said, sliding consciously into lyric poetry. "See you at eight."

"Just one other little thing," she said. "My name is Mona Gray—or is a girl's name the last thing you find out?"

Chapter Three

RIGHT AFTER LUNCH I drove up to Cone Hill again to visit the widow for a second time. The butler opened the door and his facial expression took a sharp downward trend when he saw it was me.

"Yes, Lieutenant?" he asked sourly.

"I'd like to see the lady jokingly referred to as your mistress," I told him. "The lady of the house."

"You wish to see Mrs. Miller?" His raised eyebrows formed an almost perfect arch.

"You get the drift," I said encouragingly.

We went through that into-the-library-and-wait routine again, but this time I didn't have to wait more than thirty seconds before Mrs. Miller made her entrance.

She wore a simple black dress with a low neckline which for sure had a three-figure price tag. If this was a widow's weeds, her mourning sure made me become electrified. About an inch of cleavage showed in the scoop of the dress which was molded perfectly to the contours of her rounded figure. It clung to her hips, and as she moved toward me it flattened over her thighs and dipped slightly between them. Her breasts jutted proudly, and looking closely, I could just make out the slight indentations of her nipples pressing against the fabric. I stopped looking when she saw I was looking.

"What now, Lieutenant?" she asked in a bored voice, like this was the second time already I'd asked for a twist of lemon instead of lime.

"I was curious," I explained. "Last night when I told you your husband was dead . . . maybe I could've gotten more impact if I'd told you it was raining outside?"

"Isn't it my own affair how I react to bad news?"

"Maybe so last night," I conceded, "but now it's my business. Today we know your husband didn't die of a heart attack—he was murdered."

"How odd!" She looked only mildly interested. "Do you know who did it?"

"I figured you might help me there," I said. "You'd want to help us catch his murderer, wouldn't you?"

"If I knew who he was I'd probably buy him a drink," she said calmly.

"You hated Wallace Miller that much?"

Her smile held all the warmth of an igloo-less eskimo winter. "I never made any secret of it," she said calmly. "Why should I start pretending now, just because he's dead? The whole marriage was a mistake from the very beginning. We weren't—compatible?—that's the polite word for it, I understand. It wasn't too long before he began to stay away from home for whole weeks at a time, and it didn't really need female intuition to know there was another woman!"

"Rita Keighley?" I prodded, remembering the terms of Miller's will.

Her lips twisted. "I never bothered to find out her name," she said in a contemptuous voice. "Or what kind of woman she was."

"You never thought of divorce?"

"No," she shook her head firmly. "It was a cold-blooded contract—I gave him social prestige and he supplied the money. I didn't want to lose Wally's money, Lieutenant, there was too much of it."

"I guess you're honest about it, anyway," I said grudgingly. "Do you know the contents of his will?"

"I haven't heard them yet." She raised her eyebrows. "Is there something I should know, as they say in those disgusting advertisements?"

"Half his estate goes to you," I told her. "The other to Rita Keighley."

"I'll contest it!" She nearly spat the words at me.

"When did you last see him alive?" I asked.

"Last night," she said. "He got home from the office around five, said he had to go out again and he wouldn't be back till late. It was a story I'd gotten used to over a long time, so I wasn't interested."

There was a polite knock on the door and a moment later the butler came into the room.

"I beg your pardon, madame," he said deferentially. "Mr. Kirkland is outside."

"Ask him to wait, Chivers," she said impatiently.

"Yes, ma'am." He closed the door gently behind him on his way out.

"If there was anything unusual about Wally last night," Mrs. Miller went on, "I can't think of it. Wait a minute—he did take a cab instead of his own car—if that has any significance."

"Did he have any enemies? You know anyone who'd want to murder him?"

"About everyone who had anything to do with him at all," she said coldly. "Wally wasn't a man, Lieutenant, he was a monster!"

"Are you putting that on his tombstone instead of the more usual epitaph? I asked politely.

"I wouldn't waste his money on him," she said flatly. "He wasted enough of it when he was alive."

"I guess this is what they mean when they talk about being honest until it hurts," I suggested.

She smiled warmly. "Why shouldn't I be honest? I have nothing to hide."

I let my eyes linger on the taut black dress for a couple of seconds, on the gentle rise and fall of her boobs. "Did he have any worries—anything special on his mind?"

Her shoulders shrugged carelessly. "I wouldn't know—we never talked much. Offhand, I'd figure an average of around ten words a day—give or take a day."

"Thanks, Mrs. Miller," I said. "I wish I could say you'd been a help."

I went out of the room and down the hallway toward the front door. On the way I passed the butler, who had another guy in tow—a tall, athletic-looking character with clean-cut features. He nodded and smiled at me as he went past, and I figured cleverly that he must be Kirkland, the guy Chivers had announced. I wondered idly just how athletic the wake would be.

The afternoon was still young, and even if I didn't feel the same way, I still had plenty of time to make a second call in Cone Hill. I drove six blocks, then cruised slowly until I found the house number Berkeley had given me, and parked on the driveway behind a blood-red Mercedes sports car.

The door chimes sounded in off-beat rhythm. Then the door opened, and I forgot the door chimes.

Standing there, watching me with an expression of patient nothing on her face, was a girl with short silver-blonde hair. She wore a black shirt that was open all the way down to her navel. There was nothing beneath it, and it only just covered the tips of her small but beautifully contoured breasts. Her taut nipples prodded the material provocatively, and each time she took a breath, the edges of the shirt shifted a fraction up the smooth inner slopes of her breasts. Her jeans fitted snugly over her hips and full thighs and formed a small but prominent V at her crotch.

Her bright blue eyes stared at me out of the elfin face, noting what I was noting, and accepting it calmly as the normal reaction of every male she'd met since maybe the age of fourteen.

"Are you all through?" she asked in a clipped voice. "Or you want I should get you a chair?"

"I wanted to see a guy named Quirk," I told her. "That was the idea before you opened the door—now it doesn't seem important any more."

When she took a deep breath the shirt rode up to the rims of her pale pink areolas before falling back again.

"You want to see Johnnie," she said slowly, "you got to have a reason, huh?"

"Sure," I said, "like I'm a cop. Lieutenant Wheeler from the Sheriff's office."

"Well—" she yawned indelicately "—I'll ask him."

She walked away from me down the hall, her thong sandals making a faint, slapping sound that provided a rhythmic beat to the taut motion of her sculptured buttocks under the stretched denim. Finally she disappeared out of sight, leaving me wondering how to get started in the one-armed-bandit game.

Maybe a minute later she was back. "You just got lucky," she told me. "Johnny can give you a whole five minutes."

"I'm honored," I said humbly.

She ignored the crack. "He said for you to come on in. The living room's down at the end of the hall. You can find your own way."

"Thanks."

She turned in the doorway, and I had one more brief, tantalizing glimpse of her denim-encased rump before she disappeared for the second time.

The living room was empty when I arrived, so I lit a cigarette and admired the display of bottles in back of the bar for a few seconds before the door opened and a guy, three sizes larger than real life, walked in.

He must have gone better than two hundred pounds stripped, and under the sweatshirt the muscles bulged ar-

THE BRAZEN

rogantly. His face had a beat-up look like somebody had used it for rock-crushing these last five years.

"What do you want, punk?" he growled at me.

"Are you Quirk?" I asked, not believing it.

"The hell with who I am!" he snarled. "It's you got to give with the—"

"Elmer!" a voice said sharply from the open doorway.

The gorilla shuffled around to look to the voice's owner, like it was feeding-time or something. "Jeez, boss!" he said plaintively. "I walk in here and this punk's lousing up the joint like he owns it or something!"

"It's O.K.," the second guy said, "Now—beat it!"

"Sure." The gorilla shuffled toward the door. "Anything you say—you know that, Johnnie! I always—"

"Sure, sure!" The second guy waited until the gorilla had gone, then walked toward me with his hand outstretched. "Sorry about that," he said pleasantly. "I'm John Quirk—and you're Lieutenant Wheeler?"

"I had your name figured for Frankenstein a few moments back," I told him as we shook hands.

Quirk was a tall dark-haired guy with a triangular-shaped face and features to match, the wide, candid eyes forming the base of an inverted triangle which also contained the sharp pointed nose, and a small thin mouth. He looked the kind of bird dog that leads its master into quicksand just for the hell of it.

"I'm sorry about Elmer," he repeated. "Nobody told him you were here and he had no idea who you were, of course. He's an ex-fighter who took too much punishment in his last fight and it's left him a little punchy. It was too bad—five years back he was within two fights of meeting the heavyweight champ and now—"

"Leave us hope his mother died while he was still young, anyway," I said.

"Sure." Quirk grinned obligingly. "How about a drink, Lieutenant?"

"That's the best offer I've had all day," I admitted. "Scotch on the rocks—a little soda?"

He went around in back of the bar and made the drinks with expert precision.

"What's it all about anyway?" he asked easily.

"A lawyer, name of Miller, Wallace J. Miller, died last night," I said. "I'm investigating."

"Wally Miller?" The face sharpened suddenly. "I knew him—a great guy!"

"His partner told me Miller was going to represent one of your employees—Shafer—who's been subpoenaed to appear at the congressional committee investigating organized gambling, and it was you hired Miller."

"That's right," he nodded. "I knew Wally's reputation as a good counselor to have in a courtroom. Nothing wrong in that, is there?"

"Nothing at all," I agreed. "I'm trying to find out if Miller had anything special on his mind—something worrying him, maybe. I figured there was just a chance you could help."

"Nothing I know of." Quirk shook his head slowly. "It looks like suicide, huh?"

"Could be," I said. "Where is Shafer now?"

"Right here." He handed me the drink. "You want to see him, Lieutenant?"

"If you don't mind."

He went out of the room and I had time to finish the Scotch before he returned with another guy in tow.

"Pete,"—Quirk gestured toward me politely—"this is Lieutenant Wheeler."

Shafer looked at me with a casual contempt and nodded briefly. He was around twenty-five, six feet tall and nicely built with it—thick, curly blond hair and the kind of sun-tanned, sleepy good looks that a lot of middle-aged matrons will spend big money to have around them.

"Just a couple of questions," I said. "Like where were you around eight last night?"

"Right here," he said in a sneering voice. "Where was I supposed to be?"

"Who else was here with you?"

"Elmer." He grinned. "You already met Elmer. He told me there was a cop in here already."

"Anybody else here besides Elmer last night?" I asked.

"Sure—Janie."

"Janie?"

"I think you already met her on your way in, Lieutenant," Quirk said politely. "My housekeeper."

I looked at him admiringly for a moment. "Some housekeeper," I muttered.

"Anything else on your mind, Lieutenant," Shafer growled threateningly.

"You'll need a new lawyer now that Miller's not around any more," I said. "Have anybody special in mind?"

"His partner—Berkeley—is taking over, I guess," he said. "Why?"

"Just curious," I said. "Now I've seen you I can understand Miller going out to drop dead someplace—I sure hope Berkeley's heart is healthy."

"You got a great sense of humor, Lieutenant," Shafer said coldly. "Watch out you don't strangle to death on it some day!"

"How about another drink, Lieutenant?" Quirk asked in a polite voice. "Or did you have some more questions first?"

"No more questions—and no more drinks, thanks all the same," I said. "You sell many machines in Pine City?"

"I sell all my machines in Nevada, but I operate out of an office here. I like the climate better."

"Since how long?"

"Since three months back."

"How come they subpoenaed Shafer instead of you?"

Quirk shrugged gracefully. "I wouldn't know, Lieutenant. Maybe because he's my sales manager. I concern myself more with the manufacturing side."

"How does he sell?" I asked, looking at Shafer. "With a gun?"

"You're a riot, Lieutenant," Shafer said with a taut grin on his face. "Just watch it you don't die laughing!"

Chapter Four

I FIGURED it was real nice of Berkeley setting me up with a list of names, and the least I could do was keep right on visiting. So I drove downtown to the Glenshire address where he'd told me Rita Keighley lived.

It was a second floor walk-up in an apartment building that had stood around so long it had gotten tired and was starting to fall apart. I thumbed the buzzer and waited maybe ten seconds, then thumbed it again. The door opened eventually and a semi-clad chick stood there looking at me with a frosty look on her face that told me I wasn't welcome.

Her dark hair had a center part, and all she wore was a peach-colored slip beneath which her trim body was outlined in sufficient detail to make my pulse quicken and to make me think that she was every man's dream of what should be waiting for him at home after a long hard day at the office—but never is. The dark tips of her fulsome breasts were thrust out toward me, and between her thighs, I could dimly make out the dark furriness of her pubis.

Her lips made a round O of surprise as she stared at me. "I was expecting someone else," she said blankly.

"Wallace J. Miller?" I queried.

"If you're one of Johnnie's boys," she snapped, "you can tell him from me that I—"

"I'm Lieutenant Wheeler," I interrupted, "from the sheriff's office."

Her lips made that O again. It was cute and maybe that was why she did it all the time.

"I wanted to talk to you about Miller," I said.

"Won't you come in?"

I followed her inside the apartment, watching with interest the way the orbs of her superb buttocks meshed slightly together beneath the slip. Her reverse cleavage was like a faintly drawn pencil line. Plunking down into an armchair, I lit a cigarette. Rita Keighley watched me with a thunderous expression on her face.

"You figuring on staying long, Lieutenant?" she asked.

"A while," I said easily. "So many questions. You want to finish dressing first?"

"Well, thank *you*, Lieutenant," she said waspishly. "As it so happens, I was about to take a shower."

"So go ahead," I said politely. "Be my guest."

She was still watching me with a sour expression. "Well, as long as you don't mind," she said.

I gave an airy wave of my hand. "I got time."

"Then don't just sit there," she said in a voice that had suddenly become nervous. "You could turn the shower on for me, anyway."

Her breasts rose and fell, and I could still see the faint furry patch between her thighs. "Well?" she demanded.

"Well, O.K." I got to my feet reluctantly. "You sure you insist?"

"Sure, I'm sure."

I walked across to the bathroom door, pushed it open, and stepped inside. It was a mistake—but right then the

THE BRAZEN

last thing I had on my mind was the bathroom. I was too busy figuring if I should wait until she'd gotten dressed again and then ask my questions, or join her in the shower and get some nice clean answers. Either way it became a strictly academic question because somebody gave the whole situation a new twist by dropping the ceiling in on my head.

Within five seconds of opening my eyes, I knew I had hit the floor with a dull thud, and I sure as hell had a dull ache in back of my skull to match it. The apartment was empty, which wasn't a surprise, but after I'd climbed painfully back onto my feet again, I saw Rita's slip draped across the couch. So maybe she had had her shower after all, I thought, with me lying unconscious on the bathroom floor.

I found some aspirin in the kitchen and took two, along with a glass of water. Then I lit a cigarette and wandered gently back into the living room. The bureau looked an obvious place to start, so that was where I started. The top drawer didn't reveal much apart from a pile of skimpy underwear, nor did the second. But the third drawer down surrendered a couple of interesting photographs.

The first one showed a smiling Wallace J. Miller with the scrawled inscription. *For my darling Rita with all my love—Wally*. And he couldn't have been kidding either —there was that six-figure legacy to prove he meant it. The second photo was inscribed *All my love, darling, from Jim*. So nobody gets to be original inscribing photos, I figured, not even James Kirkland. I recognized his smiling face O.K.—the clean-cut profile, the college boy type who'd been waiting to see Mrs. Miller while she was telling me how crazy she hadn't been about her late, unlamented husband.

I sat down on the couch carefully, not wishing to widen the hole I'd already gotten in my head. I thought about Rita Keighley. She had opened the door expecting someone else—one of Johnny Quirk's hoods maybe—then invited me inside the apartment, all the while quite unself-consciously displaying all she had beneath the flimsy pink slip. She had inveigled me into the bathroom, slugged me over the back of the head, and run out. In what? Wearing what? Nothing at all?

There was something wrong with that, my beat-in skull insisted—sure, she was still standing over by the couch when I opened the bathroom door and that meant it couldn't have been Rita who slugged me. It had to be someone else, somebody who'd hidden in the bathroom when I pressed the buzzer. Whoever that somebody had been, they must have had good reason for not wanting me to see them—I fingered the back of my head painfully —one hell of a good reason!

By trying hard I could remember what happened fifteen minutes back even if I couldn't achieve total recall. I'd opened the bathroom door, stepped inside, and somebody had slugged me. But when I'd regained consciousness I'd been lying on the living room carpet. . . . I turned my head slowly and saw the bathroom door was now closed. Query: Who closed it and why? Answer: Open it, you lamebrain, and find out. If I kept up this kind of deductive logic I'd be walking around with a spy-glass and tape measure next—and in no time I'd be slammed behind bars on a peeping rap.

Fearlessly I opened the bathroom door and switched on the light. After I'd made sure there was no maniac still poised behind the door with a blunt instrument in his hand, I even more fearlessly strode inside.

Rita Keighley hadn't run out of the apartment. She was right there in the bath, stark naked, with her head pillowed against one end. I knelt down and took a closer look. She was dead—maybe before she even knew about the hundred thousand dollars. The cold water faucet leaked slightly, and a slow, steady procession of glistening drops splashed down onto the big toe of her left foot.

Polnik looked at me and shook his head sorrowfully.

THE BRAZEN 31

"It's a crime, Lieutenant—killing a beautiful girl like her!"

"Sure," I grated. "They even got a name for it now—murder, they call it."

"How did they croak her?" he asked, still grieving. "I didn't see no marks on the body or nothing."

"Doc Murphy's in there finding out right now," I said. "If you want, I'll give you even money it's curare."

"Like she was strangled?"

"It's a poison," I explained. "A deadly poison—one scratch is enough."

Doc Murphy came bustling out of the bathroom with a bright grin on his face. I figure he sees so many corpses he acts so agresssively alive the whole time in sheer self-defense. But there are times when he hams it up a little too much and this was one of them.

"What have you got here, Wheeler?" he boomed at me. "A conspiracy to stop me sleeping nights?"

"Don't kid me you can ever sleep nights—with your conscience!" I told him.

"This one was in the bathroom anyway—nice and hygienic," he grunted. "You want to guess what killed her?"

"Surprise me!"

"Those little brown men in sarongs sure get around," he said happily. "The autopsy will prove it, of course, but I guess it's curare all right—the only mark on her is a faint scratch across her neck."

The buzzer sounded sharply and Polnik jumped like he'd just been scratched by a little brown man.

Murphy looked at me interestedly. "You expecting a caller, Al?"

"No," I said. "Aren't you?"

"I haven't called the morgue yet," he said. "Don't tell me they're getting clairvoyant on me at my time of life!"

"Maybe it's the Sheriff," I said. "Did you call him after I called you at the office, Sergeant?"

"No, Lieutenant," Polnik shook his head firmly. "I figured I'd let you tell him."

"Thanks," I said bitterly. "I guess there's one obvious way to find out—I'll go open the door."

"Yeah," Polnik said eagerly. "Maybe she's a real classy broad, huh, Lieutenant?"

"Broad?" I said wonderingly. "Who?"

"Sure," he nodded impatiently. "The one the doc's talking about all the time—this Clair Voyant!"

"You ought to be ashamed of yourself," I said severely to Murphy. "You being a married man and all."

"I figure it's his metabolism," Murphy said, looking admiringly at Polnik. "He doesn't have any."

The buzzer squawked impatiently for the second time as I walked across the room, and the moment before I opened the door an impatient fist rapped sharply on the outside panel.

"Open up in there!" a male voice called hopefully. "It's me, honey, your golden-haired boy back from the wastelands of Cone Hill. Open up! I don't care if you don't have any clothes on—it's cold out here."

I opened the door and simpered a little. "I bet you say that to all the girls."

James Kirkland stood there, his clean-cut jaw sagging a little as he stared at me. "What—what—" he stammered.

"If it's so cold out there, why don't you come inside?" I asked reasonably.

"But where's Rita?" he gurgled.

"She's right here," I told him.

He stepped past me inside the apartment and I closed the door and followed him into the living room. When he saw the other two, he stopped and looked questioningly at me.

"This is Doctor Murphy and Sergeant Polnik," I made polite introductions. "Gentlemen, this is Mr. Kirkland."

"What goes on here!" He looked at me with a confused expression on his face. "You—you're Lieutenant Wheeler, I saw you up at the Miller house this afternoon!"

"That's right," I said comfortingly.

THE BRAZEN

"I thought you said Rita was here?"

"Sure she is—in the bathroom."

He looked at the bathroom door, then back at me. "What is this—some kind of gag?"

"Why don't you take a look for yourself?" I suggested.

He looked at me uncertainly for a moment longer, then walked slowly into the bathroom. For the next thirty seconds there was a silence with bells on, then he came walking out again, slowly like an old man. His face was pinched and white and he looked suddenly older.

"Who did it?" he asked hoarsely.

"That's what I'm paid to find out," I said. "Maybe you can help."

He shook his head slowly. "I don't know anybody who'd want to kill Rita—what harm did she ever do anybody?"

"Maybe she was a suicide, huh?" Polnik said helpfully.

"That's crazy!" Kirkland said violently. "She was perfectly happy—we were going to be married."

Murphy cleared his throat loudly. "You mind if I call the meat wagon, Al? The way things are, what with the autopsy and all, I won't get home before four in the morning already!"

"Sure," I said absently. "Go right ahead."

Kirkland closed his eyes tight shut as "meat wagon" hit him right where he lived. I offered him a cigarette and he shook his head mutely, so I lit one for myself.

"What do you do for a living?" I asked.

"I'm a manufacturing chemist," he said dully. "What's that got to do with—"

"You answer the questions—I'll ask them," I said. "That way we'll get along fine. In business for yourself?"

"No—I work for Morgan and Scheer. They've got a plant just north of the city."

"How long had you known Rita Keighley?"

"Five, maybe six months." He took a long, shuddering breath. "Lieutenant! After the—autopsy—can I claim her body? She doesn't have any folks, not that I know of, anyway, and I—"

"If there's nobody else to claim her, there's nothing to stop you doing it," I said. "How did you first meet her?"

"I had an apartment in this building up until a month back," he said. "We got to meeting on the stairs—you know how it is?"

"Lieutenant!" Polnik erupted like an overslept volcano. "I got an idea. Maybe it was an internal triangle, huh? Two females—you get it? This Keighley woman, and then this Voyant broad?"

"That's pretty deep thinking, Sergeant," I told him in an awed voice. "I'll need time to digest it."

"I've got a stomach pump when you need it, friend!" Murphy said in a choked voice. "Why don't you take him out on the night-club circuit and make a fortune?"

"Doc," I pleaded, "why don't you take the Sergeant into the bathroom again and show him exactly where that scratch is? Maybe he can figure out how it happened—or something?"

"Why, sure," Polnik said expansively. "Give the Lieutenant time to catch up with my thinking yet!"

I waited until the bathroom door closed behind the two of them, then concentrated on Kirkland again.

"What did she do for a living?" I asked.

"She wasn't working at all the last three months." There was a tortured look about his eyes like he'd spent the last five years trying to probe the inner subtleties of Zen Buddhism—or maybe he'd eaten a bad oyster Kilpatrick.

"Before that she was a private secretary."

"Who was her employer?"

"Miller—Wallace J. Miller."

"Why did she quit?"

"I—wouldn't know about that."

He lit a cigarette, his hands shaking slightly. "Couldn't we leave this for a little later, Lieutenant? Seeing Rita like that—dead—I can't even think straight!"

"Your lying is lousy, too," I said mildly. "Miller left her a hundred thousand in his will. How about that?"

"That much?" He didn't sound real surprised.

"Maybe she was the best stenographer he ever had," I suggested. "Or maybe she was the best lay he ever had and that's why she quit working three months back—he didn't want her wasting energy."

"All right!" Kirkland shouted suddenly. "So Miller kept her!"

"And this was the girl you were going to walk to the altar with?" I asked incredulously. "With her all dressed up in white and all?"

"I loved her!" he groaned. "You wouldn't understand that, would you? I was crazy about her."

"Sure," I said. "All you needed was one small fatal accident to be arranged for Wallace J., and then you and Rita could live happily ever after on the hundred grand he'd so thoughtfully provided for her."

He looked at me blankly. "What the hell are you talking about?"

"Don't play it naive—the college boy bit is all worn out," I said. "Miller left half his estate to Rita and half to his wife. His partner figures that comes out around a hundred grand a share. The girl and the money, Kirkland—tell me two better motives for murder."

"I never knew about the money," he quavered. "I swear it!"

"Big deal."

"If what you said is true—would I have killed Rita?" he demanded passionately.

"I don't see why not," I said honestly. "If she used you to kill Miller, then after you'd done it and she knew the hundred grand was heading her way, maybe she told you goodbye? That would leave you facing a murder rap with no girl and no share of her legacy either. It's the kind of situation that disenchants people fast."

He shook his head hopelessly. "Either you're crazy,

Lieutenant, or you're just picking on me because I'm the nearest guy available. Is that it?"

"You were in the Miller house this afternoon to see the grieving widow," I said. "What for?"

"She wanted to see me, that's why. She called me around lunchtime and said it was urgent."

"Was it?"

Kirkland's face had the anguished look of the pimply adolescent facing his moment of truth with an irate father, not knowing what the girl has said already.

"I went out there to see her around three months back," he said finally. "The first time I discovered Rita was Miller's mistress, I was nearly out of my mind so I went to see his wife, figuring she could help me break it up. But she wasn't even interested when I told her about it—almost had me thrown out of the house!"

"What did she have on her mind today that was so urgent?"

"When I saw her, she said she was worried how Rita was fixed now that her husband was dead," he said. "But a little while after she'd called me she'd heard Rita didn't have to worry. She was sorry for wasting my time—it didn't make any sense to me then. I can see it now—she'd heard about Miller's will and the money he'd left Rita."

"Where were you last night?" I asked, for a change of scenery.

"Here—with Rita."

"From what time?"

"Around seven, I guess."

"When did you leave?"

"Just before eight this morning—I drove straight out to the plant."

"Is there anyone who can verify that?"

"Only Rita," he muttered.

"And she's dead!"

Doc Murphy and Polnik came back into the living room, both with identical expressions of bewilderment on their faces.

THE BRAZEN

"The sergeant figures if we can prove this Clair Voyant has a heavy suntan and wears a sarong, we've got the whole case sewn up," Murphy said in a hollow-sounding voice. "Right now, I believe it!"

"Why not?" I agreed. "Find the three foot cigarette-holder she's using as a blowpipe and we can go straight to the D.A. for an indictment!"

I turned back to Kirkland again. "Do you know anybody who'd have reason for wanting Rita Keighley dead?"

"No, I don't." He was vehement about it. "She never hurt anyone in her whole life!"

"You know a guy named Quirk—Johnnie Quirk?"

"No—I've never heard the name even."

"O.K.," I said. "That's all for now, Kirkland."

He looked at me, not believing it for a moment. "You mean I can go now?"

"Leave your address with the Sergeant first," I said, "so we know where to find you if we want you again."

I lit a cigarette while he spelled out his address slowly and Polnik wrote it laboriously into his notebook. There was a quick tattoo on the door, then the boys in their white coats came in to take care of the body. Kirkland passed them on his way out, and his face paled again. By the time he made the front door he was almost running.

"Tail him," I told Polnik as soon as the door had closed behind him.

"Sure, Lieutenant!" Polnik lunged briskly toward the door, then pulled up short. "All night?"

"When he looks like he's holed up someplace for a while, call in and I'll fix it so there's somebody to take over," I said.

"Jeez! Thanks, Lieutenant," he said emotionally. "It's my wedding anniversary today and the old lady's having the usual wake. If I don't make it sometime tonight she'll get lonely—not having anybody to throw the empties at."

Chapter Five

I GOT INTO THE OFFICE bright if not early the next morning and found Sheriff Lavers sitting at his desk with his glasses perched on the end of his nose, busy reading the headlines.

"You look like the art work in a two-page advertising spread for Fathers' Day," I told him. "Underneath it says in big black type, 'Do right by Father on *his* day—buy him a new set of teeth.' "

"If somebody asked you to do right by Mother on *her* day," he growled, "which one would you choose?"

"Touché!" I said. "Which is French for 'Get that goddamn knife out of my throat.' You've heard about Rita Keighley?"

"There are a few people left around this office who consider murder an important enough event to report to me," he said coldly. "Even if the lieutenant investigating it doesn't."

"I was busy, Sheriff." I made a vague, all-embracing

38

gesture with my hands. "I never even had time to stop for a cup of coffee."

"How about taking time out to give me a few of the details?" Lavers asked in a honeyed voice. "Or would you rather I returned you to Homicide with 'Reject' rubber-stamped on your forehead?"

"By a happy coincidence, sir," I said quickly, "I was about to give you the detail in detail."

It took maybe fifteen minutes to bring him up to date. This was one time there was nothing I needed to leave out—unfortunately—so I didn't.

"Kirkland went straight back to his apartment last night," Lavers said. "Carver took over from Polnik for the night shift, and now Polnik's back there."

"Fine," I said politely.

"You have a good friend who's maybe a journalist too, Wheeler?" he asked suddenly.

"Sheriff," I said reproachfully, "you know I don't have any friends."

"Somebody does," he snarled. "Somebody's run off at the mouth and I'd like to get my hands on them right now! It's plastered all over the front page this morning. I guess you were too busy reading the ads to pick it up."

"What's plastered all over the front page?"

"The sudden deaths of Wallace J. Miller and Rita Keighley," he snapped. "Within twenty-four hours of each other. It says she was his personal secretary until three months back, then hints pretty broadly what she was after. There's also a very broad hint that both of them were murdered and a lot of pointed questions like what is the Sheriff's office doing, and why have they drawn a veil of secrecy across the two deaths. The people demand to know—and that kind of crap!"

"Not me," I said truthfully. "Some newspaper asks you what the Sheriff's office is doing and next thing I know, you're asking me the same thing. I got enough grief of my own without advertising for more."

"I guess so," he admitted grudgingly. "But I wouldn't put it past you all the same, Wheeler."

"I don't deserve your confidence, sir," I said modestly, "but thanks anyway."

"What about this curare?" He got his teeth back into the original problem.

"Maybe we don't have to worry about the little brown men after all," I told him. "Maybe a manufacturing chemist can get hold of the stuff—and that's what Kirkland is when he's not busy making a threesome with a secretary and her boss."

"Sounds like you've got something there." The Sheriff brightened a little. "How did he react when you tossed the question at him?"

"He didn't."

"Poker-faced killer, eh?" Lavers scowled ferociously. "*Them* I love!"

"He didn't react because I didn't ask him," I explained carefully.

"You didn't—"

"I figured it was a little premature to ask," I went on quickly before his ulcer hemorrhaged. "He was jumping enough already without that. I'd rather wait awhile and see what he does first—and we've got a tail on him to find out."

Lavers grunted sourly. "Maybe he'll spend his time feeding curare to another half-dozen people."

I thought maybe it was time to change the subject. "What do you know about Quirk—and his sales manager, Shafer?" I asked him.

"I wondered when you'd get around to them," he said, then took his time about lighting a cigar while I waited with what some other guy called the minor form of despair disguised as a virtue and called patience.

"Quirk makes slot machines and sells them in Nevada?" Lavers puffed a dense cloud of blue smoke toward me. "My guess is he sells them a lot of other places too— even in states where gambling is illegal."

THE BRAZEN 41

"That figures," I said. "Buy why are they calling Shafer as a witness before the investigating committee, and not Quirk?"

"The way I hear it, Shafer is the boy with the hard sell—he uses plenty of muscle as the clincher," the Sheriff said. "He beat a murder rap three years back—the Nevada court claimed the victim was a reluctant customer but they couldn't prove it. If that committee hauls in Quirk, no matter what testimony they confront him with, he'll use the obvious out—the tactics his salesmen used were without both his permission and knowledge. They hit Shafer with the same testimony and it's that much harder for him to duck."

"Sure," I said. "What's Quirk doing in Pine City right now?"

"I wish I knew for sure," Lavers said savagely. "He set up this sales office three months or so back. It's all quite legal as far as I can tell. He doesn't carry any stock or samples, and his salesmen operate only in Nevada. We can't disprove it, anyway."

"It doesn't figure," I said obviously. "By any kind of logic that office should be in Nevada."

"There are a couple of stories I picked up around," he said. "The Vegas grapevine says he's facing tough competition through the whole state—a couple of the bigger boys got together and they're squeezing him out fast—so he moved himself and his office back into California for health reasons. There's also a rumor he's short of cash—real short; and with Shafer, his ace salesman, subpoenaed by the committee, he's in real trouble all the way round. They say he's owing fifty grand or more to the Syndicate for machine parts and if he doesn't pay real soon they're going to collect the hard way."

"Where do you get this kind of information, Sheriff?" I asked admiringly. "Weekend poker parties?"

"I'm not like you, Wheeler," he leered at me happily. "I've got friends!"

The exit line was his. I went through into the outer office and admired the honey-blonde head bent dutifully over a typewriter. Five seconds later Annabelle lifted her head sharply and glared at me.

"I can always feel you looking at me," she said. "Like I'm just out from under a cold shower and you're counting the goose pimples!"

She was wearing a black-and-white dress, which would have made for a demure effect, except that Annabelle's got the sort of figure that would make her look sexy in a packing crate.

"I figure on you, goose pimples would look real nervous," I said generously. "Like little pink rosebuds and all."

"You remind me of Pavlov's dogs—only you've got a conditioned reflex about sex and not food!" she said icily. "Or maybe you never even heard of Pavlov?"

"Didn't he play tenor sax with the Finnigan Quintet a few years back?" I asked cautiously. "Sure—I remember him now—he ate so much food he got fat and his dogs were killing him all the time."

"Finnigan's quintet?" she moaned helplessly.

"Don't sell Finnigan short!" I warned her. "He had those guys' reflexes so conditioned that any time he twitched an eyebrow even, they were into the fifteenth bar of 'Muskrat Ramble' already!"

"Just go away, please, Al-honey?" she pleaded. "Leave me and my goose pimples to condition our own reflexes."

"When you come to realize," I went on remorselessly, "that the fifteenth bar of Muskrat Ramble is almost out of town—well! You can figure it for yourself just how much mileage those cats covered at one jump when Finnigan twitched—"

"I can't stand any more!" she whimpered. "Go out and spoil somebody else's day!"

"Well, all right," I said in an injured voice. "If you insist."

The phone rang and I answered it because I was

nearest and Annabelle looked busy having some kind of private hysterics.

"That you, Lieutenant?" A wood-splintered voice asked.

"Yeah," I said. "How you making out, Sergeant?"

"I've been watching that guy Kirkland's apartment house since eight this morning," Polnik said plaintively. "It's eleven-thirty already and he don't come out yet. Looks like he's staying in bed or something. What should I do, Lieutenant?"

"Keep right on watching the apartment house," I said tersely. "Maybe he'll change his mind later."

"If you say so, Lieutenant," he said moodily. "But it's getting monotonous."

"Just keep watching," I told him, then like a flash saw my chance to do a good deed for a lousy day. "You heard Carver's report about last night?" I asked, keeping it casual.

"He told me nothing happened when I took over this morning," Polnik said glumly.

"That Carver," I sighed. "What a tight-mouth he is! I bet he didn't even tell you about the cab that arrived around two-thirty A.M.? With Kirkland down on the sidewalk to meet it and all?"

"He told me nothing!" Polnik grunted.

"Well, they'll have to leave sometime—all three of them," I said. "Make sure you don't miss them when they go—maybe he'll go along with them."

"Who's them?"

"The three girls he's got up there," I said patiently. "I think they're having a party."

"What sort of party?" Polnik asked suspiciously.

"Oh, Sergeant, what do you think?"

"You mean a sex party?"

"Is that what you think?"

"What are they?" he asked in an impressed voice. "Hookers?"

"Maybe, maybe not."

"Jesus!"

"So maybe you should go up and join them," I suggested. "Kirkland must be starting to flag by now."

There was a sharp clunk in my ear as Polnik hung up on me. I would have stayed around the office longer, and cheered up Annabelle some more—but right then she looked like the only thing that could reach her would be a three-stage rocket. I went out to the car instead, and drove downtown to the offices of Berkeley and Miller, attorneys-at-law.

It was a sunny morning, and behind the receptionist's desk, Mona Gray looked as fresh and as bright as a Kansas cornfield. "Wonderful to see you, Lieutenant," she said warmly. "But aren't you about eight hours early?"

"I'm getting through my work quickly today," I told her. "So I can rest up this afternoon to get ready for our date. But let us not get sidetracked. Is Berkeley home?"

"In his office," she said. "There's no one with him. You can walk right in if you want."

I knocked gently on the door, then walked inside the office. Berkeley looked up from his desk with an expression of mild surprise.

"Good morning, Lieutenant," the words came with the usual rush. "This is a surprise." The shiny, patent leather eyes probed me for concealed weapons all the time.

"Just wanted to check a couple of points, Mr. Berkeley," I said politely, and eased myself down into the nearest moulded chair.

"Of course. I said for you to call on me at any time at all, Lieutenant, and I certainly meant it, yes, indeed! Now,"—he leaned his elbows on the desk and pyramided his fingers—"how can I be of service?"

"You read the morning papers?"

"Yes, yes, I have. About Rita Keighley's death you mean, of course?" He pursed his lips and shook his head slightly. "I confess I'm confused! I presume she was murdered as poor Wally was murdered, yes?"

"Sure," I said. "You never told me Rita was his personal secretary until around three months back—"

He blinked rapidly. "No, no I didn't. You're absolutely right, Lieutenant." His face twitched into a painful smile. "You'll have to forgive me for that—habitual caution of the legally trained mind, you understand? Yesterday it didn't seem to have any real significance and I didn't want any scandal about my late partner, Lieutenant. Not good for a legal practice, not good at all!"

"Rita was a busy girl," I said. "She had another boy friend besides your late partner—a guy named Kirkland. You know him at all?"

"Kirkland?" His full, almost feminine lips pouted as he thought about it. "Not that I recall, no."

"Kirkland knew all about Rita and Miller," I went on. "He even went to see Mrs. Miller one time—figured maybe she'd help him break it up but she wasn't interested."

"That's amazing, Lieutenant, amazing." He drooped pathetically in his chair. "All these things going on right under my nose and I never knew, never dreamed . . ." He raised his hands then let them drop onto his desktop in a fatalistic shrug. "Well, there you are, Lieutenant. Most days I'm in court, trying to help a client and I guess a man gets too busy—"

The ham in him was beginning to rasp irritably on my nerves. I lit a cigarette and inhaled deeply.

"Mrs. Miller didn't get along with her husband," I said abruptly. "Maybe they spoke at Thanksgiving and Christmas, but they weren't what you'd call real friendly. This I have from Mrs. Miller herself; he married her for social prestige and she married him for money."

"Gail has been very frank with you, Lieutenant," Berkeley said nervously, "very frank!"

"It's possible she could've preferred his money all by itself," I suggested. "Then later still, preferred not to share it with Rita Keighley. . . ."

His eyes bulged. "Are you suggesting that Gail killed Wally and then the girl!"

"What do you think of it—as a theory?"

"It hardly seems possible . . ." His head jerked all ways as he figured the odds with the concentration of a guy putting his shirt on a long shot. "I don't know—no—I couldn't hazard a guess even. You've overwhelmed me, Lieutenant!"

"If anything should happen to Mrs. Miller, now that Rita's already gone," I said, "what would happen to Miller's estate?"

"That's purely an academic question, surely?" he said in a shrill voice. "Nothing is going to happen to Gail!"

"But if it did?" I snapped. "Who gets the money then?"

Berkeley pulled an immaculate white linen handkerchief from his top pocket and dabbed his forehead gently.

"Well, it so happens—in that most unlikely event—it would come to the partnership."

"Meaning you?"

"Meaning me," he said unhappily.

"That's nice," I said comfortably. "Of course, you have no worries—"

"I'm certainly glad to hear you say that, Lieutenant!"

"—just so long as Mrs. Miller stays alive," I finished.

He bounced up from behind the desk and for a couple of seconds I waited for him to grow another twelve inches—standing up he somehow looked even smaller than when he was sitting down.

"You certainly have a gift for putting things bluntly, if I may say so, Lieutenant!" He was shaking gently in no breeze. "If you'll excuse me now, I'm running late for a lunch appointment. Was there anything else you wished to say before I go?"

"Goodbye?" I suggested helpfully.

Chapter Six

AFTER LUNCH I drove up to Cone Hill again and pulled up in the drive of the Miller house. I didn't expect the butler would be pleased to see me, so I wasn't disappointed—frightened maybe, but not disappointed.

"Good afternoon, Lieutenant," he said from a great height. "Mrs. Miller is in the pool at the moment. I doubt—"

"Have faith!" I told him. "The day of the butler will come—it's just that cops are first in line." I pushed past him gently into the hall. "Don't bother announcing me— I'll make it a big surprise."

I walked quickly down the hall, figuring that even in Cone Hill the most likely place to find the swimming pool was in back of the house. A few seconds later I walked out onto the back terrace, and there it was.

Mrs. Miller was stretched out on a reclining chair at the side of the pool. She was topless, and her nipples stood erect from their surrounding pink, faintly puckered areolas, as if straining up toward the life-giving sun. Her abbreviated briefs were so flimsy that the hair of her delta traced a faint pattern against them. Her body glistened with suntan lotion.

The widow had her eyes closed against the sun and she didn't bother to open them when I walked up to where she lay and stood there looking down at her.

"What is it, Chivers?" she asked brusquely.

"It's just, well, things were so different with my last employer—Lady Chatterley," I said wistfully.

Her eyes opened wide and she looked at me coldly for a few seconds. "I've been meaning to have that filter system fixed," she said finally. "Then I won't be bothered any more by the things that crawl out of it all the time!"

"I came to offer congratulations," I said.

"On what?"

"You're richer by a hundred thousand, since last night."

She stood up in an undulating movement, and her breasts surged a little and resumed their well-contoured shape.

"You mean Rita Keighley? I read about it in the morning papers."

"Sure," I agreed. "She's dead—like your late husband."

She didn't bat an eyelid. "Is it true what the paper hinted—she was murdered?"

"I don't know," I lied. "I haven't seen the autopsy as yet. Where were you last night?"

"Are you suggesting I had anything to do with her death?"

"Let's face it," I said, "you're a prime suspect, Mrs. Miller. Rita Keighley was your husband's mistress and stood to get half his estate—and now she's dead you get it instead. I never saw a better motive for murder."

"I won't tolerate this!" she snapped. "I'm going to complain to the county sheriff."

"Why not Johnny Quirk? He's a man of direct action," I suggested.

"Don't be ridiculous!"

"You do know Johnnie Quirk then?"

She glared at me savagely like she wished I was bound hand and foot and she held an oyster knife. "I've met Quirk," she said. "I wouldn't say I know him."

"He was a client of Wallace J.," I said. "Your husband was going to represent a guy named Shafer—Quirk's sales manager—before an investigating committee."

"I did hear some talk about it." She shrugged her sleek shoulders. "What has Quirk got to do with Rita Keighley?"

"I haven't figured that out yet," I admitted.

She walked toward the house. "If you don't mind, Lieutenant, I'm going to get dressed!"

"I do mind," I said honestly, "but I guess there isn't much I can do about it."

"The next time you call, I'd prefer you let Chivers announce you!" she said regally.

"I'll give you five minutes to put some clothes on," I snarled, "and be back here so you can answer all the questions I haven't asked yet. If you don't want to play it that way, all right—I'll take you downtown to the Sheriff's office and we can start over."

"You wouldn't dare!" she gasped.

"Try me?" I grinned nastily.

She took a deep breath, and her superb breasts surged again. "I'll be back in five minutes."

She walked toward the house with a dignified air. The black briefs hung low over her buttocks to reveal more than an inch of reverse cleavage into which the material made a slight dip.

The butler appeared on the terrace soon after Mrs. Miller had disappeared. He set up a small table and pulled two comfortable-looking cane chairs up beside it.

"What would you care to drink, Lieutenant?" he asked bleakly.

"Why, Chivers," I said excitedly, "you mean the day of the cop has come already?"

"Mrs. Miller suggested I make you a drink while you're waiting," he said blankly.

"Just bring a bottle of Scotch, ice and soda," I said. "It will save running in and out all the time with fresh drinks."

The look on Chivers' face would have stopped a clock, but he returned with a tray of the essentials and put it down on the table carefully, managing to avoid looking at me during the operation, then went back inside the house again.

I made myself a drink—the whisky was the blue-blood brand that never bottles a drop under thirty years old—and sipped it reverently, wondering if it's exporting their whisky that makes the Scotch a dour race.

Mrs. Miller returned to the terrace. I checked my watch and saw it had taken her four-and one-half minutes. When I saw that all she had done was throw a terry robe around herself, I wondered why it had taken her so long. The robe came down to about mid-thigh, and the top of it was open enough to show the inner flanges of her shining breasts.

She relaxed into one of the cane chairs and crossed her legs idly so the hem rode up to the tops of her thighs, and I caught a furtive glimpse of a small triangle of black material between them. Then she straightened the robe over her thighs, and the triangle was gone.

Her black, black hair had warm, sunny tints through it that were reflected in her eyes as she looked at me, a hesitant smile on her lips.

"I'm sorry I was rude," she said. "There's no reason why we can't be friends, is there?"

"You answer my questions and we'll wind up real chums," I said.

She made herself a Scotch on the rocks, then leaned back into the chair again, cradling the glass between the palms of both hands. "Good," she said in a purring, contented kind of voice. "Fire away!"

"The last time I was here, Kirkland arrived just as I was leaving," I said. "What did he want?"

"I asked him to call and visit with me," she said easily. "I was worried about the Keighley girl—I knew Kirkland was crazy for her and wanted to marry her even though she was owned by my husband. With Wally dead I wondered how she'd get along—she might need help. I thought Kirkland could tell me how she was fixed. But then, of course, by the time he got here you'd already told me Wally had left half his estate to her, so I didn't need to worry."

"It was a nice thought, anyway," I said over-politely. "You must be one of the newer-type wives."

"It wasn't a nice thought at all," she answered, ignoring my sarcasm completely. "She knew what it was like living with Wally and so did I. So naturally she had my sympathy—anyone who went through that ordeal had my sympathy!"

"But divorce would've been a bigger ordeal in your book?"

She stretched her arms above her head lazily. "I like this house, Lieutenant," she murmured, smiling dreamily. "I like the pool, the Bentley in the garage, the servants, the three closets it takes to hold my wardrobe..."

"The money—you told me already."

"So if anyone got a divorce it would have to be Wally," she said silkily. "All it would cost him would be a six-figure cash settlement. But living apart from me in the same house never worried him—I guess Rita Keighley was the reason why."

"That's why Kirkland got no reaction at all when he busted in here and told you about Rita three months back?"

"That's right," she nodded absently.

I made myself another drink. The sun was hot, the cane chair comfortable, the widow exotic—if I was still in my right mind, how come I was still a cop?

"Did your husband ever talk about his work at all?"

"Wally?" She smiled pityingly at me. "He never talked at all—about anything—to me, anyway."

"You still can't think of one good reason why anyone should want to kill him?"

"I couldn't get past his personality," she said. "That was enough reason for anybody who knew him!"

I finished the drink, put the glass back on the tray, and stood up.

"Leaving already, Lieutenant?" She looked up at me, shading the mocking expression in her eyes against the sun. "Just when we were getting to be real chums, like you said!"

I leaned down toward her, resting my hands on the arms of her chair so that my face came close to hers.

"I'm leaving, Mrs. Miller," I agreed. "I only came along for the ride and now I'm dizzy. You don't mind if I tell you I think you're lying in your teeth?"

Her arms came up and twined around my neck, pulling my head down until our lips met. Her mouth was open, and I could feel her tongue pushing against mine. There was a hot, ruthless passion in her kiss that would have singed the soul of an evangelist—what it did to mine was nobody's business but my own. Her robe fell open and her breasts pressed hard against my chest. I moved my hands down inside her robe, and cupping her firm buttocks, pulled her tightly against me. There was a soft throbbing in my groin, a quickening flow of blood which filled my yard and made it strain against her pelvis. Then, around the time I figured we were just getting to know each other, the fire went out. She put her hands against my chest and pushed me away abruptly.

I straightened, and the life quickly ebbed from my prick, leaving it limp and sulking over its lost pride.

"If you have to leave, Lieutenant—" The mocking smile on her face widened as she watched me with a collector's interest. A dull ache began to spread in my groin.

"I'm leaving," I said huskily. "And I still think you're lying in your teeth."

THE BRAZEN   53

She wagged her finger at me. "You're just saying that so you've got an excuse to come back."

"Why should I come back?"

"Can't you guess?" She looked at me archly. Her robe was still open, showing her full breasts in all their glory. "Make it tomorrow night," she said evenly. "I'll see the servants are out for the evening."

I looked down at her ripe breasts with their upstanding tips, at the rounded smoothness of her bare thighs, and the low-slung black briefs that only just covered her mound, and figured all I needed was just a little willpower and I could tell her to go jump in her own pool. Then I sneaked a second look at her briefs, and saw the thin fringe of curly hair peeking above them. It was a mistake.

"Around eight?" I asked.

I was on time for my date with the redheaded Mona Gray and we had an expensive dinner in candle-lit intimacy, then got up to my apartment around ten-thirty.

"You sure you invited me in just to hear your sound equipment, Al?" she asked as she walked into the living room.

"What else?" I said innocently. "Can I make you a drink?"

She sighed happily. "After the imported wine and the candles, you can make me something exotic."

I went along with that. She looked exotic enough herself, and it was only fitting. She was wearing a long black dress that was scooped low in front and even lower at the back. She wasn't wearing a bra, so that her boobs moved with a lazy rhythm of their own. I wondered idly if she was wearing anything at all beneath the dress which, with one quick look, you knew the designer had just been doodling when he created it.

"How about that drink?" she asked, cutting right across my idle speculations.

"Coming right up," I told her and went into the kitchen.

I made the usual for myself and put equal parts Scotch

and Irish on the rocks for Mona—at least a whisky drinker would rate that as exotic.

Mona was sitting on the couch when I got back, looking very relaxed. I just hoped the tab for the imported Riesling had been worth-while. She took the glass from me with a cautious look in her clear gray eyes.

"I was just remembering this is the kind of situation my mother warned me about," she said.

"I never knew your mother," I remembered. "If I had she might still be here."

She winced. "I love a modest man," she said. "If we're going to talk about you all the time, I'd rather hear some music. That's what I came here for after all—isn't that right? To listen to your fabulous sound equipment. I'm what you might call an audio buff."

"What would you like to hear?" I asked.

"Anything you like. I'm sure your taste is impeccable."

I looked at her doubtfully. "You having me on?"

She waved her hand. "Select, select."

"O.K., I'll select."

I selected something with softly throbbing drums and plaintive woodwinds, in keeping with the exotic tone that had been set for the evening. As the music started, and began to work up to a slow frenzy, I went back to the couch and sat down close, but not pushing it, to Mona. She sipped her drink, then looked at me reflectively.

"What do you call this?"

"Exotic," I said. "What do you call it?"

"I'll let you know later."

Five minutes later she handed me her empty glass to match mine and her eyes had a dreamy look in them when I returned to the couch.

"Sst!" she hissed commandingly when I started to make conversation because I thought I should say something to break the silence—anything at all, like what the Ayatollah was doing for Christmas, and who would be the next President of the United States.

"What did I say?"

THE BRAZEN

"I'm listening," she said in a dedicated voice. "The jungle beats, the fantastic rhythms. Doesn't it stir your blood, Al?" Give you a tingle?"

"A tingle—yeah."

"So there you are."

"No conversation then?" I asked.

"No conversation. Just the jungle beats."

"Fuck the jungle beats."

"Primitive, Atavistic Al."

The music finished about the same time as our drinks. I clapped my hands down on my thighs. "Yeah, well—" I said, leaving everything open.

"More music," she demanded. "More drums. I love it. It goes right through me. Heats the blood, and brings out the basic passion."

Encouraged, I found another cassette and slipped it into the player, and as the jungle drums and woodwinds swirled around us once more, settled back down on the couch next to Mona, close but not too close. Around an hour and three drinks later, the music stopped, and the only sound was the slight hum of the five speakers built into the walls. After some moments Mona seemed to shake herself back into the present from whatever jungle paradise the throbbing music had transported her. I wondered how much of those basic passions of hers had figured in her thoughts.

"That was great, Al." She sighed ecstatically. "Wonderful." She shook her head. "Oh well, I guess I should be going home soon. It's getting late." She gave me a warm smile. "Thanks for a lovely evening, Al. It's been fun."

"Sure," I said sourly. "Such nice clean fun."

"I have to get some sleep," she said apologetically. "You know how it is for a working girl—up early in the morning."

"Yeah," I grunted. "I guess it's quite inspiring, working for a criminal lawyer."

"It's very interesting," she said in a neutral voice. She

held her empty glass out to me. "I guess I will have one for the road."

She got it so fast even the whiskey was out of breath. I sank down on the couch beside her again, clutching my own drink in a nervous hand.

"Thanks," she said absently. "You know, Mr. Berkeley is a funny kind of guy as a boss. I liked poor Mr. Miller a lot better."

"Berkeley is a nervous character—he never stops twitching each time I talk with him," I said. "It doesn't seem right, a criminal lawyer having nerves like that—out of character somehow. Has he always been that way?"

"I don't know," Mona said helpfully. "I started the day Rita Keighley left and I worked for Miller most of the time."

"He was going to represent Shafer at the gambling hearing, wasn't he?" I asked casually.

"So he was—I guess Berkeley will handle it now. You see some screwballs in that office at times, Al! Shafer's one of them—it scares me to death just looking at him." She giggled suddenly, "There was another one this afternoon—real drama! Said it was a matter of life and death that he saw Berkeley right away. Didn't even wait for me to call his office—just kept on going and crashed straight in. I thought poor little Berkeley would have a heart attack, honest!"

I tried to keep the look of polite interest on my face, while I wondered why the hell I hadn't gone to a movie in the first place.

"I mean it was real tense," Mona went on. "He shouted something like, 'O.K., Berkeley! So you had me figured for the fall guy!' Then poor old Berkeley tried to hush him up but he had no chance. The other guy went right on at the top of his lungs, something about he didn't do it but they thought he did and asked him a hell of a lot of awkward questions and they could pull him in again any time he liked. They would for sure, he said, once they got around to the plant—"

"The what?" I nearly dropped my glass.

"The plant," she repeated. "I don't know what kind—he didn't look the type to grow orchids."

"I'll strangle that Polnik with my bare hands!" I growled.

"Huh?"

"Never mind—what else?"

"Then Berkeley slammed the door shut and I didn't hear any more," she said in anticlimax.

"That's too bad."

"Isn't it?" Her eyes sparkled wickedly. "You're supposed to be a cop, Al—I bet you can't make any more sense out of it than I did."

"What will you bet?"

"Ten dollars!"

"Be a shame to take the money," I said smugly. "Every word of it makes sense to me. Not only because I'm a cop—I guess my unbeatable deductive powers and genius I.Q. have got something to do with it, too."

"Why, Lieutenant Wheeler!"

"You think I'm kidding?" I sneered. "I could even name the guy who was doing all the shouting."

"That's impossible," she said flatly.

"I'll give you twenty-to-one odds I can name him," I offered. "How much do you want to bet? Put your money on the line—let's see something solid to back up your big mouth."

"Why—you!" She quivered in fury. "I'll bet fifty dollars you can't."

She was near busting out at the seams with the anticipation of cutting me down to dwarf-size, and I figured she was hooked.

"O.K.," I yawned. "So you stand to win a thousand bucks—like real spending money. But if I win what do I get? A measly fifty, that's all."

"Don't try and crawl out of it now, Wheeler!" She snarled, like a tigress on the prowl for a new mate, having just eaten the old one. "You can't welsh on a redhead with Irish blood in her veins!"

"I'm not welshing," I said calmly. "Just trying to figure some worth-while stakes on both sides. How about winner take all? Make it a real bet and I'll double the odds so you stand to collect two thousand."

"And—even though I know you can't—you somehow cheat me and win?" she asked suspiciously. "What do you get?"

"Winner takes all," I said blandly.

"Winner takes . . ." Her cheeks reddened suddenly. "You mean—me?"

"What's the matter?" I sneered. "The Irish blood take a sudden transfusion?"

"I'd like to—" She made a concentrated effort and simmered down a little. "Insults are cheap, Al Wheeler! You need a lesson and you're going to get it right where it hurts—in your pocketbook. I know what's going on in your miserable little mind. You think you'll get off the hook by frightening me out of the bet, don't you?" She tossed her head back in the kind of gesture that would've given Freud enough incentive for ten years' research.

"Well, you don't scare me one little bit! I accept the bet—I get two thousand if you lose and if I lose, you get me. O.K. Go ahead—name him!"

I breathed on the fingernails of my right hand, then rubbed them gently against the lapel of my coat. "James Kirkland?"

Her face changed color rapidly from red to white then back to red again while she stared at me, her eyes bulging.

"You—you couldn't know!" she said weakly. "How could—but it's not possible—"

"It's a kind of mental telepathy," I told her. "I can tune in on people's minds and that makes it easy. For the last ten minutes I've been tuned in on your wave length and if you don't mind me mentioning it, some of the words you've been thinking—"

She got to her feet in one quick movement and grabbed

THE BRAZEN

her purse from the arm of the couch. "Well," she said, smiling nervously, "I really have to go now. Thank you for the night out, it's been—well-different anyway."

I let her get two paces past me, then grabbed her elbow and swung her around so she was facing me again.

"The way I heard it, the redheaded Irish just never welsh on a bet," I said accusingly.

Her lips trembled for a moment, then she shrugged her bare shoulders resignedly. "I guess you heard right," she whispered.

I took her in my arms, and I could feel her body soft and pliant against my own. Her lips returned the pressure of mine and our tongues met briefly. I moved my hands down from her waist and slid them lightly over her firm buttocks. Gradually, I could feel the last of the resistance melting away from her, and she began to writhe sinuously against me. The jungle passions were beginning to stir, and I could almost hear the drums throbbing in the background. A long time later I let go of her reluctantly.

"Well!" She took a deep, shuddering breath. "Well, well, well." Her voice was uneven. "Say, you *are* pretty versatile for a cop."

"That was the overture," I croaked. "Now let's have the first movement."

"I have a feeling you're going to be a Shylock about this bet." She smiled tremulously, "You'll insist on collecting all you've got coming—right down to the very last pound of my flesh!"

Out of nowhere it hit me the moment she stopped speaking. Maybe it was a delayed reaction to that imported wine, or maybe the Scotch I'd drunk since we got to the apartment. I knew there was no percentage in trying to figure the cause—the important thing was the result and that always came out the same—remorse. This I get at the damnedest times; for me it's like hives and dandruff are for other people—hits when you least expect it.

"I just remembered," I told her gently, "you're a working girl and you got to get up early in the morning. I'll take that short, sharp interlude of passion as full payment of the bet—I'll do better even and drive you home."

I lit a cigarette while I waited ready to cut short her joyous and tearful thanks which I wanted no part of—it would be like turning a knife in the wound. They seemed a long time coming so I finally sneaked a look at her in case she'd lapsed into traumatic shock.

She was just standing there, glaring at me with a baleful glitter in her eyes, while the corners of her mouth were turned down in complete contempt.

"I'll never understand it," she said in a brittle voice. "All night you've been giving me a big buildup—for this? Shit! The intimate dinner complete with candlelight, the soft lights, and tall drinks in your apartment. The jungle rhythms—all calculated to create a cozy mood." She shook her head slowly, and there was a wondering look in her eyes. "Then the master stroke of an experienced and expert tactician—pressuring me into a sucker bet you knew you'd won before you even made it. So you won—with an unconditional surrender, no less—and now for no reason you chicken out. So what is it with you?"

"I figured for the first time in my life," I muttered hoarsely, "I was being decent."

"Oh, no!" She laughed for a few seconds, then stopped abruptly as she leaned forward and kissed me with a brazen frankness that blasted the remorse to hell and gone. While I was still catching up, she moved away gently, and looked at me again, but this time it was different.

"Al," she murmured in a tender, affectionate voice—the kind a loving mother uses to reproach her teen-age son after he'd just confessed to dynamiting City Hall.

Her hands moved deftly and surely, and a moment later the black dress was lying in a crumpled heap on the floor. All she was wearing was a tiny pair of black briefs. I gaped at her, at the small erect nipples that stood out from her magnificent breasts, at her gently rounded pelvis, her thighs, and the tiny black triangle between them.

THE BRAZEN

Then the tiny briefs were whisked off, and she was wearing nothing at all. I took a deep breath, and there was a faint humming sound in my ears.

For a timeless moment she stood motionless, confident in the flawless perfection of her figure. Between her shapely thighs her pubis was small and even, with a wispy tuft of red hair drawn in over her slit. Then she took a slow, languid step toward me.

"What are you waiting for, Al?" Her voice was low-pitched and vibrant. "Isn't it time you collected your winnings?"

I didn't need any more encouragement than that. My yard was already twitching and stiffening, and it took me about ten seconds flat to get rid of the clothes that restrained it. By the time I threw my briefs onto a chair, it was rock solid.

We came together on the couch, our bodies writhing and twisting around each other, our legs entwining. Our hands were everywhere, stroking, caressing, fondling, prodding. Her lips and tongue moved down over me, from the base of my jaw to my nipples, then my navel. The touch of her fingers as they closed lightly around my straining prick was cool. Then her lips were down there, closing around the bulbous head, and the tip of her tongue was working against it. My own hands moved up the insides of her smooth thighs, to the moist, pulsing sponge that crowned them. I could smell her scent, light and subtle, as I put my mouth against her.

Then she was beneath me, her legs drawn up and parted, and I was deep inside her, my shaft lunging in right to the hilt. She moved against me, her hips lifting from the couch, her legs clamping me in a tight embrace. She moaned more loudly and her head rolled from side to side. The sensation was flowing freely as our bodies pounded each other, and then as it came in a tremendous rush, she gave a loud cry and went rigid beneath me. Her fingernails raked my back and her cries echoed in my ears.

Then she slumped, and I slumped on top of her, drained and breathless.

Some time later, as we lay side by side on the couch, sharing a cigarette, I said, "Oh boy, I think I hit the jackpot."

"You sure did, lover," she murmured contentedly. "You sure as hell did."

Chapter Seven

IT WAS SO EARLY it was obscene when I dropped Mona outside her apartment building next morning. After a quick goodbye which didn't last more than fifteen minutes I drove four blocks and found a diner open for business. The guy in back of the counter had the bleary-eyed look of a codfish, caught two days back and left too long in the hot sun.

"Eggs benedict and a cup of coffee," I told him.

"Huh?" he grunted.

"Make sure it's breakfast coffee," I added. "I don't want to wind up on a psychiatrist's couch like that slob in the ads—all through drinking dinner coffee in the morning. You have to watch these things."

"Jeez!" He scowled at me like I was from the sanitation department and bitching about last week's lipstick thick on the cups.

"Eggs benedict and a cup of breakfast coffee," I repeated, slowly so it had time to penetrate. "Hurry it, huh?

I've got a lunch appointment at one, downtown, and I'd like to make it—that means you only got five hours left."

"It's coffee!" he said in a brooding voice. "You drink it now so it's breakfast coffee. Come back tonight you get dinner coffee. It's still the same goddamn coffee, ain't it?"

"I wouldn't be surprised," I said.

"Twelve hours a day, six days a week, I stand on my goddamned feet in this joint, trying to make a buck!" he said bitterly. "All the time it gets worse—you know that? Only last week a guy comes in and has me build him a sandwich—four kinds of salami, two kinds of liverwurst, ketchup on each layer and a base of chopped onions—ten lousy minutes it takes me on one sandwich, then he walks out on me because I don't got no marshmallow to top it off!"

"Tough!" I sympathized.

"There are some guys get their kicks out of making things tougher—if they aren't bad enough already." He picked up a long, thin-bladed carving knife and drove it violently into the counter where it stuck quivering right under my nose.

"Then you got to come busting in here," he snarled, "and you want *breakfast* coffee yet! You want I should label the coffeepots? Yeah—I guess you'd figure that was real fine!"

"So just pour it and I'll drink it," I said.

"All right! How you want the eggs?"

I saw the bright, murderous gleam in his eyes just in time. "As they come," I said hastily, "as they come!"

They came around twenty minutes later and I shouldn't have waited. I got back into the car wondering if I'd survive the drive out to Morgan and Scheer's chemical plant, and figured I had a chance if I kept my eyes shut. It didn't look like it was going to be my day at all.

I arrived at the plant sometime close to nine-thirty and talked with the guard on the gate. He figured both Morgan and Scheer died a long time back—he'd been working for the company the last twenty years and they were only a memory when he started—but the vice president in charge of production was a guy named Allison, and him I could see.

Ten minutes later I was sitting in a plush chair belonging to the vice president's office. Allison was a gray-haired, intelligent guy in his late fifties. We exchanged a few pleasantries then got down to business. I gave him a brief rundown on the two murders and the autopsy findings, then told him one of his employees was under suspicion.

"Curare?" Allison looked shaken. "Of course we use it here, Lieutenant—in processing tubocurarine, a muscle relaxer. Which of our employees is under suspicion?"

"Kirkland," I said. "James Kirkland."

"He has charge of the processing plant," Allison said heavily. "It hardly seems possible—he's got the makings of a brilliant biochemist!"

"Maybe he's not doing real bad as a murderer, either?" I said brightly and Allison winced.

"I sincerely hope this won't involve the company in any unpleasant publicity, Lieutenant," he said anxiously.

"And I hope to live to a virile old age," I said. "Maybe we'll both get lucky."

"He'd only need a minute quantity of the drug, of course," Allison said. "We manufacture under strict government control, but it would certainly be possible for a man in the position of trust that Kirkland holds to obtain that minute quantity."

"Is he working in the plant right now?" I asked.

"I'll check." He picked up the phone.

I lit a cigarette while I waited until he hung up about half a minute later.

"No, Lieutenant." He shook his head. "Hasn't been in the last two days, either. His assistant said he called in yesterday morning and said he'd picked up a virus infection that would keep him home for a few days."

"Thanks a lot, Mr. Allison," I told him. "You've been very helpful."

"What shall I do if he does show up for work?" he asked anxiously before I got to the door.

"I'd have him transferred to a less lethal operation someplace in the plant," I said. "You make aspirin here?"

I drove back into town—that part of town where Kirkland lived. Halfway down the street I saw what I was looking for—the living monument to stupidity, the only living monolith in captivity, the ape masquerading as man in the guise of a sergeant of police—Polnik.

He had a hurt look on his face when I parked at the curb, then got out and walked toward him.

"Must be a great party in there, Lieutenant," he said in a sour voice. "Those broads don't even come out yet."

"Like they're different from Kirkland," I said in a restrained voice.

"Huh?" Polnik blinked at me.

"Yesterday afternoon Kirkland was in Berkeley's office," I snarled. "How did he get past you? With a false beard?"

"I watched the place all day," Polnik said earnestly. "So help me, Lieutenant, he never come out that front door!"

"What about the back door?"

"Back door?" he croaked. "You never said nothing about a back door, Lieutenant!"

He was right, of course. I hadn't mentioned the possibility of a back door and it was my fault. Who the hell did I think I was, anyway, expecting Polnik to think?

"Never mind," I said wearily. "Let's go see if he's home now."

We stepped into the front hall of the apartment building and an overweight female in a sleazy, fur-trimmed robe made a kind of elephantine dance toward us. From the look of her bleary eyes and red-veined face she was obviously seeing the fuel crisis through in a boozy haze.

"What do you want?" she asked suspiciously in a furry voice to match the robe. "I'm the owner here."

"Police," I told her. "Sheriff's office—we want to see Kirkland."

"I haven't seen him in a couple of days," she said and sniffed loudly. "What's he done?"

"We just want to ask him some questions," I said patiently. "What's his apartment number?"

"Fourteen—first floor up," she said. "I'll show you the way."

She was three stairs up already before I had a chance to tell her not to bother—and then it was too late. We followed her up and she stopped outside the apartment and gestured toward the door marked 14. "In there," she said in a heavy, conspiratorial whisper which sounded louder than a wild shriek. I knocked on the door and waited—knocked some more until it was obvious I could wait all day and nobody would bother opening it.

"You think he's holed up in there?" the fat horror asked eagerly. "Maybe with a gun?"

"I think maybe he's out," I said tersely. "You got a back entrance to the building?"

"Sure," she said. "Opens out onto the alley."

"Nobody told me, Lieutenant!" Polnik said in a reproachful voice.

"You can't trust nobody these days," I agreed. "You lot a master key to the apartment?" I asked the woman.

"Sure—you want to take a look inside?"

"Yeah." What was the use?

"I'll go get it!" She waddled energetically back toward the stairs.

Polnik pulled a face that made him look even more repulsive. "Holy Christ!" he growled. "After her, even my old lady looks good."

"Yeah," I agreed. "Stay around her too long, and a guy would start wondering about the percentage in staying heterosexual."

"Huh?" The Sergeant stared at me doubtfully. "I'd never have figured you for one of those, Lieutenant," he said in a surprised voice.

"Heterosexual means normal!" I snarled.

"I get it!" He heaved a vast sigh of relief. "And nobody could accuse you of being that, huh, Lieutenant?"

I was saved from an answer or bloody mayhem, or maybe both, by the sound of the heavy creaking on the stairs that announced the return of Lady Macbeth. There are a lot of fancy phrases about breath and the way it comes—in deep sighs, quick gasps, short pants even. But this was the first time I ever heard it come in hysterical wheezes. It sounded like somebody had punched the keyboard of an organ, with all the stops pulled out.

"Here's—the—key!" she announced in a succession of baying yelps, like a short-winded bloodhound hot on the scent.

"You should take it easy," Polnik told her seriously, "or one of these days you'll drop dead on the stairs and they'll need a mechanical shovel to get you out of here!"

I turned the key in the door, then walked inside the apartment. The living room had as much character as a teen-age rock star. The one personal touch was a photo of Rita Keighley on the table, autographed, *I love you, Jimmy!—Rita*.

"Maybe he's shacked up in the bedroom with her?" a rumbling asthmatic wheeze queried in my ear.

"Not unless he raided the morgue," I said coldly. "Who told you to come in here, anyway?"

"I own the building!" she spluttered excitedly. "I got a right to know what's going on!"

There was no future in arguing with her right then, so I walked quickly across to the bedroom door and opened it. James Kirkland was shacked up in the bedroom all right, but there was nobody with him. He was alone in the ultimate sense of the word.

He lay sprawled across the bed on his back, his eyes wide open with a blank stare of final betrayal. Congealed blood stained the right side of his head and the washed-out bedspread underneath. There was a gun on the floor directly beneath his limp right hand.

I heard the sharp, gurgling intake of breath directly behind me and turned around in time to see Lady Macbeth's eyes roll upward as she tottered backward on her heels. Polnik made a frantic sideways leap just in time to get the hell out of the way as the colossus passed the point of no return and crashed to the floor with a thud that shook the whole building.

Polnik smiled proudly as he looked down on the prostrate ruin at his feet.

"Jeez, Lieutenant!" he said gratefully. "I got out from under just in time, huh?"

At six that night the citizens were enjoying the warm night air, while inside the Sheriff's office the temperature was rapidly sliding down past freezing point.

Lavers sat behind his desk scowling at me moodily while he chewed a cigar into small fragments.

"Let's go over it once more—for the last time!" he barked. "You hear me, Wheeler—the last time?"

"I hear you good, Sheriff," I said coldly.

"I'll even tell it the way you tell it," he conceded generously. "Rita Keighley stopped being Miller's secretary to become his full-time mistress—right? Then Kirkland falls for her real hard and he's still crazy about her even when he hears about Miller, right?"

"Love conquers all," I agreed.

"But not for too long," Lavers said. "After a while, Kirkland got jealous and then he got impatient. The Keighley girl valued all the material comforts Miller provided—the kind of money Kirkland made was no substitute. Somehow she found out about the will Miller had made, leaving her half his estate and she told Kirkland the good news.

"Sooner or later he saw all his troubles would be fixed if Miller died—he'd get both the girl and the money. He had easy access to a rare poison through his work at the chemical plant, so he took the curare and killed Miller! It's as simple as that, Wheeler!"

"Fine," I agreed, "right up to this point. Now tell me why he killed Rita—and balled up both his motives for killing Miller. With Rita dead there was no girl and no money."

"Panic, that's why," Lavers said confidently. "After he'd killed Miller the girl panicked. He must have been in her apartment when you arrived, and hid in the bathroom. The last thing he wanted was you to find him with her, so he clobbered you—it wouldn't be hard for a boy scout, never mind a full-grown man!"

"I got clobbered by a girl scout once," I said reminiscently. "She never did give me a chance to explain I was only practicing for my trail-blazer badge."

"Then Kirkland saw the girl would fall apart once any cop started questioning her," Lavers continued with enthusiasm. "She'd lost her nerve completely—and that made him panic, too. So he killed her—just like that."

"Then came back to the apartment a half-hour later, pretending he thought she was still alive?" I said in a wondering voice. "Christ, with an acting talent like that, why isn't he making a fortune in movies and not wasting it at Morgan and Scheer?"

"He could've gotten his nerve back, figured that was his best alibi—to pretend he was calling on her, not knowing she was dead!" Lavers snorted.

"O.K.," I said resignedly. "After that he goes home and thinks about it—gets so depressed with the whole deal that he blows his brains out finally?"

"I don't see why not. Like you said, he'd lost everything and gained nothing by two murders. Wouldn't you feel like blowing your brains out, Wheeler?"

"Doesn't everybody first thing in the morning?" I asked.

"I'll make a statement in good time to catch the morning editions," Lavers said almost happily, "and that's that!"

"Kirkland busted into Berkeley's office yesterday after-

THE BRAZEN 71

noon yelling he wasn't going to be the fall guy," I said. "What did that mean?"

"That's some garbled story you heard from Berkeley's secretary!" Lavers grunted. "I don't believe it—have you checked with Berkeley?"

"I haven't had time yet," I told him. "For sure, he'll deny it anyway."

"The case is closed!" Lavers glared at me. "Don't you forget it, either."

"When Rita Keighley opened the door of her apartment to me, she said quote If you're one of Johnnie's boys you can tell him from me unquote. Johnnie meaning Quirk—who else? So there was a connection between Rita and Quirk—there was a connection between Miller and Quirk."

"Sure," Lavers grated. "We know Quirk hired Miller to represent his so-called sales manager, Shafer, at the committee hearing on gambling. Quirk probably saw the Keighley girl around the office when she was still working there—she was a nice-looking girl, wasn't she? So Quirk had been bothering her for the most obvious reason a man can bother a girl—I don't have to explain that to *you*, Wheeler?"

"All right—you've got all the answers," I admitted. "How about the never-loving widow who's gotten rid of a husband who was a bore and his mistress who was going to inherit half his estate. She knew Kirkland. He came to see her when I was up at the house. It all looks a little too convenient for me. And how about Berkeley? He picks up his late partner's share of the business for free if both beneficiaries under Miller's will should die, and he's halfway there already."

"I'll worry about him if and when Mrs. Miller drops dead," Lavers said wearily.

"Twenty-four hours," I said. "That won't make any difference. Just give me another twenty-four hours to nose around a little more. If I don't come up with anything new by then, I'll give up."

"If I agree, will you get the hell out of my office right now?"

"Sure," I said coldly. "You know me, Sheriff, I'm the sensitive type. I can sense when I'm not wanted."

He checked his watch deliberately. "You've got till a quarter of seven tomorrow night!"

"I'm gone already," I promised.

Chapter Eight

THE DOOR of the Cone Hill house opened and the widow stood looking at me, making a nice change from the butler.

"I'm even punctual," I said. "It's right on eight."

She wore a pale blue robe that offered a teasing glimpse of the inner slopes of her breasts rising from the deep cleavage that divided them. Her lips parted in a slow smile as she looked carefully into my eyes.

"I see you remembered," she said evenly. "I'm glad you were on time—I was starting to get bored all by myself, alone in this big house."

I followed her through the hall and into the living room; we finished up at the well-stocked bar that ran half the length of one wall.

"I'm glad I've graduated from the library," I told her. "A thirst for knowledge is just fine, but who can drink a book?"

"Wally never even tried reading a book," she said. "You make the drinks?"

"Sure," I said promptly and moved in back of the bar.

"An old-fashioned for me," she said. "I'm just an old-fashioned girl at heart."

I made the drinks while she lit a cigarette and looked at me again, her cold dark eyes making me twitch a little like a bug under a microscope.

"We should get onto a first-names basis," she said crisply. "Calling a man 'Lieutenant' when there are just the two of us in the house cramps my style. My name is Gail."

"Al," I said.

"Why don't we make ourselves comfortable on the couch?" she suggested. She led the way, and once again I found myself admiring the slinky movement of her buttocks beneath the robe.

I took my drink with me and joined her on the couch, my pulse rate stepped up a little as I sat down.

"How's the investigation coming along?" she asked idly.

"We keep on getting new developments," I told her. "Like another body."

"Someone else has been murdered?" She stiffened her body unconsciously as if to ward off a blow. "Who?"

"Kirkland," I said. "Exit the college boy bit—but he wasn't murdered, he suicided. Blew his brains out sometime last night."

"He must have had a reason?" Her body relaxed again into its normal symphony of curves.

"The Sheriff has a theory." I went on and gave her a fairly detailed rundown—it was curare that killed both her husband and Rita Keighley—Kirkland had access to the poison—Lavers' ideas on the motivation for both murders.

Her glass was empty by the time I'd finished. I took it with me across to the bar and made us both fresh drinks.

"It's the Shcriff's theory, you say?" Shc bent hcr hcad to light a cigarette, then looked up at me again. "But not yours?"

"It leaves too many gaps for me," I said. "And we don't know for sure that Kirkland did kill himself yet—not until the doctor's finished his autopsy and the lab boys are all through."

"But you just told me he did."

"That was how it looked." I took the drinks back with me and sat down on the couch, a little closer to her this time, close enough for our knees to touch.

She sipped some of her new drink, then shrugged her shoulders delicately. "You just don't want to let go of your prime suspect—me!"

"That's a shrewd observation, Gail," I said admiringly. "You can even drop those words 'prime suspect' and you're still absolutely right!"

"That subtle approach of yours is irresistible, Al!" There was a tart flavor to her voice. "Wally used to excel at that kind of dialogue—I guess that's how he overwhelmed his little stenographer in the first place."

I winced. "Sorry—I didn't realize subtle dialogue and an oblique approach were necessary. The way I had it figured, you invited me here tonight with the assurance the servants wouldn't be home—and the way you put it, I figured conversation of any kind would only be a drag."

"You must have misunderstood me," she said in a slightly bored voice. "I was just being polite. I thought you had a lot more questions and I'd give you a chance to ask them when we wouldn't be interrupted."

"And I see you got yourself nice and ready for the occasion," I said, lifting the hem of the robe between my fingers and drawing it a short way up her bare thigh.

"I'm wearing this because it's comfortable." She brushed my fingers away with an impatient gesture. "Don't do that. It makes me nervous." She flattened the robe over the exposed part of her thigh.

The buzzer sounded, surprisingly loud inside the room. Gail Miller put her glass down on the small table, then stood up.

"You're expecting company?" I asked.

"No." She shook her head. "Only you—and you don't qualify under that heading."

She walked out of the room and I got that rear view again. The soft material of her robe emphasized the slow, sensual roll of her hips and the classical orbs of her buttocks.

I heard the murmur of voices in the hall, then a few seconds later they came into the living room. Gail came first, followed by Johnnie Quirk. Behind him came the punch-drunk Elmer, still looking twice as large as life and around three times as repulsive. A couple of seconds behind them, judging her entrance with a fine sense of timing, came Janie the housekeeper.

She wore a black shirt which tightly molded the outline of her small, conical-shaped breasts in arrogant detail, and the same pair of tight-fitting jeans. Her eyes were hidden behind a pair of dark glasses, and there was a giant-sized emerald ring on one finger.

Quirk's head lifted a fraction when he saw me, like a birddog again, and I almost looked to see if his tail stood out in a straight, horizontal line behind him. Then he smiled politely and nodded. "Good evening, Lieutenant."

"Are you installing a one-armed bandit in the butler's pantry?" I asked curiously.

His face darkened. "I was a client of Miller's—you know that. I figured the right thing to do was to call on his widow and offer my sympathy—that's why I brought my housekeeper along with me. I wouldn't want Mrs. Miller to misunderstand my motives. I don't appreciate your sense of humor, Lieutenant!"

"Who does?" I agreed and climbed out of the couch onto my feet.

"Leaving already?" Gail Miller said casually. "Let me walk you to the door."

I walked past Janie on my way to the door. Behind those dark glasses, I couldn't tell whether she was looking at me or not—she didn't say anything or give any sign of recognition. I wondered for an idle moment if Quirk had

THE BRAZEN 77

a key and maybe she'd just stand there forever unless he wound her up again.

"How's your investigation coming along, Lieutenant?" Quirk said as I came level with him. His voice was friendly again. "Making any progress?"

"Mrs. Miller can give you the detail," I said. "You were a friend of Rita Keighley's—why didn't you tell me?"

"Rita Keighley?" He frowned then shook his head. "Not me, Lieutenant."

"That's what she told me," I said.

"I can't figure out why she'd say that." He laughed shortly. "Maybe I should feel flattered?"

"Yeah." I kept on going, past Elmer's flattened face, and I felt his beady eyes staring at me malignantly.

"You took a dive in the tenth," I said suddenly when I was real close. "You just stopped and lay down—I saw it with my own eyes."

"That's a lie!" he said hoarsely. "Where did you see it?"

"All over." I sighed heavily. "Every fight it was the same. Most times you'd dive before the other guy even connected—it got real monotonous!"

"You're a dirty, lying—" He almost foamed at the mouth.

"Shut up!" Quirk said coldly. "He's riding you—the Lieutenant has a lousy sense of humor!"

When we reached the front door, Gail Miller looked at me scornfully. "The trouble is there are so many of your type!" she said in a sneering voice. "Little men who hide behind a uniform or a badge. I bet you think you're real brave, sounding off like that, knowing if either of them had even lifted a little finger, you'd have called out four carloads of police and had them tossed into jail!"

"If you don't know already," I said patiently, "Johnnie Quirk is in the rackets, and Elmer is his muscle. Talk to them any other way and they'd figure I was sick or something. Maybe I am—I'm real sick of you right now."

"Get out!" she said tautly. "Get out of my house!" She jerked the door open wide. "And don't come back without a search warrant."

"You're a tease, Gail," I said sadly, "and also a woman—and they're the very worst kind!"

The door rocketed shut behind me as I stepped out on the porch. By the time I got into the car the frustrations inside me had come to a quick boil. Visiting with the widow I'd figured might get me some new information along with an exciting evening—and I'd gotten neither. Three out of the twenty-four hours Lavers had given me had gone already and I didn't even know where to start looking.

I drove out of the driveway into the street, thinking sourly about Quirk, his housekeeper, and his goon. Then I remembered he also lived in Cone Hill and right now he was out visiting. I had to do something to get rid of the frustration and maybe that was the answer—take a look inside his house while he wasn't there. It was a stupid idea—I didn't know what I was looking for, and if there was anything worth finding Quirk wasn't the guy to leave it lying around anyway—but right then the idea seemed good because it gave me something to do.

I drove past the house five minutes later and parked the car half a block farther down on the other side of the street, then walked back. There were no lights showing in the front of the house as I walked up the driveway, so it looked like an elementary exercise in housebreaking. I tried the windows along the side of the house. The third one down was unlocked and slid upward easily so I threw one leg over the sill and climbed into the room.

It was pitch dark inside. I waited for a couple of seconds listening but there was no sound. My eyes gradually got used to the dark and I could make out the dim outlines of the furniture. I moved forward and bumped into the hard edge of a desktop in the center of the room; then my fingers located the metal base of a lamp and pressed the switch.

THE BRAZEN

Maybe I'd gotten lucky for a change, finding Quirk's desk without even trying. I sat in the chair behind it, lit a cigarette, then pulled open the lefthand top drawer. At the same time I heard a click and the overhead lamp suddenly flooded the whole room with harsh, glaring light. My insides flipped painfully, like the first time I realized there was a practical reason for girls being different.

"All right, punk," a sneering voice said. "Put your hands on the desk nice and slow and maybe you'll live a little while longer!"

He stood in the open doorway, wearing a black silk robe over lemon silk pajamas. The thick, curly blond hair was rumpled, giving him a boyish look, only the cold glitter in his eyes and the gun in his hand were out of character.

The next time—if there ever was one—I had frustrations, I'd take them straight back to the apartment and drown them in Scotch, I figured bleakly. Frustrations had given me a hole in the head where my memory used to live. I'd forgotten all about Pete Shafer and now it looked like he was all set to give me a hole in the head where all of me lived—period.

He walked toward me slowly, a tight grin on his face.

"You should be laughing, flatfoot!" he said. "You're the cop with the great sense of humor, isn't that right? Don't you figure this whole situation is real funny?"

"I'm not sure yet," I told him. "Check with me tomorrow."

"You got a search warrant, of course?"

"I'm the forgetful type," I admitted sorrowfully. "For sure I left it on the table in my apartment—it won't take thirty minutes to go get it."

"Now that's a real shame." He shook his head in mock sympathy. "Breaking in like that and committing a felony."

He came up to the edge of the desk and lifted the phone with his free hand, while the other hand held the gun pointing directly at my face in a dedicated, unswerving steadiness.

"Johnnie's over at the Miller house," he said casually as he dialed the number. "I got the feeling he won't like this, sweetheart—not at all."

There were a few seconds' silence and I could hear the steady beep of the widow's phone, then a tinny, feminine voice answer.

"Like to talk with Mr. Quirk, please," Shafer said and waited a few more seconds. "Johnnie? It's Pete. Guess what just crawled in through a window and was busy going through your desk. The cop! . . . Yeah, that's right—Wheeler. . . . No, he's still here—I got a gun pointing right into his face. . . . No, no warrant—I guess it was strictly his own idea. What do I do with him?"

The grin slowly faded from his face as he listened carefully. "You're sure?" he said soberly. "Yeah—I guess there's no reason why not. I'll take care of it, Johnnie." He hung up the phone gently and looked at me again.

"Can I go now?" I asked him. "Does Quirk feel like giving me a break if I promise I'll go straight from now on?"

"You're not going anyplace, flatfoot," he said softly, "not anyplace at all."

"You're going to keep me here—maybe chained to the wall?" I said, grinning weakly.

"I'll give you a rundown—I can use the practice," he said coldly. "I'm up in my room in bed, but not asleep, when I think I hear someone moving around in here. So I grab Johnnie's gun—I know he keeps it in his bureau—and come looking. I switch on the light and see a guy at the desk. He takes a shot at me and I shoot back automatically. His slug misses me and ends up in the wall right beside my head. My slug ends up in his guts and by the time I get to him, he's dead. Believe me, I'm amazed when I find out the guy burglarizing the place was a cop!"

"You don't think you'd get away with it?" I sneered.

"We time it right." He glanced at his watch. "Ten minutes from now Johnnie will be coming up the driveway—just in time to hear the two shots, and he'll have Janie and the muscle with him, two more witnesses. All I got to do is shoot you, then use your gun to put a slug into the wall. They'll find your fingerprints all over the window—and that desk. It's a breeze, my friend."

I had the nasty feeling he was right. Lavers would shake his head and figure that's what happened when a cop got too unorthodox—only a screwball like Wheeler would think of burglary as a natural extension of a cop's duties.

Shafer slid a pack of cigarettes out of the pocket of his robe and shook one onto the desk in front of me. A moment later he dropped a book of matches beside it.

"Help yourself, copper," he said. "But real slow, huh, so you don't make me nervous?"

"Sure." I picked up the cigarette and lit it, wondering why this particular one should taste so much better than all the others when I've been smoking the same brand these last five years.

Shafer checked his watch again. "You got eight minutes still, copper. Feeling nervous?"

"Who wouldn't?" I said. "Just for my own curiosity— did Quirk kill Miller? Or was it you?"

"You made two bum guesses already!" The sneering grin split his face again. "With what you got coming, that makes you a three-time loser?"

"O.K.," I said. "So neither of you killed him—then what's the connection?"

"Miller was going to hold my hand in front of that committee—you knew that already," he said impatiently.

"There's got to be a bigger connection," I said. "What the hell—in five minutes I'm a cadaver!"

He shrugged his shoulders negligently. "This I don't get at all, copper. If Johnnie made a different kind of connection with Miller he don't tell me nothing about it." He looked at his watch again. "Four minutes you got."

"Maybe there's one small thing I should mention," I said politely, "like what every torpedo should know."

"I told you the first time we met you'd die laughing," Shafer said. "Go right ahead—for another three and a half minutes I can take it."

"Thanks," I nodded gratefully. "It's just that I'm not carrying a gun."

"When I see a cop in nothing else but a union suit—then I'll believe he's not carrying his gun," he snapped. "You need to try harder, punk!"

"It's on the level," I insisted. "I was inside the Miller woman's house when Quirk came calling and busted up a sweet little romance—you don't believe me, call him again and check."

"He already said you were there," Shafer scowled. "It don't prove nothing."

"Well, what do you think?" I said confidently. "There were other things on our minds. Christ, we were only just getting down to it when Johnnie and the others arrived. Almost, but not quite. So O.K., we were all set for an intimate evening. You think I carry a gun to that kind of assignment?"

His mouth twisted viciously. "Keep talking," he snarled. "Now you got two-and a-half minutes left."

"No gun means no slug in the wall close to your head," I said reasonably. "It means you can't say self-defense anymore. The way it'll stack up, you shot an unarmed man who also happened to be a police lieutenant. They'll call it murder, Pete, and Quirk will have a sad look on his face when they put you away for life."

"You're lying!" A fleeting doubt showed in his eyes for a moment. "Open your coat!"

"The hell with you," I said pleasantly.

"I'll give you three seconds!" he snapped.

"All this time you got to give away—you keep on giving me minutes and now it's seconds yet! I get a pain in the ears from listening, Shafer. The only way you're going to prove I'm lying is the hard way—you got to shoot me first to find out."

His face whitened under the heavy tan and for a while there, I figured I'd made my biggest and final mistake. But he didn't pull the trigger even though his finger quivered with the temptation. His face smoothed out again and he managed a tight grin. "O.K., wise guy," he said. "I'll wait for Johnnie—he'll be back any time now."

"Fine," I said casually, "and while we're waiting I'll just call the Sheriff's office and let them know where I am."

I started to reach for the phone with my left hand before I'd finished speaking and my fingers closed around the instrument before Shafer reacted.

"Drop it!" he snarled.

My gamble paid off—instead of simply pulling the trigger, he smashed the gunbarrel down across my wrist. I was concentrating so hard right then I didn't even feel the pain. My right hand jerked the .38 Police Special out of the belt holster and lifted it above the level of the desktop.

I saw the sudden fear in Shafer's eyes and knew I just didn't have the time to wait and see if now he'd have the right reaction and shoot. I triggered the .38 three times in succession because with only the width of the desk separating us, I wanted to be sure he was very dead.

At that range the impact of a .38 slug must have equaled a hit by a ten-ton truck—three ten-ton trucks. Shafer's gun dropped onto the desktop and the fear in his eyes suddenly lost its urgency as he crumpled onto the carpet. I moved around the desk fast and took a close look—all three slugs had hit him in the chest and now he wasn't going anyplace except to a refrigerated drawer in the morgue.

I figured I had to keep moving fast because any moment now Johnny Quirk, Janie, and the muscle would be walking into the house. I wrapped a handkerchief around his gun, lifted it, and aimed carefully at an invisible spot about six feet up on the wall directly behind the desk, then pulled the trigger twice before I dropped the gun back onto the desktop again and returned the handkerchief to my pocket.

The sergeant who answered my call at the Sheriff's office came awake fast when I told him I'd just had to kill a guy in self-defense and for him to call the Sheriff and let him know where I was and what happened. As I hung up, I heard the sound of a car coming up the driveway.

Chapter Nine

"WE HEARD the shots O.K., Pete—but five? How many slugs does it take to—" Quirk's voice died abruptly as he stepped past the open door into the room and saw me standing by the desk.

Then it played like the script of that old, tired movie everybody's seen before. Cut from medium shot of Wheeler standing beside desk to close-up of Quirk's face registering blank surprise. A moment later he looks down at something on the floor—cut to close-up of Shafer's body, then back to Quirk, now registering bewildered horror as he comes to realize . . .

Janie and the muscle came into the room behind Quirk and went through the same routine—only if Janie registered any emotion behind those dark glasses it didn't show.

It was the overweight, punchy Elmer who reacted first. He came across the room toward me, his huge fists clenched and looking like business.

"You killed Pete," he growled deep in his throat. "For

that I'm going to tear you apart, punk!" His beat-up face contorted into the kind of mask an African witch doctor would trade five wives for gladly.

I lifted the .38 until the barrel pointed directly at his massive chest. "Relax, Elmer," I told him. "You'd only embarrass the morguekeeper—he'd need to cut you in half first to fit his storage."

Elmer came to a sudden stop, his face blurred with indecision—then he took another look at Shafer's corpse and obviously made up his mind to stay right where he was.

"You killed Pete?" Quirk said in a wondering voice. "How in hell did that happen?"

"I still can't figure it myself," I said blandly. "He must have been a psycho. Knowing the rest of you were visiting with Mrs. Miller, I figured it was a good chance to stop by and ask him a couple of questions. He invited me in here, told me to sit down over there behind the desk—acted real friendly. I'd hardly asked the first question when he blew his stack."

"You lousy, lying—" the muscle exploded.

"Shut up, Elmer!" Quirk said sharply. "I want to hear this—hear it good!"

"Yeah—" I edged a little more of the bland quality into my voice, enough, I hoped, to rasp against his nerve-ends like coarse sandpaper. "He started babbling something about he wasn't going to take any more of this persecution—that committee was crowding him hard enough and now me. There was a real crazy look in his eyes—he was almost screaming by the time he finished—then he suddenly pulled a gun and fired two shots at me. They missed by that much—" I held my thumb and index finger close together so they almost touched "—so I didn't get a choice. Either I shot back or he wasn't going to miss the third time."

"Pete fired two shots at you?" Quirk repeated in a dull monotone. "I guess that means the slugs must be around here someplace?"

THE BRAZEN

"Sure." I pointed to the wall behind the desk. "Right there about six feet up. How they came so close and still missed me, I'll never know."

"And Pete opened the front door to you, then asked you in here, huh?"

"That's right." I grinned at him happily. "You don't figure I'd burglarize the house, do you, Johnnie?"

He closed his eyes tight for maybe five seconds, then opened them again slowly. "I guess somebody should call the police, Lieutenant."

"I already have," I said smugly. "Should be here in a few minutes."

Janie looked around the room in agitation. "I need a drink," she said in a wan voice. "Any law against it, Lieutenant?"

"Not if you make me one, too," I said.

She walked across to the bar with quick, nervous strides, her pert backside swinging gently beneath the denim.

"You got it all figured out, haven't you, copper?" Quirk said bitterly. "One of these days you'll get too goddamned smart and I'll be right behind you, waiting for it!"

"Suit yourself, Johnnie," I said mildly. "Who gets promoted to sales manager now there's a vacancy—Elmer?"

Janie came back from the bar, a glass in each hand. She stopped directly in front of me.

"Scotch on the rocks—O.K.?" She held out a glass toward me.

"I wouldn't bitch about a dash of soda," I said gallantly. "Not after I mussed up your nice clean carpet with Shafer, and everything."

"Huh?" the dark lenses retained their opaque blankness.

"If you're the housekeeper around here, don't you get to clean up the mess?" I asked interestedly.

Her mouth curved slowly into an appreciative smile,

then she turned around and took the other drink across to Quirk.

"How about that, Johnnie?" She gurgled with laughter as she gave him the glass. "You never said nothing about cleaning up the joint when I signed the contract."

"Shut your stupid mouth!" he said viciously. "I'm in no mood right now." He jerked his wrist suddenly so the contents of the glass splattered over her face.

She turned away from him in a slow, careful movement, taking off the dripping sunglasses as she looked at me again. Her face was completely devoid of expression—only the bright blue eyes burned with an intense flame.

"You were right, cop," she said. "I do get to clean up now. Only Johnnie's such a gentleman he don't like coming straight out with it, so he gives me a hint."

"That Johnny," I said. "Always making with the bright ideas—like Shafer told me, he's a real smart boy!"

"Cut the clowning and get out of here!" Quirk snarled at Janie. "Or you'll be a carhop again before you know it."

She inclined her head in a curiously gracious gesture, then walked out of the room, closing the door gently behind her.

"We gonna stand here all night?" Elmer demanded.

I heard the squeal of tires as a car entered the driveway.

"You've been such a good boy, Elmer," I told him, "you get to open the front door to the rest of the cops."

He glared at me for a moment, then swung around and stomped out into the hall. A short time later, Polnik came into the room, followed by Doc Murphy and one of the crime lab boys toting a camera.

"The Sheriff had to go out of town sudden-like, Lieutenant," Polnik explained. "Won't be back till morning."

"O.K.," I said. "It only needs a clean-up job anyway—the story will keep for Lavers until morning."

THE BRAZEN 89

"Do you have a license, Wheeler?" Doc Murphy asked interestedly. "I thought humans were out of season?"

"When you've dug those three slugs out of him, Doc," I said lightly, watching Quirk's face while I spoke, "I'd like them for my souvenir collection."

Johnnie's face went white, then he turned away quickly and went across to the bar.

"You're just a ghoul, Wheeler," Murphy said good-naturedly. "You want I should mount the skull on a small trophy pedestal?"

"Shut up, both of you!" Johnnie shouted suddenly from the bar. "That guy was a friend of mine!"

"Pardon me," Murphy said politely and went on with his cursory examination.

"Don't take it so hard, Johnnie," I said in a soothing voice. "Friends like Shafer you can get any day of the week."

"I'll get you for this, Wheeler," he said, almost choking on the words. "Like I said, one time you're going to make a big mistake—and when you turn around I'll be right behind you!"

"That's what they call a friend in need," I said gratefully. "Which reminds me—Shafer's going to need a funeral?"

"I'll take care of the details," he whispered. "You take care of yourself from now on, cop."

I turned around and saw Polnik looking at me curiously.

"The punk with the big mouth?" He made it a question. "You want I should book him for anything, Lieutenant?"

"Like what?"

"You name it, I got it," he said confidently.

"Not right now, but I appreciate the offer," I thanked him. "I want pictures of the body before it's moved—and there are two slugs in the wall over there." I pointed out their exact location. "I want pictures of those holes before you dig the slugs out. That's about it—I've had a long hard day so I'll leave you the detail."

"Sure, Lieutenant," Polnik said, nodding placidly. "You don't get to find the Voyant woman yet?"

I goggled at him for a moment, then remembered. "Not yet, Sergeant," I said confidentially, "but I'm still working on it."

"I'd sure like to meet that one," he sighed heavily. "Her in a sarong and all!"

It was a quarter of midnight when I pushed the buzzer outside Mona Gray's apartment. Maybe it was kind of late to visit without calling first, but I figured I needed some relaxation and where else could I get the kind of relaxation I needed? I had to press the buzzer three more times before the door finally opened.

Mona stood there, a wide yawn on her face, rubbing her eyes sleepily. She was wearing a flimsy nightdress that was not quite opaque and which clung to her in the right places. I could see the heaviness of her breasts through it, and the outline of her thighs. She stopped rubbing and her eyes opened wide. "You!" she said. "I should have known."

"You should be careful who you open the door to, dressed like that," I said. "I could have been your friendly neighborhood rapist. Or is it a party?"

"Who said anything about a party?" she wailed despairingly as I stepped inside the apartment and closed the door behind me fast.

"That's what happens when I'm around," I said modestly. "Suddenly it's a party."

Mona walked into the living room with me, staying close behind.

"What do you want at this time of night?" she moaned. "Oh Jesus, maybe you better not answer that. I'm still sore and bruised all over."

"I'll go and make us a drink," I said.

"Ah, well, here goes my early night." She gave a long sigh, then collapsed onto the couch.

THE BRAZEN

I found the Scotch in her kitchen. I made a couple of herculean drinks, then carried them back into the living room. Mona had both eyes closed, so I leaned down and gently prodded one nipple like I was pressing an elevator button. Her body jerked, then she opened one eye and looked at me with long-suffering patience.

"What the hell?" she complained huskily. "If I call a cop you'll only walk back in here again."

She took the glass out of my hand as I sat beside her on the couch, tasted the drink cautiously, then looked at me with a wondering expression on her face.

"This is another of your exotic drinks?"

"Just Scotch."

"Yeah?" She drank a little more. "Hey, you're right. Terrific. Really something."

I swallowed some of my own drink and relaxed, feeling it light a mellow bonfire in my veins.

"I had a long hard day," I said somberly, "and the evening only got worse. You know something? I needed somebody to come home to—somebody with a sympathetic, not to say hot-blooded, disposition. You may not believe this but you're the only one I know.

"How lucky can I get?" she said acidly.

"The sympathy bit doesn't get a play?"

"Not in my theater," she said determinedly.

"I shot somebody tonight—in self-defense," I said. "Then I got ulcers trying to make it look like self-defense. How about that?"

"If you've got ulcers, give up Scotch," she snapped. "which might tame your imagination, too."

"That sucker bet of yours, Kirkland,"—I kept right in there, pitching—"he killed himself sometime last night— we found the body in his apartment this morning."

This time she turned her head and looked at me with her eyes wide open. "On the level?"

"Sure," I said honestly. "And so was the self-defense bit."

"Who was it?" she asked breathlessly.

"Shafer."

"Tell me about it!"

So I told her about it in detail, maybe kind of skipping over what I thought were inessential details, like the contours of Gail Miller's boobs and the way her robe had slid seductively across her high buttocks.

"Gosh! I'm sorry, Al," Mona said warmly when I'd finished. "I figured you came up here because you didn't have anything better to do, and I was mad at you for it—it wasn't exactly a compliment to me. Let me get you another drink." She grabbed the empty glass out of my hand and disappeared into the kitchen.

She was back in no time, pressing the new drink into my hand and the warm length of her thigh against mine.

"I've been a bitch, Al!" She kissed me gently on the lips. "Let me make it up to you?"

"You know I'm a soft touch," I said happily. "I never could resist an offer like that." Just in time I caught the warning signal in her eyes. "From you, that is, honey!" I added quickly.

"Keep it that way!" she cautioned me. "Do you really think it was Kirkland who murdered Mr. Miller and that poor Keighley girl?"

"No," I said. "But right now I don't have any other candidate to take his place—and it's beginning to worry me."

"What about Miller's wife—his widow, I mean?"

"Sure," I said. "Then what about Berkeley? His motives are as good as hers. And what about Quirk, or maybe his muscle-boy—his housekeeper even? It doesn't need any physical strength to poison someone. What about you?"

"Me?" Her voice suddenly jumped an octave.

"I'm only kidding." I patted her thigh in what started out as a reassuring gesture and finished up altogether different.

"Don't make jokes like that, Al, please!" she gasped. "It scares me to death."

THE BRAZEN 93

"You remember seeing either Shafer or Quirk around the office much?" I asked her. "Was it only Miller they talked to—or Berkeley as well?"

Mona thought for a moment, and my hand did a little more roaming, moving up her thigh unerringly to where it all mattered. Suddenly, she clamped her hand down on mine. "For Christ's sake, don't distract me." She tightened her grip on my hand still more. "I can remember them coming into the office a few times, but I guess I never paid too much attention. I'm sure it wasn't only Mr. Miller they saw each time—they would have seen Mr. Berkeley too."

"How about Kirkland?"

"The only time I ever saw him was the one I told you about—when he rushed in and started shouting at Mr. Berkeley."

"Mrs. Miller?"

"I don't ever remember seeing her around the office."

"It was only a thought anyway," I said regretfully.

"If there was only something I could do to help!" Mona said earnestly. A wicked gleam suddenly glowed in her eyes and her lips parted in a brilliant smile.

A moment later she squirmed out of my grip, walked across to the light switch, and flicked it off. That left only the soft illumination of one shaded lamp that stood on a small coffee table all by itself in the far corner of the room, and which silhouetted her figure beneath the gauzy nightgown she was wearing.

She came halfway back to the couch and stopped, her face was in shadow and I couldn't tell anything by the expression. Then she bent forward, and taking the hem of her nightgown, lifted it over her head in one quick movement, and tossed it onto the couch beside me. The glow from the light softly burnished her body. Between her legs the wispy tuft of her delta looked as if it were on fire.

She came across to the couch, and leaning over me, began to unbutton my shirt, pulling it away from my chest then bending over me to give each one of my nipples a light nip between her teeth. Then her mouth was glued wetly to mine, and as our passions began to throb, I thought I could hear the jungle drums again in the background.

I lay passively back on the couch while she undressed me, taking her time about it. Her movements were slow, deliberate, and I lifted myself slightly from the couch to make it easier for her to take off my briefs. She eased them down over my rampant yard, which she took in her hand, as straddling me, her legs wide apart, she lowered herself down onto it, her moist, warm sheath enveloping it completely.

"You think I can be a help, Al?" she asked in an artfully innocent voice as her body began to move over me.

"Maybe you can at that," I said in a choked voice, letting her take the initiative all the way.

Chapter Ten

I PATTED the honey-blonde curls on top of Annabelle Jackson's head in a brotherly gesture as I went past her desk.

"Good morning, honey-chile," I said cheerfully. "What's cooking with you? and don't give me any of that southern fried chicken crap!"

She lifted her head and looked at me in amazement. "What makes you-all so bright and happy this morning?" she asked blankly. "After what happened last night I'd have figured—or maybe you just hadn't shot a man in weeks and it was getting you down—is that it?"

"Well, well," I said fondly. "If it isn't good old Annabelle Freud, I do declare!"

"For a moment I wondered," she said in a detached voice. "Excuse me for being a drag, but the Sheriff's been in his office since nine-thirty waiting for you—and as it's now ten-thirty . . ."

"I was detained," I said, "and that's the best reason for being late."

"Oh!" she said flatly. "I should have known—now I get the hilarity and love-thy-nieghbor kick this morning. You've been out loving some special neighbor and you're still hungover!"

"It makes a guy nervous after a time," I explained. "I mean working in this office and never even denting that 'No pass' line of yours. Next thing he knows he'll lose all his self-confidence and wind up getting married!"

"No girl in her right mind would marry you, Al," Annabelle said easily. "Who could face up to all those lonely nights?"

I was still trying to figure an answer when I walked into the Sheriff's office. All I could see for a moment was a thick cloud of cigar smoke, but I knew somewhere in back of it there had to be a county sheriff.

"Been resting up after last night's violent exercise, Wheeler?" the familiar voice barked at me.

"No, sir." I sank into the nearest chair. "But it's real nice of you to think of it."

The smoke cleared a little and I could see his face, which made me wish the smoke had stayed right where it was.

"Polnik's told me the story already," he said. "But I'd like to hear it again from you."

I told it the same way I'd told it the night before—that I'd called on Shafer to ask a couple of questions and he'd invited me into the house. I knew Lavers just wasn't the kind of sheriff to encourage burglary among his assistants so I was really doing his ulcer a favor by not telling him the truth. He listened in stony silence while I told him about Shafer having a persecution mania—and how he'd finally pulled a gun on me, then fired a couple of shots that fortunately missed me, forcing me to shoot in self-defense.

"No witnesses," Lavers said. "There were the two slugs from his gun in the wall to substantiate the story. I guess I don't have any choice but to accept it."

THE BRAZEN

I managed to stop myself from thanking him, and just sat there with what I hoped was an alert look on my face.

"Have you seen the autopsy report on Kirkland?" he asked after a long, brooding silence.

"No, sir," I said, carefully polite.

"Of course you haven't had the time yet," he said almost jovially. "You've been much too busy shooting people! When you have a few minutes to spare, you should read it, Wheeler—you'll find it interesting."

It was his idea of fun and I didn't want to spoil it for him, so I still sat like there was no special rush to do anything this year. Lavers tapped his gold pencil idly on the desktop for a while until he couldn't stand the suspense any longer himself.

"There were no powder burns on the side of his head!" he said finally.

"So it wasn't suicide?"

"Not unless he had an arm ten feet long!" he snapped.

He clamped the cigar back between his teeth and glared at me. "Go on—say it!"

"What?"

"You were right and I was wrong. If you hadn't talked me into giving you another twenty-four hours on the case, I'd have given the story of Kirkland as the killer who suicided to the papers last night. And I'd be sitting here this morning with egg all over my face!"

"Maybe I should go back to the apartment house and ask some questions about the callers Kirkland had the last couple of days," I suggested tactfully.

I shook my head regretfully. "I wish I knew, sir."

"Polnik's doing that already," Lavers said. "And now it's a triple murder—who did them, Wheeler?"

"You must have a shrewd idea at least by now."

"No," I said truthfully. "If there's a new Murder Incorporated started up in business, I wouldn't be surprised."

"Don't hold out on me!" he grunted. "You can do better than that."

"Not right now, Sheriff," I told him.

"All right," he said coldly. "That twenty-four hours is still good. If you don't come up with something definite by seven tonight, I'm going to swallow my pride and crawl into Homicide and scream for help!"

"It's your privilege," I said.

"I'm hoping it won't be necessary," he said soberly. "It won't help any of us. Seriously, Wheeler, you're telling the truth—not holding out on me?"

"I'm not holding out on you, sir," I assured him.

"Is there anything else I can do to help?"

"If there is, I can't think of it," I said, "but thanks for the thought."

I went back to the outer office where Annabelle searched my face hopefully for bruises and looked disappointed when she couldn't see any.

"Haven't found your murderer yet?" she asked.

"I was just figuring," I said. "Maybe it's an inside job—one of those least-probable-suspect capers. You get around much in a sarong, carrying a blowpipe in your dainty little hand?"

"Maybe it's high fashion in Waikiki," she said sweetly, "but in li'l ole Virginny where I come from, they'd figure right off a girl was ailing and feed her hot molasses until she started wearing white cotton dresses again."

"They could blame it on the hot sun," I said absently. "The sudden heat—hey? That gives me an idea!"

"Hang onto it quick, honey-chile," she said excitedly. "With you, this doesn't happen very often."

"I'm going to make like that li'l ole sun," I said, "and turn on some heat. How about that?"

"Oh, brother!" Annabelle shook her head sadly. "You're real sick!"

I walked into the offices of Berkeley and Miller around coffee-break time, and couldn't reconcile the coolly efficient receptionist behind the desk with the hot-blooded redhead who'd made my breakfast coffee that morning.

"I missed you," Mona said in a soft, purring voice. "You know I haven't seen you in a whole two hours?"

THE BRAZEN

"I just dropped by for another cup of coffee," I said hopefully.

"Screw you, mister," she said. "Go buy your own lousy coffee."

"Is this the way you talk to the man who—"

"O.K.," she said hastily. "I'll see what I can do about it—was there anything else?"

"How's Berkeley this morning?"

"About the same." Her gray eyes searched my face curiously. "Shouldn't he be?"

"I just wanted to talk with him awhile," I said. "Announce me, huh?"

I lit a cigarette while Mona called through to his office. Then she put down the phone and nodded. "He said for you to go right in—Lieutenant."

"Thank you, Miss Gray."

Berkeley smiled at me as I came into his office, and for a startled moment I thought I almost saw a twinkle in the glistening dark eyes.

"Good morning, Lieutenant." He spoke with his usual fast diction. "Come to needle me some more?"

I sat in the nearest moulded chair and looked at him for a while without saying anything. He sat behind his desk, the smile still on his face, showing only an expression of courteous attention.

"You heard about Kirkland?"

"I read about it," he said.

"He didn't suicide, he was murdered," I said flatly. "But whoever killed him sure tried hard to make it look like suicide."

"This is most interesting," he said. "But why tell me?"

"Your partner, Miller, and his girl friend, Rita Keighley, were both murdered by a poison called curare," I said. "You've heard of it?"

"It's featured in a number of romantic adventure novels I read in my youth." He smiled again. "I always associated it with the Amazon."

"Whoever killed him wanted it to look like suicide for a

very special reason," I went on. "That way, they figured the cops would believe Kirkland was the murderer who shot himself before he was arrested."

"Oh?"

"Kirkland was a manufacturing chemist—he worked in a processing plant which used curare. My guess is whoever masterminded the murders only used him to get their hands on the poison, and killed him when he threatened to cop out because he figured I had him tagged as the killer."

"Why would Kirkland agree to get the poison in the first place for your mastermind? That would make him an accessory to murder."

"He wanted to marry Rita Keighley," I said. "She was Miller's mistress and she didn't want to give up the luxury he provided and have to live on Kirkland's salary. My guess is Kirkland jumped at the opportunity to get rid of Miller—it also meant Rita would inherit half the estate, which took care of the financial problem, too."

Berkeley leaned back in his chair and yawned delicately. "This is all very interesting, as I said before, Lieutenant, but why bother telling me?"

"The last time I was here you said you didn't know Kirkland," I reminded him. "The same afternoon he busted into your office shouting that you had him figured for a fall guy. Maybe you can explain this?"

He looked faintly amused. "Where did you hear this story about Kirkland coming here?"

"I have an eyewitness," I said easily.

"Of course—the charming Miss Gray," he said quickly, nodding. "She's an excellent worker, too. I'm sure she told you that story in all sincerity and thought she was telling the truth—and so she was, except for one minor discrepancy."

"Like what?" I waited for the punch line.

"The man's name wasn't Kirkland," Berkeley said in a tone of polite regret. "It was Birkman—a small-time shill who keeps trying to convince me his boss framed him this time and he's as innocent as a newborn babe. I only agreed to handle his defense in the first place because I felt sorry for him, and now I'm beginning to feel sorry for myself. However—it was Birkman who was in here that day, Lieutenant, very definitely Birkman!"

"Miss Gray will go on the witness stand and swear it was Kirkland."

He shrugged his shoulders. "I will swear it wasn't—and produce Birkman to prove it."

"Maybe I should have a talk with him right now and clear the whole thing up?" I said idly.

"Oh, no!" His mouth hardened. "I don't want you getting anywhere close to Birkman, Lieutenant!"

"Why—because he doesn't exist?"

"Don't forget I'm a criminal lawyer—I have some idea of how law enforcement officers work! You get to him and you'll try bribing him to forget he was anywhere near this office that afternoon. You'll offer to get the indictment against him dismissed if he'll just play ball!"

"I never make that kind of deal," I said truthfully.

"I salute your ethics, Lieutenant!" he said in a half-sneer.

I leaned forward in the chair a little. "Ethics I don't have," I said. "Only a sense of justice. It bothers me if a shill doesn't get what he's got coming. It bothers me even more if a murderer doesn't get his comeuppance. I'll stand on a killer's toes just to crowd him a little more—maybe crucify him even—but no deals!"

"Nevertheless," Berkeley said crisply, "I'll keep Birkman on ice until I need him. Are you all through now?"

"All but," I said. "This case has one unique advantage for a working cop—there's been three murders and each one narrows down the list of suspects. Right now I'm left with Mrs. Miller, Johnnie Quirk and you."

"I think you're out of your mind!"

I grinned at him, baring my teeth a little. "And you've got such small feet, Counselor!"

"This is an attempt at deliberate intimidation!" Berkeley said coldly. "Get out!"

Mona looked at me with questioning eyes when I got back to the reception desk.

"I respected your confidence, honey," I told her. "Like I told Berkeley your story about Kirkland shouting he was framed that afternoon."

"Ho, hum!" She shrugged fatalistically. "So I find another job."

"He says you made one mistake—the guy's name was Birkman, not Kirkland."

"Maybe you're my one mistake," she said, "but Kirkland was definitely his name. Nice-looking guy, fresh-faced, strong shoulders."

"That was Kirkland," I said happily. "Tell me something—you ever see Berkeley in court."

"Just once. Why?"

"How was it?"

"Terrific! You forget he's only a little man—defending a client he gets to be around six and a half feet tall. Cool as ice and deadly like a rattlesnake. I'd hate to be on the stand when he's cross-examining!"

"Some of the best fighters are that way," I said. "Tense, jumpy, before they get into the ring—but the bell goes and they change instantly into a cool, efficient fighting machine."

"So?" Mona prodded.

"So I figured, for a criminal lawyer, Berkeley was out of character when I saw him in his office and each time he was so nervous he couldn't stop twitching. But now it looks like he's always that way outside the court—but inside he's like you said just now—cool as ice and deadly like a rattlesnake."

"I'm not following you," Mona said tersely. "Maybe it's me, and I'm just not thinking straight any more."

"This morning, Berkeley isn't nervous any more," I explained, "and he isn't in court, either."

"Well, all right—don't tell me!"

THE BRAZEN

"I figure it means he's already in there fighting," I said cautiously, "and maybe I'm the guy who didn't hear the bell go!"

I was halfway toward the front door when she called my name.

"Yeah?" I turned back and looked at her vaguely.

"When do I see you?"

"I'm not sure, honey," I said. "I'll call you."

"You're not giving me the brush-off, are you?" she asked icily. "The old 'don't call me—I'll call you' routine?"

"Not me, honey," I assured her. "I'm getting to like the way you're helping me."

She smiled involuntarily. "So make sure it stays that way."

"Don't worry about it," I said.

"And take care of yourself," she said anxiously. "Don't go shooting any more people—next time they mightn't miss!"

"What do you think I am?" I asked in a horrified voice. "A hero?"

Chapter Eleven

QUIRK'S OFFICE was eight blocks south from Berkeley and Miller, so it only took five minutes to get there, and another ten to find a parking space.

The reception area was ultra-modern, with lots of bamboo and wrought iron, and a well-stocked bar in one corner of the room.

There was no one in sight when I walked in, but a few seconds later a door opened and a blonde woman with a bosom that defied the imagination writhed across the floor toward me.

She was about the blondest blonde I ever saw, and her skirt was stretched tightly over her pelvis and pneumatic hips. Her slightly chubby face was smooth and unwrinkled, the overfull lips pressed into a petulant pout.

"Can I help you?" She raised her blackpenciled eyebrows a fraction. The carefully modulated voice was so artificial it started me wondering about that bosom again.

"I want to see Mr. Quirk," I told her.

THE BRAZEN

"He's busy right now." Her baby blue eyes had a completely blank look. "Do you have an appointment?"

"Just tell him I'm here," I said patiently. Lieutenant Wheeler, from the Sheriff's office."

"Please sit down while I inquire," she recited.

I relaxed into one of the cane chairs and watched the unnerving roll of her Junoesque hips and buttocks. By rights she belonged in some enchanted wood, gamboling naked by the side of a stream, giving inspiration to the ancient Greeks while the pipes of Pan played in the background.

Quirk came into the room, his triangular face somehow even more so—the nose looked sharper, the lips thinner. His wide eyes were bleak and hostile as he stared at me.

"What the hell do you want?" he rasped.

"I figured it was time we had a cozy chat," I said, friendly-like. "Draw up a chair, Johnnie."

"Be a waste of time," he said tautly. "We got nothing to say to each other, cop!"

"You're wrong," I said. "This is a good time to open up our hearts, Johnnie, seeing we're all alone."

"Elmer's in back," he snarled. "All I got to do is yell once, so don't try leaning on me!"

"Cool off," I said mildly. "All I want is for us to have a little chat, man-to-man, like we were buddies even."

"Make it short," he said. "I got better things to do."

"O.K.," I agreed. "Since we're all alone we can be frank about the things we know already—like I busted into your house last night and Shafer caught me flat-footed, then called you for instructions. You told him how and when to knock me off—but at the last throw I got lucky so it was Pete that wound up in the morgue and not me."

"For the record I don't know what you're talking about," he said. "But—just for kicks—let's say I did. So what?"

"I was just filling in the background—the stuff we both

know," I told him. "Now we can get to the stuff *you* don't know."

"Like what?" He machine-gunned the words.

"Like Pete Shafer being so sure I was going to be dead in a few minutes, he got expansive," I said. "Confidential, even. He didn't mind answering my awkward questions right then because he figured what was the harm in talking to a corpse?"

"My guess is you're bulling me, cop." He stared down at me intently. "But even if you are on the level, it doesn't mean a horse's shit. Pete's dead already."

"Sure," I nodded. "I don't have anything I can use as evidence—and Pete wasn't that close to you anyway. But he was close enough to give me a picture—something I could work on, and that's what I'm doing right now."

"Is that all you got to say?" he asked impatiently.

"That's about all," I said, and stood up. "I got a personal interest in you, Johnnie, ever since you ordered me dead. I'm going to tie a three-count murder rap so tight around you that the jury won't even leave the courtroom!"

"You come in here and waste my time just to tell me that?" He laughed harshly. "I knew you was stupid—but not that stupid!"

"I just wanted you to know," I said as I moved toward the door. "It won't take me very much longer—another Johnnie. Once you're indicted, you won't have a snowball's chance in hell."

He watched me all the way to the door, his mouth working savagely.

"You remember what I told you, cop!" he shouted after me suddenly. "I'm going to be right behind you all the way!"

I opened the door and stepped out into the corridor.

"You hear me—cop!" he screamed.

I closed the door behind me gently, then walked down to the elevator. It wasn't a new theory—you turn on the heat and something starts to boil. You keep applying

THE BRAZEN 107

pressure until something snaps. I just hoped I hadn't made a bad mistake and gotten hold of a piece of rubber that would bend until it couldn't bend any more, then snap—right back in my face.

When I got out onto the street I walked half a block until I found a drugstore. I went into the phone booth, dialed the number, and heard the phone ring twice. Then a pleasantly familiar feminine voice said, "Berkeley and Miller."

"Mona—this is Al Wheeler."

"What's this? another coffee break?"

"I want you to do something for me."

"I'm not that kind of a girl—in office hours anyway." She gurgled wickedly. "Like what?"

"Call this number," I gave her the phone number of Quirk's house in Cone Hill. "A woman should answer—"

"Natch!" Mona said tartly.

"Relax—she's Quirk's so-called housekeeper! If a man answers just hang up, but I'm almost sure she'll answer. Ask for Quirk and she'll tell you he's out. Then say maybe she can help you—you're trying to locate your friend, Gail Miller, who isn't answering her phone, and she told you if she wasn't home she was almost sure to be at Mr. Quirk's place."

"What then?"

"She'll say Gail Miller isn't there or she'll hang up or she'll say a couple of rude words," I said. "It doesn't matter."

"It sounds crazy—but then you are crazy," she said reflectively. "O.K. I'll do it right away—don't forget you owe me a favor."

"Name it," I said.

"Please, Lieutenant!" she said in a shocked voice. "Not over the phone!"

I went back to the car and drove out to Cone Hill, keeping my fingers crossed that the housekeeper was home and had gotten Mona's call. With Quirk and his muscle in the office, she'd surely be alone in the house.

I parked five houses past Quirk's place, then walked back. The up-tempo chimes played for me again when I pushed the button, and soon after the front door opened and there was the housekeeper.

This time her shirt was deep-water blue, and opened all the way down the front. Her nipples prodded the thin fabric, and her crotch bulged provocatively beneath the tight-fitting jeans. Her huge emerald ring glittered in the sunlight.

"Hi, Janie," I said brightly.

"Johnnie's not home," she said, and started to close the door again.

I leaned on it a little until there was enough space to let me walk into the hall. "That's O.K.," I told her. "I'll wait."

"He won't be home until tonight," she said flatly.

"No hurry."

She followed me into the living room, her boobs moving easily beneath the open shirt.

"I see you cleaned up in here just fine," I said, looking at the carpet.

"Either you're crazy—or you didn't come to see Johnnie," she said slowly.

"You're real smart, Janie," I said.

"Smart enough to give you just two minutes to get out of here," she said. "Or I'll call Johnnie and have him come home and toss you out!"

I sat down on the couch and lit a cigarette. "Even if he came it would take him a half-hour to get here." I smiled at her. "Why don't you sit down and relax? Or is the housework piling up? I guess even all those little domestic chores are better than working as a carhop, huh?"

Her eyes glittered brightly. "You're real cute," she said viciously. "Like poison ivy."

"You're real cute too, Janie," I said. "That's why I bothered to take time out for some friendly conversation right now—before it's too late."

"What's that supposed to mean?"

THE BRAZEN

"That you can't win, sugar," I said sadly. "Either way you're the loser."

"Lots of words," she said irritably, "but they make no sense."

"I figure I'll have Johnnie in jail waiting trial on a murder rap before tomorrow morning," I said evenly. "Where will that leave you, Janie?"

"I'll wait and see—thanks!"

I shrugged my shoulders. "I don't think I'm wrong but let's say I am. So Johnnie doesn't get stuck with any kind of rap—what happens then?"

"You're the wise guy—you tell it!" she snapped.

"He's real friendly with Gail Miller right now," I said. "But he's still only warming up—he's going to give her the big rush anytime now—right up to the altar."

"Now I know you're crazy!" she said.

"Gail Miller's a beautiful woman," I said. "Any guy would go for her."

She smoothed the front of her shirt complacently, letting her hands run down her tautly curved hips. "Shit, that kind of competition don't worry me at all. I know a few tricks. I know how to keep Johnnie happy."

"Yeah, but Gail Miller's got something that Johnnie wants real bad and he'll have to marry her to get it."

"Like what?" she asked contemptuously.

"Like money—and Johnnie needs money real bad. She's a widow, remember? And her former husband's estate is worth a good deal."

She sank slowly into the nearest chair and bit her lower lip with sudden savagery.

"The way he treated you last night—tossing that drink in your face," I prodded. "Didn't you get it? That was the kiss-off! You may be loads of fun around the house, honey, but Johnnie isn't going to be around long to enjoy it unless he pays off the Syndicate what he owes!"

For a short time she just sat there, then suddenly jumped up onto her feet again and walked over to the bar.

"I need a drink," she said dully. "How about you?"

"Thanks," I said. "I could use one."

I looked around the room, but the best scenery was that pair of tight denim jeans stretched over her rounded rump. Wistfully, I stripped the jeans away in my mind, and thought how useful it would be to have a live-in housekeeper with a body like that. I wondered how much housework actually got done around the place. Then I began to ponder the definition of the word "housework". It offered a great many possibilities.

She carried the drinks back with her to the couch and sat down beside me. I took the glass from her hand, feeling its icy coldness as our fingers touched momentarily. She tilted her own glass to her lips and drained it in one swallow. Then she turned her head slowly and looked at me. The glitter had gone from her eyes, leaving them dull and lifeless.

"You got to have an angle," she said slowly. "So what is it?"

"It's simple," I said. "Johnnie Quirk is a bastard. I figure he's a murdering bastard, but at this moment I can't prove it. Maybe you can."

She took a deep breath that pushed the tips of her small but firm breasts tighter against the thin shirt, then looked at me steadily. I waited while the seconds ticked by interminably and she never moved a muscle. After what seemed like a life span, she suddenly relaxed and smiled at me as she shook her head slowly.

"It was a nice try," she said easily. "You had me going there for a while—but no dice! Even if I did know it was Johnnie—and I don't—it would still be no deal."

"You have a reason?" I asked her.

"There's nothing in it for little Janie." She leaned her head comfortably against the back of the couch. "I never made a no-profit deal yet and I don't figure on changing now."

"You'd rather let Johnnie walk all over your face and get away with it?"

"He hasn't tried it yet," she said confidently. "If he does, I can handle it myself."

"I wish you luck, Janie," I said sincerely. "Only my guess is you'll need more than luck—discretion maybe? If I'm right about Johnnie, he's killed three people already—and if you make like real trouble, then one more killing won't worry him at all."

I got up from the couch and started toward the door.

"Thanks for nothing!" she said coldly. "And close the door behind you on the way out, huh—cop!"

The six blocks to the Miller house didn't take any time at all. I parked on the driveway, then walked up onto the porch and pressed the buzzer, hoping I'd have better luck with the widow than I'd had with the housekeeper.

Then the door opened and the butler looked at me bleakly, like I was a mortician calling for the body at the wrong address.

"Even on a hot day, Chivers," I said with sudden, poetical inspiration, "you still give me the shivers!"

"Most amusing, Lieutenant," he said smoothly. "I always think a juvenile sense of humor is so appealing in an elderly man."

"Second childhood is a passing phase," I snarled, "like butlers. I want to see Mrs. Miller—is she in the pool?"

"I'm afraid Mrs. Miller is out," he said with a faint note of triumph in his voice. "She didn't say when she'd return. Shall I tell her you were here?"

"I don't see why not," I said morosely. "It's a free country!"

On the way back to the office I remembered I hadn't had any lunch yet and it was mid-afternoon already, so I took time out at a coffee shop for a steak. It was around four-thirty when I walked into Lavers's office and sat down opposite his happy, snarling face.

"Well?" he asked brusquely.

"I've had a hectic day, Sheriff," I said wearily. "This brainwork is worse than legwork yet!"

"Brainwork?"

"Real subtle stuff," I assured him. "Applying psychological pressure in a steady increasing tempo the whole time. Now all I can do is sit back and wait for somebody to break."

"You mean you've got some chick lying on a couch somewhere, all tied up waiting for you to come back to take advantage of her?" he said blankly.

"I was talking about suspects," I said coldly. "If you don't mind me saying it, Sheriff, at a crucial time like this I'd have figured you would keep your mind off sex."

The bright red flush spread across his face so fast, I watched interestedly to see if this time the veins would burst—but they held, if only just.

"The suspects?" His voice shook slightly. "That's something, I guess—I didn't even know you had any."

"Just three," I told him. "Mrs. Miller, Quirk, and Berkeley."

"They'd better break fast," he snorted. "You've got around two and a half hours left."

"That's what I wanted to talk to you about," I said quickly. "I'd like an extension—until the morning?"

"You got twenty-four hours already," he said. "Tomorrow morning you'll want two more weeks—months, probably!"

"Only tonight," I said. "You know damned well if you try and turn the case over to Homicide at seven in the evening they won't even start to look at it before the morning anyway."

"Maybe not," he admitted. "Have you made any real progress—or are you just stalling, Wheeler?"

"I'm not stalling," I said. "The way I pushed them today, if something doesn't break before morning it never will. So if I've goofed come tomorrow morning, you can give it to Homicide with my blessings."

THE BRAZEN 113

"I'll do more than give them just the case," Lavers said with a nasty finality in his voice, "I'll give them back you along with it!"

"O.K." I nodded agreement. "So we've got a deal?"

He lit a cigar with frustrated ferocity, then looked at me through the dense smoke. "Polnik didn't come up with anything from that apartment house where Kirkland lived. It's got two entrances as you know, and nobody who lives there saw anyone coming or going from his apartment."

"Christ, I can't understand it," I said gloomily. "A pretty girl walks down the street and everybody notices her. A guy can tell everything about her, the size of her boobs, and the way her ass wiggles. They can spot flying saucers in the sky. But make it simple, like seeing somebody go in and out of a small apartment building, and you never find one eyewitness."

"You must have some idea by now who the killer is," the Sheriff said.

"My guess is it's a little more complicated than just finding the actual killer," I said.

Lavers closed his eyes tight. "That's all I need," he said in a quivering voice. "If you're still here after I count five and open my eyes again, I won't be responsible for my actions."

"Let's face it, Sheriff," I said, halfway out of the office already. "You never were."

The phone rang on Annabelle Jackson's desk as I closed the Sheriff's door behind me. She answered it, then looked across at me. "It's for you, Al." She kept her hand over the mouthpiece. "One of your little playmates, by the sound of it," she said icily. "All hot and breathless, and probably lying there with nothing on, just waiting to hear the husky virility in your voice."

"My!" I looked at her wide-eyed. "With that kind of imagination you should be in advertising." I took the phone from her and said, "Wheeler."

"Al?" The voice was low-pitched and intimate.

"Yeah?" I said.

"This is Gail Miller—I'm so sorry I was out when you called at the house this afternoon!"

"Think nothing of it," I told her.

"I was going to call you anyway," she went on, "and apologize for being so rude to you the other night." Her voice caressed my ear with a sensual quality I could almost feel. "Can you ever forgive me?"

"Sure," I said. "Maybe it was something you ate."

She laughed gently. "I had that coming! Seriously, I'd like to apologize in person, Al. I was wondering—are you doing anything tonight?"

"Nothing special."

"I'm so glad!" she breathed heavily and I waited for the crackling noise as the insulation melted all the way down the wire. "Why don't you visit with me—say, around eight? I'll give the servants another bonus and send them out for the night, so there'll only be the two of us. Then I can make up for my rudeness to you without having to worry about being disturbed." She was silent for a few seconds and I listened to that heavy breathing again. "I'll do anything to make things right," she added for the clincher.

"It sounds great, Gail," I said warmly. "I'll be there."

"I'm so glad—oh—maybe you'd better bring a toothbrush?" The click was so gentle I didn't realize she'd hung up until five seconds later.

"What do you use for bait?" Annabelle asked as I replaced the phone on the cradle. "Three-dollar bills?"

Chapter Twelve

SHE WORE the same robe she had worn last time, showing just the same area of cleavage and thigh. "Come right in, Al." She held the door wide open for me.

I walked into the hallway and she closed the door, then threw her arms around my neck and kissed me with an uncontrolled open-mouthed violence you always hope for but so rarely find. The robe fell open, and I felt the pliant warmth of her body pressing eagerly against me, her rubbery breasts flattening against my chest, her pelvis writhing against me, her lips moving against mine in an urgent, demanding intensity of passion. There was a familiar stirring in my groin as I dropped my hands to squeeze her firm buttocks, and for a fleeting moment I wondered if Wallace J. Miller ever had such a homecoming during his domestic career—then I didn't have the capacity for thinking any more.

When she finally took her arms from around my neck, pulled her robe together and backed away, she was trembling uncontrollably.

"I need a drink," she laughed shakily. "We haven't even got to the living room yet."

The living room was all set up with just one light over the bar—the bottles nicely grouped, the ice bucket full and glistening. Gail went over to the couch while I made the drinks. When I joined her she was half-lying across one corner of the couch, showing a long section of bare thigh which went almost all the way up to her crotch. A fraction of an inch more and there it would be, opened to my unabashed scrutiny.

She smiled lazily as she took the drink. "Am I really forgiven for being so rude, darling?"

"You're forgiven," I said. "Here's to our new understanding—the new era!"

She lifted her glass. "I'll drink to that!"

I watched her while she drank, the raven-black hair making a soft frame for the unblemished oval of her face. Even in the semi-darkness of the room, her white, delicately-textured skin shone with the pearly luminescence I'd noticed the first time I ever saw her.

She looked at me, suddenly conscious of my gaze, and smiled brilliantly. "Why don't we have a cigarette? We've got the whole night ahead and I wouldn't want it spoiled by a little over-eagerness, h'mm?"

"You're so right, honey," I agreed politely and fumbled in my pockets for a pack of cigarettes.

After I'd lit the smoke for her, she sighed contentedly and lay back against the couch with her eyes half-closed.

"This is where we should have a little light conversation," she said in a lazy voice. "You know any good starters?"

"Shoptalk, that's all I know," I said apologetically. "It's a sure sign of a wasted life."

"That'll do fine," she urged. "Tell me about the investigation and everything!"

"Just remember you asked for it," I said. "Once I get started it needs a heavy truck to stop me."

"You can't bore me, Al," she said warmly. "It simply fascinates me—every little detail!"

"O.K." I cleared my throat in a fast warm-up. "I only got around to figuring the obvious sometime this afternoon. You get this kind of problem once in a long while when you can't see the answer because it's been staring you in the face the whole damned time!"

"So I'll take your word for it," she said easily. "What was the obvious answer?"

"All the time I'd been looking for a murderer," I said, "and that was putting things the wrong way round—I should have been looking for a conspiracy."

"Conspiracy?" she sounded puzzled.

"Sure. Every suspect had a first class motive for murdering your husband," I went on. "Somebody who was real smart could see that all they needed was a little organization. So the Brain started to get organized. If your husband died, his partner had the chance to buy his share of the partnership at a high price—maybe he'd join the conspiracy if he could get it for nothing.

"His wife only married Miller for his money and didn't even speak to him any more—maybe she'd join the conspiracy if it meant she was free of him and collected most, if no all, his money in a nice lump sum.

"His mistress had a boyfriend who wanted to marry her—with Miller out of the way he was free to go ahead, and the money he'd left her in his will would solve their financial problems—so they were hot candidates for the conspiracy.

"Then there was his client—Quirk—who'd hired him to represent his sales manager at a congressional hearing on gambling. Quirk was desperate for money—he owed the Syndicate plenty and knew they'd come to collect soon and if he didn't pay they'd kill him inside twenty-four hours. For money, Quirk would do anything including joining a conspiracy."

Gail sat bolt upright, staring at me with startled eyes. "I think you're out of your mind!" she gasped.

"I told you it needs a truck to stop me now," I said briskly. "So the Brain went ahead and it worked the way he'd figured it would—they all joined the conspiracy. Kirkland had the first job, to get the curare, then somebody else had the job of administering it to your husband.

"It worked fine—Miller was dead as the conspiracy had planned, but then, for Kirkland, it went wrong. The Brain had told him it would be taken as a natural death—a coronary occlusion—but the police found it was curare and that made it murder. It was obvious to Kirkland that it wouldn't take them too long to connect the poison with him and once they found he had access to it, they'd nail him as the killer. He was so worried he had to come and tell you all about it while I was still in the house.

"My guess is the Brain didn't really kid himself the police wouldn't find the poison in Miller's body—he only kidded Kirkland they wouldn't. Rita Keighley had lost her nerve from the moment Miller died, so Quirk was around to threaten her into keeping her mouth shut. But that was only to give the Brain time for the second stage of the operation—to have Rita killed."

"I'm not going to listen to any more of this!" Gail said wildly. "You're insane!"

She started to get up from the couch, but I grabbed her wrist and pulled her back again, holding on tight.

"You're going to hear the finish, honey," I said gently. "Even if I have to twist your arm off! Stage three of the operation was to murder Kirkland but make it look like suicide—the Brain had him tapped for the fall guy from the start. The police would discover his strong motive for killing Miller and also that he had both the means and the opportunity. They'd think Rita Keighley lost her nerve and Kirkland had to kill her to stop her from talking. Then he realized he'd lost everything—the girl and the money she would have gotten from Miller's estate—so he shot himself."

The overhead light came on suddenly with a startling brilliance that dazzled my eyeballs for a moment.

"A fascinating theory, Lieutenant!" a masculine voice said smoothly. "Just who do you think was the Brain?"

I looked around and watched them walk into the room—the immaculately dressed lawyer who wasn't quite a midget, Johnnie Quirk with a gun in his hand, his muscle, Elmer, lumbering along just behind him with a dull gleam of anticipation in his eyes—and finally Janie in her tight-fitting jeans and open shirt.

"You, Mr. Berkeley," I said politely. "Who else could be the Brain?"

"I'll accept that as a compliment." He inclined his head in a sardonic gesture. "You had it figured out pretty well from what I heard, Lieutenant. Have you tagged the hatchetman yet? The one whose job was to dispatch Miller and the girl?"

"You don't mention Kirkland in the same breath as the other two," I said, "and that figures. Handling a gun needs some experience so knocking off Kirkland would be a pro's job, and that means Johnnie-boy."

"True," Berkeley looked like he was enjoying himself. "Now you can go for the jackpot question—who killed Miller and the Keighley girl?"

"It's the kind of deal that needs something special in personality," I said. "You got to have the temperament for it—who else but the widow who didn't weep?"

"No!" Gail said violently. "It's not true! I didn't kill them, I didn't!"

She jerked her wrist free of my grip in a sudden, violent movement, and ran blindly across the room.

"What a pity!" Berkeley said in a very sincere voice. "You missed the big prize by only that much, Lieutenant!"

"You'll have to convince me of that," I told him.

"I'll do even better"—he chuckled softly—"I'll arrange a personal introduction for you."

The room was suddenly quiet. I dug a cigarette out of the pack on the couch beside me. I heard a faint rustling sound which had to be very close for me to hear it at all—the intimate rustle of denim. I lifted my head quickly and looked straight into a pair of vivid blue eyes, and a moment later her jeering laugh sounded harshly in my ears.

"I'm real glad you warned me about Johnnie, lieutenant," Janie gurgled. "You know—like he'd killed three people already! I figured that meant there were two he hadn't even told me about, but when I asked him straight out, he said it was only one—you must have gotten confused about the two I killed!"

"It's not important, honey," I snarled. "You all rate equal in this kind of deal. One gets sent up for a life stretch, you all get sent up for a life stretch. It's real democratic."

"I want to work him over a little," Elmer said thickly. "Just give me five minutes, huh, boss? He's the punk what knocked off Pete, and me and Pete we were buddies—maybe a couple of minutes, huh, boss?"

"We don't have the time!" Johnnie said coldly. "You think I don't want a chance to cut a lousy cop down to size?"

"Let's have no more of this childishness, gentlemen!" Berkeley snapped in an old-womanish voice. "It's vital that he's not marked in any way—I thought I made that clear."

"Sure, you did, genius," Janie purred in a soothing voice. "You don't have to worry about a thing—I can handle it."

I grinned up at her ruefully. "You sure handled me this afternoon, Janie! I figured I got real close to swinging you my way. How did you keep from busting out laughing?"

THE BRAZEN

"Don't let it throw you—cop!" she said icily. "I didn't think you were funny—just pathetic!"

There's nothing like truth for hitting right where it hurts—the Wheeler ego sighed gently the moment before it crumbled into dust.

I didn't feel like watching Janie's sneering face any more for a while, so I looked at Berkeley instead.

"For my own curiosity," I said. "How do you split on this? You get the half-share of the partnership for free. How about Miller's estate—the two hundred thousand?"

"I need a drink!" Gail said suddenly in a loud voice, then stumbled across the room toward the bar.

"An even split," Berkeley said, ignoring the interruption. "Straight down the middle as they say—half to me, and half to Johnnie. He takes care of Janie out of his share, although—" he looked at her for a quick moment with an almost embarrassed expression on his face— "I think she deserves a bonus and I intend to see she gets it. A rare combination of beauty and efficiency such as hers demands tribute!"

"Why—you darling little man!" Janie cooed delightedly, missing the painful twitch that momentarily distorted his face. "I think you're real generous!"

"Hey!" Gail said loudly from in back of the bar. "What about me?"

"You'll be taken care of, naturally," Berkeley snapped. "Haven't you had that drink yet?"

"Got to have some soda," Gail mumbled. "Know it's in here someplace." Her head disappeared below the counter and then there was the tinkling sound of bottles being banged against each other.

Berkeley shrugged irritably. "I never thought she'd just disintegrate this way! Not that it matters now."

"What the hell are we standing around for?" Johnnie asked harshly. "Let's get it over and get out of here!"

"You're right, Johnnie," Berkeley said soothingly. "Dead right!"

"What makes you think you're going anyplace?" I asked.

"You think there may be something to stop us?" the lawyer asked politely.

"I spent the whole day trying to squeeze you into pulling some caper like this," I said coldly. "When Gail called me and made the date for tonight it proved you'd panicked. You think I didn't talk it over with the Sheriff—that there aren't men staked out all around the place?"

"A nice try, Lieutenant." Berkeley smiled, his dark eyes beaming approval. "But I took the trouble to find out a great deal about you—and your reputation as a lone wolf. We double-checked, naturally. Since seven-thirty tonight, Johnnie and Elmer have been out checking the area within a half-mile radius of this house. It won't be a big surprise, Lieutenant, if I tell you there's no police officer within a half-mile of the house—and there hasn't been since seven-thirty?"

"Kill a cop and you're dead," I said. "You ought to know that by now, Berkeley!"

"I agree!" he answered. "But we're going one better—we're going to kill a cop—and then the cop's killer. That will make for everything nice and neat—tidied up already before the county sheriff even gets here."

"What in hell are you talking about now?" I snapped.

"Being a smart, courageous cop," he smirked at me, "you finally tracked down the killer in her own house—but then it went wrong. Maybe you were over confident—maybe you forgot it only takes a scratch of curare to kill almost instantly. They'll find you dead on the couch with a scratch down the side of your face—and the killer dead beside you with what must have been a self-inflicted scratch down her face. Neat, don't you think? no loose ends."

"The widow gets to play the big part and winds up dead beside me?" I asked.

THE BRAZEN

"What!" Gail's head reappeared suddenly above the bar counter.

"I hate doing this." Berkeley turned toward her and spread his arms appealingly. "But Gail—baby!—we need you!"

She put a hand to her mouth and bit down hard on the first knuckle, her head starting to shake uncontrollably.

"You—wouldn't?" she whispered.

"You should hurry that drink, baby," he said genially. "Or you won't have the time."

Johnnie came over to the couch and rammed the barrel of his gun against the side of my head.

"We don't want to shoot you, punk," he said tautly. "But you try anything and we'll have to!"

"Where do you carry the curare? In your fanny?" I snarled at Janie.

She moved around directly in front of me and I saw the hot, off-key excitement suddenly flare in her eyes, and I knew she was sick—crazy sick.

"I've got it right here." She joined her hands together and fiddled with the emerald ring for a moment. Then I saw the stone had been opened outward, and in the socket of the ring there was a tiny steel point. "Neat— yes?" She bent forward over my legs, bringing the ring slowly toward my face. I watched the sharp point coming steadily closer and felt the sweat beginning to roll down my face.

"Just one little scratch," she cooed. "It won't hurt a bit."

"Stop!" Gail shouted in a cracked voice. "Or I'll shoot!"

I caught a quick glimpse of her out of the corner of my eye. She was still standing behind the bar but now she had a gun in her hand, which jumped convulsively each time her whole body trembled.

"Put that down, you little fool!" Berkeley said sharply.

"The way you are right now you couldn't hit a crosstown bus three feet away from you."

"I mean it!" Her eyes were black sockets in her chalk-white face. "Stop it or I'll shoot!"

The pressure of the gun barrel against the side of my head eased off suddenly and I figured Johnnie was slowly angling the gun for a shot at her. Then I looked back at Janie and saw the curare-tipped point of the ring was poised motionless less than a foot from my face. Her face was contorted in a snarl and she was breathing quickly with an unpleasant rasping sound through her wide open mouth. The glazed look in her eyes told me she wasn't going to stop now, for Gail or a squad of marines.

"I said don't move, Johnnie!" Gail said hysterically. "Drop your gun!"

"Take it easy, honey," Johnnie said in a soothing voice, "Nobody's going to hurt you. If you just put down that—"

What was needed right then was some fast action, and I figured another two or three seconds would be too late. I slammed my knee up into Janie's stomach and saw the sudden pain mirrored in her eyes for the split-second before her head dropped onto her hand. Almost without stopping, her head jerked upward again frantically and naked fear drove the pain from her face which showed a thin red scratch-line under her cheekbone. Then she slumped down onto the floor as a gunshot exploded just above my head, followed by two more shots that sounded farther away.

I dived headfirst over Janie's limp body and rolled desperately when I hit the floor, clawing the .38 free from the belt holster. My head banged sharply against a chair leg a moment before my body was brought to an abrupt stop by the other leg, and I finished up on my left side with the gun clutched firmly in my right hand.

A slug slammed into the upholstery two inches above

my head and the shock suddenly brought my worm's-eye view into sharp focus. The immediate view of Johnnie's gun pointing straight at me had more than enough interest and I concentrated on that alone. Without stopping to think I grabbed my right wrist with my left hand to steady it and pulled the trigger three, maybe four times. I could see his snarling face in fine detail, and then the next second it wasn't there any more—it just disappeared and all that remained was a red-stained blur.

I climbed to my feet, noting vaguely that Gail hung limply across the bar counter, her head dangling in the air. Berkeley was sitting on the floor, screaming like a scalded child, with one hand clasped to his shoulder. Then with a sudden prickling of my scalp I remembered Elmer and looked around frantically, but he'd disappeared.

My spine started to turn rapidly into liquid as I skittered across the room, looking for him with a nervous trigger-finger. I found him after what felt like two hours and was maybe ten seconds. He lay peacefully where he'd fallen on the carpet, behind a heavy armchair—I hadn't seen him in my moments of panic because I'd been looking for a guy standing up. There was only one thing wrong with Elmer—the back of his head had been blown off.

Berkeley was screaming thinly. The volume had cut down but the high-pitched keening note he'd found and held onto whipped my frayed nerve-ends fast along the road of no return. I nudged his ribs with the toe of my shoe ungently and told him if he didn't shut up I'd put a slug into his other shoulder—and halfway meant it. It must have sounded good because he suddenly stopped and for a moment I wondered optimistically if he'd choked to death.

I lifted Gail's head, expecting to find a couple of bullet holes in her face at least, and discovered the sticky furrow a slug had plowed across her hairline, knocking her out cold—but otherwise she was fine. It took no time at all to lift and carry her across to the couch. Trying to explain what happened to Lavers on the phone took a hell of a lot longer. I finally got rid of him with the old gag of breaking the connection when I was speaking—the hopeful theory being that no one believes you'd deliberately cut yourself off.

Berkeley had crawled to the nearest armchair and was now sitting in it, still nursing his shoulder and whimpering a little. I made three drinks and gave him one. Gail was still out cold so I left hers standing on the bar counter, and drank the third myself.

"How did Elmer get the back of his head blown off?" I asked Berkeley.

"Gail!" he quavered. "I think she aimed at Johnnie and—"

"That figures," I said. "How about you?"

"Johnnie—the fool!" For a moment his righteous anger made him forget the pain. "He saw Elmer killed and I guess he lost his nerve for a moment as he pulled the trigger!"

"Maybe it proves even a Brain can't think of everything," I said tritely.

Gail moaned softly, so I took the drink over to the couch as she opened her eyes and stared up at me.

"It was only a scratch," I told her. "You didn't get shot—the slug knocked you cold."

She sat up slowly and I pushed the drink into her hand. "You'll feel better after that," I said hopefully.

"Quirk?" she asked softly.

"Dead," I said. "So are Janie and the muscle. Berkeley's got a shoulder wound."

"I talk tough," she smiled wanly, "but once I get near any real violence I go to pieces."

"You did all right with that gun," I said. "Where did you get it?"

"It belonged to Wally—that's kind of funny when you

THE BRAZEN

think about it. He always kept it on the bottom shelf behind the bar. I suddenly remembered it and made the excuse about needing a drink to get over there."

"You saved my life," I told her. "I'm very grateful."

"But it won't make any difference—will it?"

"You'll have to stand trial along with Berkeley," I said. "I'll do my damnedest to see it does make a difference."

"Thanks." Her mouth twisted into a poor imitation of a smile. "Maybe it'll make the difference between thirty or forty years in the penitentiary even?"

I had a nasty feeling she could be right, so I changed the subject fast. "One thing still bothers me—why did Miller call and make a date with me in that bar the night he died?"

"I think he overheard me talking on the phone to Berkeley," she said dully. "We were discussing the Kirkland-Rita Keighley setup in relation to the plan for killing Wally. I think he'd been suspicious for a while that something was going on around him, and he heard enough that time to make him real worried."

"Whose idea was it to use the curare?"

"Berkeley. All the ideas were his—he was the real brain behind the whole thing!"

I looked across to the armchair where he sat—holding tight onto his glass with one hand, the other arm limp. The little whimpering sound still mewed from his lips every now and then, while a steady stream of tears ran down his face and salted his drink.

He looked up suddenly and caught my eye. "Lieutenant, what do you think will happen to me?"

"I wouldn't know," I told him. "You're the brain—you figure it out for yourself!"

Mona held the top of her robe together and looked at me proudly. "You should get a citation, at least, for this," she said.

"Not from the way the Sheriff was talking when I left

the office this morning," I said cautiously. "Like he was mad about something."

"I still think you were very clever," she said stoutly. "And brave with it."

"That reminds me." I checked my watch. "It's two-thirty already—I should be going."

"There's something else I want to know," Mona said determinedly. "How did you feel when you went to Mrs. Miller's house knowing all the time it was a trap and once you were inside the rest of them would try to kill you? I mean, well you could've easily had lots of men hidden close to the house so all you had to do was yell and you'd be out of trouble—but you didn't."

She sighed fondly. "That's what bugs me, Al honey! Where do you get that kind of cold courage?"

"It's simple," I said bitterly. "You just have to be stupid—like me. No, that's not right—it isn't simple. To get real stupid the way I am, you got to work on it."

"What are you talking about?" she asked blankly.

"I had Gail Miller figured as the one who did the actual killing," I said painfully. "I never even thought for one moment that the rest of them would show up. I figured it would be just the two of us and I could take her on my own for a couple of reasons—she only weighed around a hundred and five—and she was a woman!"

I hauled myself off the couch. "I'm beat—and strictly in the square sense of the word," I mumbled. "See you tomorrow, honey."

"Al?" She sounded shocked. "You're not leaving?"

"Like I said—I'm beat," I said firmly. "There comes a time in every guy's life when he's just got to go to bed—and sleep!"

I could feel the cold, hurt silence behind me as I tramped slowly out of the living room into the tiny entrance hall. There was nothing I could do about it anyway—whatever I said, Mona would still be hurt and I was too tired to argue.

THE BRAZEN

I was reaching for the door knob, when she called my name softly. I lowered my hand and turned back into the room. Her robe was lying in a pool at her feet, and she seemed to rise up out of it like Aphrodite emerging from the waves, completely naked. Her pink nipples were taut and she slowly ran her hands down her smooth flanks.

"I still want to help, Al," she said meaningfully.

"And help you shall."

"You deserve it. Call it a reward, if you like."

"Call it anything."

I moved back into the room with the sudden joyous certainty that there comes a time in a guy's life when he realizes he's ten years younger than he thought he was.

THE
STRIPPER

Chapter One

THE CROWD ON THE OTHER SIDE OF THE STREET WAS thickening fast when I parked outside the Starlight Hotel. It was a pleasant, lazy kind of afternoon—a hot sun in a cloudless azure sky, with a gentle breeze rolling in off the Pacific Ocean.

It was a time to laze on a beach, or sit in a shady bar and listen to the gentle clunk of ice cubes in a tall glass. A time for dreaming, when everyone felt good just to be alive—and maybe in the whole of Pine City there was only one exception. The girl stood out on a ledge fifteen stories high, getting ready to jump.

Inside the lobby a bunch of uniformed cops from the Sheriff's office kept the curious crowd clear of the elevators. I rode up to the fifteenth floor and found the right room with no trouble at all. Sergeant Polnik greeted me inside the door with a worried frown corrugating his sloping forehead.

"Lieutenant Wheeler," he said hopefully. "Cheez! I'm sure glad you got here! The Sheriff's going nuts hanging out the window and all—still trying to talk some sense into that crazy kid out there."

An agitated character with protruding eyes and a pencil line of twitching mustache thrust himself in front of the Sergeant.

"You have to stop her, Lieutenant!" he gabbled almost incoherently. "We can't have young women using our hotel for suicides—the publicity will be murder!"

"Why don't you make up your mind?" I suggested politely, then placed the flat of my hand against his chest and nudged him out of the way.

Sheriff Lavers was sitting on the sill of the open window, his back twisted painfully as he talked with the girl who stood outside on the ledge. The sight of his tight-stretched pants was tempting but I firmly resisted the impulse, out of a reluctant respect for authority and an even greater reluctance to lose the pay check I've grown used to at the end of every month.

"I guess if she didn't jump when she saw *his* face," I said loudly to nobody special, "we got nothing to worry about any more."

The Sheriff's heels jarred onto the floor, then he turned toward me, his face a mottled color.

"So you finally got here, Wheeler," he grunted. "See if you can talk any sense into that girl out there—I can't!"

"She's a psycho?" I asked.

"Not like you'd figure," he said in a worried voice. "No hysterics, no nothing. The way she's acting, you'd figure the Girl Scouts were having their annual cookout, or something!"

"Did she give you a reason for wanting to jump?"

He shook his head. "Like I said, she just don't make any sense. Her name's Patty Keller and the only thing worrying her right now is what time you've got!"

"She's not worried about how much time she's got?" I queried.

"Either way I wouldn't know," Lavers said heavily. "See what you can do with her, Wheeler."

THE STRIPPER

I sat on the sill he'd recently vacated and looked out, then down—and it was a big mistake. The massed crowd on the sidewalk was only a collection of pinheads; for a moment I watched the toy automobiles being pushed along the street by an invisible hand, then vertigo caught up with me fast. As I turned my head quickly, I saw the girl standing about six feet away with her back pressed against the outside wall. The ledge was no more than eighteen inches wide, and the gentle breeze off the ocean suddenly turned sinister as it plucked at the hem of her skirt.

She didn't look any more than twenty at most—a thin-featured face and mousey-colored hair—and she didn't look nervous even. Her blouse was kind of sloppy and the hem of her skirt a couple of inches too long. Maybe she was a misfit like her clothes, and this was her big problem that one step forward could resolve for all time.

"Hi," she said quickly in a bright, eager-to-please voice. "I'm Patty Keller. Who are you?"

"Al Wheeler," I told her. "You're wasting your time out there, Patty, the cross-town buses don't come this high."

"That's very funny," she said gravely. "You're a police officer, I guess?"

"A lieutenant," I admitted. "You got a big problem or something, Patty?"

"Or something," she agreed. "What time have you got, Lieutenant?"

I checked my watch. "Five of three—you expecting company?"

"Now I get it." She smiled wisely. "All part of the psychology, is it? Put the subject at ease. Crack a joke or two. A bit of comedy always helps—right?"

"You're much too smart for me, Patty," I said sincerely. "But you got it wrong. I'm representing the street cleaners. They don't want the job of cleaning up what's left of you after you hit the sidewalk."

Her face paled a little. "That's—that's horrible!"

"Sure it is," I agreed. "So do them a big favor and come back inside, huh?"

She shook her head determinedly. "I'm sorry, Al, this is something I have to work out for myself!"

"You sure I can't help?"

"There's nothing you can do to help!" she said in a voice so casual that it made the finality of rejection almost brutal.

"Then maybe I can get you something—a cigarette—a cup of coffee?" I sounded stupid to myself even, but "keep them talking" was the tested theory.

"No, thanks." She looked straight down for a moment. "There's an awful lot of people—TV cameras and all, I guess."

"Sure," I said. "And all of them want just one thing, Patty—for you to come back inside this window! You do that one little thing and you'll make thousands of people throughout the city feel good—make them feel life really is worth living after all!"

"What time is it?" she asked abruptly, and that did up the philosophy real neat.

"I just told you—it's almost three." I took another look at my watch. "Three on the button—and what the hell difference does it make anyway?"

It wasn't the kind of question that you expect an answer to, but for a moment she looked like ten thousand bucks *and* a vacation in Rio hung in the balance. Suddenly the frown of intense concentration cleared. She took a deep breath and for the first time smiled at me with genuine warmth.

"I guess you're right, Al," she said easily. "It would be stupid to disappoint all those people down there, wouldn't it? I'll come back inside now."

"It sure would," I said fervently. "Remember, you got all the time in the world—so just take it easy. Keep your back hard against the wall and kind of slide toward me, huh? One little step at a time will be plenty."

Patty Keller nodded, then slid her right leg toward me,

THE STRIPPER

keeping her back pressed taut against the wall. Her first step brought her maybe a foot closer to the window. I twisted my body around, straining toward her with my arm outstretched and that cut down the distance between us to four feet. In back of me, I felt the Sheriff's large hands clamp down onto my legs, and that made me feel a little better.

"You're doing just fine, Patty," I said. "A couple more steps and—"

She'd already taken one of them while I was talking, and was about to take the second. Her right leg slid forward again and her ankle was almost within reach of my hand—almost. Then she moaned softly and her left leg stayed right where it was.

"O.K.," I yelped frantically. "Take a rest, honey, you got all the time in—"

Her face suddenly contorted grotesquely. Her knees seemed to buckle, and she swayed forward, then bent in the middle like a jackknife, overbalanced, and plunged. I made a desperate grab for her ankle and missed by not more than six inches, losing my balance at the same time. It was only Lavers' iron grip around my knees that saved me from falling out the window.

Her drop to the sidewalk fifteen floors below couldn't have taken more than two or three seconds. For much longer I could hear ricocheting in my head the sound that accompanied it—half moan, half scream, like something out of the primeval forests before people were born.

I got into the office around nine-thirty the next morning, and Annabelle Jackson—the Sheriff's secretary and the most likely reason I'll lose my mind—lifted her blonde head and smiled happily like I'd just broken a leg or something.

"Doctor Murphy is with the Sheriff right now," she said in her soft southern accent. "They're both waiting for you, Lieutenant, and my guess is you should have an alibi ready!"

"That's right neighborly of you to tip me off," I said gratefully. "One of these days I'm going to do you a big favor. I'm going to pick out my own burial plot ahead of time so you can go and stomp on it whenever the fancy takes you."

"What fancy?" she said sweetly. "Maybe I couldn't be bothered. Did you ever think of that?"

It was a sobering thought that held my attention all the way into the Sheriff's office, and then from the look on Lavers' face I obviously had other things to think about.

"Sit down, Wheeler," he growled. "This may take a little time!"

I sat in one of the visitor's chairs and looked at Doc Murphy and he looked right back at me, so to break the monotony I looked at the Sheriff and the same thing happened.

"What are we expecting?" I ventured finally. "Fallout?"

"Patty Keller," Lavers said, "the girl who jumped off that hotel ledge yesterday afternoon."

"She didn't jump—she fell," I corrected him. "She was on her way back inside when she got sick and—"

"You said that yesterday," he interrupted rudely. "I figured it was the usual Wheeler reaction. What female could possibly commit suicide when she was favored by a personal appearance of Nature's gift to her own sex—?"

"You're jealous, Sheriff!" I interrupted him with equal rudeness. "Just because you've gotten fat and—"

"All right!" He bit the end off a cigar, then shoved the black cylinder into his face. "That was yesterday—Doctor Murphy's finished his autopsy since then."

"She fell fifteen stories onto a concrete sidewalk and you need an autopsy to establish the cause of death?" I wondered out loud.

"Why don't you concentrate real hard, Lieutenant?" Murphy asked amiably. "See if you can come up with one intelligent answer. You said she got sick and that made her fall. Expand that a little, will you—as a personal favor?"

"Since when would I want to do the mortician's friend a personal favor?" I said. "She was edging her way back to the window when she suddenly groaned—her face was all screwed up like she was in agony. Then her knees buckled and she doubled up and overbalanced. That's about all there was to it."

Murphy looked at the Sheriff and nodded wisely. "It adds up, all right."

"You two are real cute," I said coldly. "So play secrets and see if I care!"

"She kept checking on what time it was—right?" Lavers prodded.

"Yeah," I muttered. "Like morning workouts at Santa Anita. . . . Hey, come to think of it, when I told her it was three o'clock, she suddenly changed her mind about staying out on the ledge—like that!" I snapped my fingers.

"Interesting," Murphy mumbled. "She was loaded with apomorphine."

"Apomorphine? Like morphine?" I said.

"No, not like morphine at all. It's a derivative, but it's not a narcotic. It's a powerful emetic. A mere trace of it can be used as an expectorant, and as little as a twelfth of a grain makes you toss up that arsenic your wife gave you in your oatmeal—but good! It produces acute nausea, vomiting, fainting, giddiness. It's hard to say how much she'd gotten, but it was enough to do the trick.

"But why in God's name would she drink something like that when she was about to take a dive off a building?" Lavers said.

"She didn't drink it—it was a hypo. Not that it matters much, except that the timing is different," Doc Murphy explained. "It's usually given that way—in the arm, not the stomach."

"Then it certainly looks like she had a little help," I said. "Most of us don't go around sticking needles in our own arms."

"*Plenty* of us do!" he corrected me. "It's a cinch—as

any mainliner will tell you, plus a lot of other people who have had one reason or another to give themselves shots."

"So maybe she'd eaten a bad oyster," Lavers suggested gloomily, "and she wanted to get rid of it, and she took the stuff, and then decided she was tired of living anyway, oyster or no oyster, so she tippy-toed out on the ledge and mulled it over for a while trying to make up her mind, and then *blam!*" He snorted. "Nuts! It doesn't make sense!"

"How long after the shot would it take for the reaction to hit?" I asked the doc.

"He scratched his head and screwed up his face. "Pretty hard to say, for me anyway—I haven't had any occasion to use it since I was a resident in the hospital on emergency call. About ten or fifteen minutes, maybe."

The Sheriff met my questioning look with a sour expression. "She called the desk and told them she was going to jump," he said bleakly. "They sent the house dick up there right away to see if it was a gag or not. I got there fast with Polnik—you took longer—" he gave me that one through clenched teeth "—I suppose the whole thing from the time she phoned the desk until she went down might have been fifteen minutes, give or take a couple."

"Was the hypodermic found in her room?" I asked him.

"No one was looking for it yesterday, and there's nothing there today. All she had was an empty overnight case with her—which figures, if you want to take a hotel room but plan to exit fast, by the express route!"

"When had she checked in?"

"Only a couple of hours earlier. No one with her, and no one called or went up to see her, as far as they know at the desk. She lived in a one-room apartment on the wrong side of Grenville Heights. Polnik should be checking it out right now. She only had one relative we can find so far—a cousin."

"Who's he?"

THE STRIPPER

"It's a she," Lavers said morosely.

"If she's under sixty and under one-eighty pounds," Murphy said in a gleeful voice, "Wheeler will come back with a whole dossier, complete to the last birthmark—and you know where you mostly find that one?"

"You're just jealous, like the Sheriff," I told him disdainfully. "You Hippocratic hypocrite!"

Lavers encompassed both of us with a baleful glare. "The cousin's name is Dolores Keller—commonly known as *Deadpan* Dolores." He shook his head in a gesture of numb despair. "This has all the signs of a Wheeler case. I guess I should realize by now that nobody can fight Fate—right, Doctor?"

"Deadpan Dolores?" I gurgled. "How come?"

"That's her name. She works as a stripper down in one of those sex palaces. You know, where it all happens, from oral sex to lesbian orgies, only I don't think she's into that part of it. She just strips, throws herself around a bit, simulates an orgasm or two—nothing serious."

"There comes a time in every man's life," I said in an awestricken voice, "when he's given his just reward."

"I sure hope I'm around when you get yours, Wheeler," Murphy sneered. "I'll do the autopsy for free!"

"Before you start," Lavers said resignedly, "I want that Jefferson case report finished up. How soon will I have it?"

"Sometime late this afternoon, sir," I said promptly. "But don't worry about it, I'll get right onto this new case just as soon as I'm finished with the Jefferson report—even if it means working on my own time tonight. You know me, Sheriff," I added, smiling modestly at him, "I'm conscientious!"

"I know you from way back, Wheeler," he snarled, "and there just ain't no justice!"

Chapter Two

WHEN NIGHT HAS FALLEN OVER THE CITY AND THE NEON signs blink and glitter along the boulevards, I get a moment of nostalgia here and there for the time when the world was young, and Wheeler along with it. It always happens to me when I'm down there among the drug pedlars, the muggers and whores of both sexes, the porno bookshops and movie houses, and I think of the days of comparative innocence when it wasn't all so blatant and a damn sight less sleazy. It was happening to me now.

The neon spelled out *Club Extravaganza*, and luridly painted signs in the doorway featured a list of the main attractions, along with a spotty selection of photographs presumably there to whet the appetite, but which had the effect on me of cold oatmeal. The erotic displays included Helga and Anna, Swedish porno-gymnasts, and Rodolfo, the stud of all time, Hispanic stallion with a weapon all of fifteen inches—dormant. There was Madame Olga and her pony, Estralita and her python, and Damien and Roger, who just kept popping up everywhere. And, of

THE STRIPPER

course, *Deadpan Dolores*. There she was, shot from a three-quarter angle, stark naked, holding up her magnificent boobs, her long legs sweeping up to the curve of her high buttocks. Her strawberry-blond hair was unruly, and her face was molded in broad planes; her overly generous mouth curved in a faintly cynical smile, while her dark eyes sparkled with about the last thing you'd look for in a stripper—intelligence. I could hardly wait to get inside and see the real thing.

I walked in through the door to a darkened lobby to be greeted by a hairy, musclebound character wearing a wrinkled tuxedo.

"I want to see Dolores Keller," I told him.

"You come to the right place, friend!" He leered at me like we were both members of the same fantasy club. "The next show don't start for a half hour yet. You want a ringside table, maybe I can fix it?"

"You hire out binoculars for a small fee, too?" I snarled at him.

His eyes narrowed and maybe an ugly expression appeared on his face, but who could tell? "Hey, listen," he rasped in a gravelly voice, "I don't know what your angle is, but if you want trouble, you got the right guy for it, friend!"

"I guess it's no use asking you to do me a big favor and drop dead," I said regretfully. "So do me a small favor and stop calling me 'friend'—'Lieutenant' will do just fine!"

I took out my badge and shoved it under his nose; if he couldn't read I was all set to spell it out, but the sudden sick look on his face said he could read just fine.

"Cripes!" he gurgled. "I'm sorry, Lieutenant, I didn't know you was—"

"We all have our problems," I sympathized. "You got that repulsive face, and I got to see Dolores Keller."

"Sure, sure!" He turned and beckoned me to follow. "Right this way, Lieutenant."

There was a blue movie showing, with two guys and a

chick displaying a lot of energy in vivid close-up, the chick not missing a beat as she took it at both ends. We threaded our way through the tables with their heavy-breathing occupants, and down a corridor to the dressing rooms. The maître d', if that was what he was, stopped outside the second door and knocked.

"Who is it?" a feminine voice asked from inside.

"Louis," he said. "There's a police lieutenant here wants to see you, Dolores."

"So send him in," the voice said coldly. "You don't expect a cop to pay the cover charge?"

I went inside the dressing room, closing the door on Louis behind me. Dolores was sitting at a dressing table in front of a mirror, doing something to her eyes. She studied me in the mirror for a long moment then turned round to look at me in the flesh. The thin robe, which had made her look more or less modest from a rear view, was wide open, and underneath she was dressed the same as in the poster outside—in exactly nothing. She didn't seem to mind in the slightest, and I guessed that figured, her body being her paycheck and all.

And what a body! It was really something, and it would have been a damn shame to keep it covered. It was superb, from the graceful line of her neck and her shoulders, the full breasts with their dark pink tips, to the length of firmly fleshed thighs and the curve of her buttocks. Between her thighs was an abbreviated wedge of strawberry-blonde hair. I started feeling an ache right there and then, but official duties had to come first.

"I'm Lieutenant Wheeler," I told her, "from the County Sheriff's office."

Her lips parted in a faint smile. "What have I done, Lieutenant?"

"It's about your cousin—Patty."

There was a plaintive squeak from a box in the corner, which sounded like it needed oiling. Dolores sprang to her feet and rushed over to the box, then knelt down and lifted a small bundle of fur in her arms.

THE STRIPPER

"Bobo!" she crooned reassuringly. "Poor little Bobo! Were you feeling all neglected down there? You know your big mommy loves you always!"

She came back to the dressing table and sat down again facing me, still holding the bundle protectively cradled in her arms. A small pointed head lifted above her forearm and the bright eyes of a pooch stared at me with insolent disdain.

Dolores smiled at me again. "Bobo hates being left out of anything—he gets awful jealous whenever I have company!" She hugged the pooch even tighter to her bare midriff. "Doesn't 'oo get jealous, 'oo naughty little Bobo, h'mm?"

The pooch gave a couple of sharp affirmative yelps, then was so exhausted it had to leave its pale pink tongue hanging out while it panted for breath.

"If the noise worries you, you can always have it stuffed," I suggested helpfully.

That revived the little monster long enough to let out a series of frantic yelps that had my nerve ends crawling for cover.

"You pay no attention to the wicked man, Bobo honey!" Dolores glared at me balefully. "He's just a horrible, cruel old policeman—and I bet *he's* jealous!"

"I was only trying to be helpful," I protested. "That way you can make it part of your act without any worries about it screwing up the show, like barking at the wrong time, or cocking its leg—something like that."

"So forget it," I said apologetically. "You were going to tell me about Patty, remember?"

"Poor kid!" Her eyes were still cold as she looked at me. "She must have had some tough breaks to jump out of a hotel window like that!"

"You know any reason why she could've wanted to kill herself?"

Dolores shook her head. "I didn't know her real well, Lieutenant. She only came to Pine City about six months back, from back home in Indiana. Her folks got killed in an auto smashup and I guess I was about the only relative she had left. We didn't get along too well—she wanted to be a dramatic actress and she figured my job was degrading or something!"

"She didn't approve of what you're doing?" I asked.

"Have you seen the show, Lieutenant?" Her dark eyes studied me levelly.

"Well—no."

"Then you can't make snap judgments, can you? I consider myself an artist, nothing common like most of these other—I class myself as an exotic dancer with something to offer. I put all my heart into what I'm doing, and that's a fact."

"I'm sure," I said humbly. "You figure Patty was maybe still emotionally disturbed about her parents' death?"

"No," she said confidently. "I think she was glad to be rid of them—they figured a girl's place was right there, down on the farm where she was born." Her eyes were reflective for a moment. "Maybe they were right?"

"How about her friends?"

"That's easy—she didn't have any."

"Nobody?"

"This may come as a big surprise to you, Lieutenant," she snapped, "but even in southern California, the lonely are legend!"

"That's a good phrase—I must remember it," I told her. "You mean she didn't have one friend?—not even a boy friend?—there was no man in her life at all?"

"It's about a month since I last saw her," Dolores admitted, "but up to that time anyway, there was no boy friend. Things had gotten so bad, she'd joined up with a lonely hearts club even. She was all excited about it—couldn't wait for her first blind date. It was real pathetic!"

From the security of her warm and intimate embrace, the pooch gave me one last stare of cynical confidence, then closed its eyes and went to sleep. The heavy sound of its breathing still persisted but at least it was longer between pants.

"You remember the name of the lonely hearts club?"

"Sure—the Arkright Happiness Club. I asked Patty if it was run by a guy called Noah Arkright because he'd be a real expert at pairing off—but she didn't think it was funny at all."

"Neither do I," I said honestly. "But I'll bet Bobo bust a gut laughing."

"You are a horrible man!" She clutched the pooch even tighter until it squealed reproachfully without waking.

"There's always something vicious about a man who doesn't like dogs," Dolores said darkly. "It's a sure giveaway."

"You call that a dog?" I asked in genuine amazement. "Honey, the only difference between your pooch and any other ego-projection is that Bobo comes fur-lined. It's not the dog I dislike, only what you've done to it."

"Why don't you get the hell out of here, Lieutenant," she asked tightly, "if you're all through with the questions?"

"I guess I am—for now," I said. "But most likely I'll be back."

I had the door half open when she spoke again, the curiosity overriding her dislike of me for a moment.

"Does it matter this much, Lieutenant? I mean, why Patty killed herself? There's nothing anybody can do about it now, is there?"

"The questions are routine," I said vaguely, then turned and looked at her. "You ever stop to think—you and your 'the lonely are legend' and all—that if you'd given her maybe one-tenth the affection you give that pooch, she might still be alive right now?"

The muscles in her face set rigid as she stared back at me; then the pooch came awake with a sudden frantic yelp and leaped out of her arms to avoid being squeezed to death.

"It's just a thought," I said politely, then closed the

door on her frozen features before she got around to throwing something.

Outside the club, I stopped to have another look at the poster of Dolores, under the red neon. I gave it a whole five minutes, but there wasn't even a twinge of nostalgia. Then I drove back home and was inside the apartment by ten.

I slipped a Barry Manilow cassette into the stereo, and made myself a drink. Sitting in an armchair, sipping my drink and letting the music wash over me, the living room walls seemed to shrink a little. I got a sudden urge to push them back a couple of feet. My time was my own. I had a choice—I could sit and drink all night by myself, or go to bed and sleep by myself. So what the hell was I being depressed about? Two drinks later I thought, to hell with Deadpan Dolores—even if I was the latest to join her legend—and went to bed.

Next morning, with bright sunlight streaming into the apartment, I felt no different at all. For a couple of seconds I considered going straight to the office but the thought of Sheriff Lavers' face when he read that Jefferson report decided me against it. A guy has to face facts and the fact was I felt lonely. A guy has to be logical and the logic was to do something about it. Don't sit around and mope, kiddo, get out there and make the real big try. Face it—if it's a lonely hearts joint you need, get out and find one.

I found the Arkright Happiness Club about an hour later on the thirteenth floor of a mid-city building—but maybe the floor was only coincidence. I knew a guy once who spent a week in Miami with his best friend's girl friend strictly through coincidence—they just happened to book the same room in the same hotel at the same time. What happened to my ex-best friend could happen to the Arkright Happiness Club, could happen to a dog even—a pooch yet—and I was back to Dolores Keller again.

Inside the office I felt kind of disappointed because it

THE STRIPPER

looked about the same as any other office—no pink plaster Cupid aiming a dart at a delicate portion of someone's anatomy, not even a vase full of hearts and flowers yet. Then I got my first look at the receptionist in back of a big desk and all of a sudden my heart sang—a little off key maybe, but definitely sang!

Her dark hair was rather carelessly styled, and she had a deep suntan to match the sultry beauty of her face. When she looked at me, I saw her eyes were alert with a kind of primitive warmth. It was no trick to close my own eyes and see her lying on a beach somewhere, her long naked body absorbing the sun and turning a deeper golden color. I could imagine the slow sensual yearnings the sun and the sand and the salt water stirred in her. I could almost see her dark nipples straining upward toward the source of the warmth, the lazy movement of her buttocks as she moved down toward the water's edge.

"Good morning," she said in a vibrant, faintly husky voice, and my daydreams popped like a burst bubble.

"Uh!" I managed, and it was some effort at that.

"Please sit down," she said as, in my mind's eye, I saw her dive cleanly into six fathoms of crystal clear water. "I'm Sherry Rand. You are—?"

"Wheeler," I muttered awkwardly. "Al Wheeler."

She smiled, and her teeth were like priceless pearls. My eyes dropped to her proudly jutting breasts beneath the thin shirt she wore, unbuttoned far enough to reveal about an inch of deep cleavage, then looked quickly again when I saw she was still watching me.

"Please don't be shy," she said in a sympathetic voice. "We have hundreds of people who come in here for the very same reason you did. They're nice people but they're lonely and they want to meet other nice people, only they don't know how to go about it. So you can see, Mr. Wheeler, you have put yourself in very capable hands."

"Yes, I can see that," I said ingenuously, giving her the old Wheeler leer.

"You seem to have gotten over your nervousness quite fast," she observed drily.

"With someone like you, how can a guy be nervous?" I said. "I mean, who would want to pass up the opportunity of a lifetime just because he happens to be nervous? Nervousness tends to make a guy fumble."

"Well, now—" Her voice was still bright but the smile was getting a little limp around the edges. "Just how can we help you, Mr. Wheeler? I imagine you're looking for a nice girl with maybe a view to matrimony—and we're here to help you find the right one! Do you have any special preferences?"

"You mean I get to lay out the measurements like a mail order for a Sunday suit?" I asked interestedly.

"We don't guarantee to find the exact girl of your dreams, Mr. Wheeler," she said carefully, "but most times we can come pretty close."

I thought about it for a couple of seconds, and although I was tempted to string her along a bit more, to give out with a few details of my feminine ideal of the moment, right down to erotic preferences, I decided it was high time to get down to business.

"There's a lieutenant tag instead of a mister," I said apologetically. "I'm a cop."

She stopped smiling and looked at me cautiously for a while. "Are you serious?" she asked at last.

"Sure, I'm serious."

"You're a police officer?"

"I know it sounds kind of stupid," I said, "but they even gave me a badge to prove it." I tossed it on the desk in front of her and she looked down at it suspiciously.

"I don't understand, Lieutenant," she said finally, a bewildered look on her face. "This is a legitimate enterprise and we've never had any—"

"Well, there always has to be a first time," I said in a consoling voice. "I just want to make some inquiries about a former client of yours—Patty Keller."

THE STRIPPER

"I guess you'd better talk with Mr. or Mrs. Arkright," she said doubtfully. "Excuse me."

I waited while she announced my presence and intentions in a hushed voice—the kind the morticians have copyrighted for when they're using the past tense—to whoever was listening on the other end of the phone. Then she hung up and said both Mr. and Mrs. Arkright would see me right away and it was through that door on my left.

So I opened the door to my left and walked into a small but neat office. This time there *was* a vase—it sat on the desk and it contained a spray of faded carnations. The flowers matched the rest of the furnishings—the drapes, the carpet, the wall paint—they were all faded. In back of the desk Mr. and Mrs. Arkright were standing like a faded photo in the family album—I had an eerie feeling that if you tapped either of them sharply on the shoulder all you'd get would be a cloud of dust.

Mr. Arkright was a little, chubby-faced guy with rimless glasses and the remains of his hair combed thinly back over his pink scalp, held in close contact by a glossy hair tonic. He wore a slightly crumpled gray suit and a gold, black, and red striped tie which was knotted absurdly tight and small against the high starched collar that left him no neck at all.

"Good morning, Lieutenant," he said in a rusty voice that squeaked a little like he hadn't been oiled in a long time. "My name is Arkright—Jacob Arkright—and this is my wife Sarah."

Sarah was tall and lean with it. Her face, all angles and hollows, was surmounted by thinning, frizzy hair that had been dyed a brilliant titian. She wore a shapeless black dress that hung on her gaunt frame like a dust cover carelessly tossed over a high-backed chair. Her eyes were a faded blue and kind of fuzzy around the edges. When she spoke, her voice had a sharp, brittle quality, like she was used to hearing evasive half-truths and she wasn't about to stand any nonsense from a police officer either.

"Sit down, Lieutenant." She pointed to a dusty chair. "Now—Sherry said you had some questions about one of our clients?"

I sat on faded cretonne, a little worn about the edges, and wondered how desperate you had to be for a little companionship to wind up in a dump like this. Sarah Arkright watched me for a moment, then resumed her own seat in back of the desk. Her husband still stood beside her, and his right hand dropped to her shoulder in a pose that put them even closer to that family album photo, circa 1927.

"Patty Keller," I said. "She was a client of yours, Mrs. Arkright."

"Patty Keller?" she repeated sharply. "I don't remember her, do you, Jacob?"

"I—think so." He cleared his throat apologetically. "A young girl who was very shy and wanted to be an actress—I do hope she hasn't gotten into any trouble, Lieutenant?"

"Didn't you read about it in the newspapers?" I asked him.

"We don't read newspapers!" Sarah snapped.

"Not in a long time." Jacob smiled at me, and with those over-white dentures, it was a mistake. "The standards of modern journalism, Lieutenant..."

"She's dead," I said coldly. "Yesterday afternoon she walked out onto a hotel ledge fifteen floors up and—"

"Suicide?" The rimless glasses magnified a kind of watery compassion in his eyes. "How tragic!"

Sarah Arkright folded her hands in front of her and pursed her lips thinly in disapproval.

"They don't have any roots," she observed calmly. "None of them do, that's their trouble today. No aim in life—all the standards have gone!"

"And Patty Keller along with them," I grunted. "Do you keep a file on your clients?"

"Of course." Jacob looked shocked at the thought of

THE STRIPPER

anyone doubting their businesslike efficiency. "Excuse me a moment, Lieutenant, and I'll get it for you."

He walked out of the office with a springy step which reminded me of the little white ball that used to bounce over song lines in one of the six shorts accompanying the feature at a Saturday matinee when I was a kid. After he'd gone I got out a cigarette and was looking for a match when Sarah spoke her sharpest yet.

"Not in this office, if you don't mind, Lieutenant! One thing neither of us will tolerate in this office is the foul smell of tobacco!"

Jacob returned as I replaced the unlit cigarette in the pack. He handed me a white manila folder, then resumed his position behind his wife's chair. The folder contained a couple of neat, typewritten detail sheets. Under the heading, "Patty Keller," was listed her address, age, occupation, interests, likes and dislikes—and it looked like somebody had done a real job on them. Page 2 was even more interesting. It was headed "Desirable Companion," and then broken down into detail under various subheadings, such as age, occupation, and financial status—all classified as unimportant. Character and interests were the things that concerned Patty: "Should be a kindly, sensitive man, interseted in the arts and live theater especially."

The harsh voice of Sarah Arkright interrupted my reading.

"As you can see, Lieutenant," she said almost smugly, "we take a great deal of time and trouble analyzing our client's wishes before we attempt to find them compatible companions. Because of this, our percentage of successful introductions is very high—more than sixty per cent of our clients finish up marrying someone they've met through our Happiness Club!"

"How many wind up dead on a sidewalk like Patty Keller?" I wondered out loud.

The last notation in the folder was of a meeting arranged between Patty and one Harvey Stern, and the date was three months back. I ignored the outraged snort from Sarah at my last crack, and looked at her husband.

"This meeting with Harvey Stern—" I prodded him. "How about that?"

"Is that the last notation on the detail sheet?" he asked, squeaking a little on the last word.

"That's right."

"Our system works this way," his wife cut in forcefully. "We study the detail sheets and if we think two clients are potentially compatible, then we arrange an introduction. We do nothing further until one—or both—of them reports back that the introduction wasn't satisfactory. In that case we then arrange a further introduction. If that's the last notation on the girl's sheet, she hadn't reported back to us at all."

"How about this Stern character?" I asked. "Did he report back?"

"I'll go get his file, Lieutenant," Jacob said quickly and bounced out of the room again.

Sarah glared at me in open hostility. "I don't see what this girl's demise has to do with us—or our club!" she grated. "I consider this an unwarranted invasion of privacy, Lieutenant!"

"That's your privilege," I said politely. "Maybe this Stern character was a sex maniac and the experience of her first date with him drove the girl to suicide?"

She was still making gabbling noises deep in her throat when Jacob materialized with a manila folder, a blue one this time.

"Blue for boys and white for girls?" I said.

He flashed those store teeth at me. "Blue and pink would have been even nicer," he said. "But we'd already started with white."

I shuddered slightly as I took the folder from his hand. "You use black for widows and gray for the divorced?"

Jacob made a faint incoherent squeak, then darted for the cover of his wife's chair. I took a quick look at the last entry on Harvey Stern's detail sheets and saw the last date he'd had through the club had been the one with Patty Keller, and the dates matched. Harvey must have been one of the foundation members or maybe he was just unlucky—that date had been about the fifteenth on his list.

"I'd like to have these files for a couple of days—if you don't mind?" I said.

"Lieutenant!" Sarah looked shocked. "Those files contain confidential information. We guarantee all of our clients privacy! We couldn't possibly—"

"They'll be marked 'Top Secret' and kept in the county sheriff's safe at his office." I smiled brightly at her, then got to my feet. "Thank you for your help, Mrs. Arkright—and you, too, Mr. Arkright. Anytime I feel lonely I'll know where to come."

Sarah's face was a color to match her dyed hair while she struggled to find the right words; the rimless glasses magnified the bewilderment in Jacob's eyes into complete confusion. I left them looking like a couple of disturbed personalities in a psychiatrist's casebook, wondering on my way out of the office how they'd look with their heads shrunken down to the size of the knot in Jacob's tie. Cute as buttons, I figured.

Back in the outer office, I stopped for a moment in front of the receptionist's desk and listened to the soft murmur of the surf and the breeze rustling through the palm fronds.

"Is something the matter, Lieutenant?" Sherry Rand asked anxiously.

I looked down at her, and there she was with her clothes back on. The beach was gone. "Honey," I confessed, "I'm real lonesome, but I don't have the price of joining the Arkright Happiness Club, and I don't feel I could be happy here, not after meeting the owners. You figure you could help out somehow?"

The primitive warmth was still lurking there in her eyes as she looked at me closely for a moment.

"I'm not sure," she said cautiously. "What did you have in mind, exactly?"

"Well—" I thought for a moment. "Maybe dinner at my place, for a start."

"Oh, yes, I know," she said sweetly. "Soft music, soft lights, loaded drinks, and a heavy rug in front of the fireplace."

I looked at her suspiciously. "How did you guess?"

"It's all part of a general pattern," she said, shrugging gracefully. "It's hardly original, now, is it?"

"How about a show then?" I asked, with sudden inspiration.

"What sort of show?" Now it was her turn to be suspicious.

"Well, I thought of something intimate. A sophisticated girl like you—"

She gave a short, harsh laugh. "Hah! That can mean only one thing. Sex. S-E-X. Am I right?"

"It could be a hoot," I said. "As long as you have the right attitude. I like a girl who has a refreshing attitude toward S-E-X."

"And is that what you think I have?" She gave me a penetrating look, and my heart started beating a little faster.

"I was sort of hoping—"

"It might be interesting at that," she broke in before I could finish. "A sex show. A glimpse into the seamier section of life in our fair city. Yes, O.K., Lieutenant. You can pick me up around eight."

"Just give me the address," I said eagerly.

Chapter Three

YOU COULD HAVE TOLD BY THE FLOWERS EVERYPLACE that it was a florist's shop even if you hadn't looked at the fancy script on the shopfront outside. A girl with thick hornrims and lank hair came forward to greet me. She wore a lilac-colored smock and flat-heeled shoes, along with a dedicated look on her face like she personally supervised the bees pollinating all summer.

"Good morning." Her voice was precise. "A corsage for a lady?—a dozen red roses?"

"Just some talk with the owner, thanks," I explained. "You think maybe he'd like a corsage?"

"Mr. Stern is very busy at the moment," she said frigidly. "And he never sees salesmen on a Wednesday, anyway!"

"An unfortunate traumatic experience with some roughneck pushing fertilizer?" I sympathized. "I'm Lieutenant Wheeler from the county sheriff's office, and I'm interested in hearts—not flowers."

She walked away from me, weaving her way around

the gigantic vases that cluttered the floor until she was finally lost from sight in a back room. I lit a cigarette in self-defense against the heavy mingled scents that hung in the shop, then saw the florid-faced guy with a pink carnation in his lapel hurrying toward me as fast as his short legs would carry him. His face was a little plump and unwrinkled, like it had a lot of massage and was well scrubbed at least three times a day.

"I'm Harvey Stern," he announced breathlessly as he stopped in front of me. "My assistant said you are from the county sheriff's office?" His voice had a bland quality to match the pink and white complexion. Cut off cleanly at the knees and standing in a pastel-colored vase, he'd blend happily with his surroundings, I figured, showing the hostess had good, if not exciting, taste in floral decoration.

"Lieutenant Wheeler," I told him. "I'd like to ask some questions about a girl called Patty Keller."

"I read about it." He shook his head sorrowfully, then removed an immaculate white pocket handkerchief and dabbed his forehead gently.

"A shocking tragedy, Lieutenant! A young girl like that with everything ahead of her—why would she want to destroy herself?"

I sighed patiently. "It's a good question and I'm trying to find an answer, Mr. Stern. Maybe you can help me."

"Me?" The look of surprise showed up a little too late to be completely spontaneous. "Why me, Lieutenant?"

"The Arkright Happiness Club," I said. "That's how you met her, isn't it?"

"Oh—that?" Stern looked faintly embarrassed. "I wonder if we could discuss this in private, if you don't mind? My office is just down there."

I followed him past glass-fronted jungles of orchids, carnations, roses, gladiolas; past pails of greenery and pots of ivy; through a small greenhouse area with benches jammed with flowerpots, and even a bunch of dwarf trees which I guessed figured prominently in the dreams of a

THE STRIPPER

pooch called Bobo. Finally we made it into Stern's office and he closed the door while my sinuses gratefully noted that there wasn't a single cut flower in the room. He moved around in back of a kidney-shaped desk and invited me to sit down in one of the molded fiberglass chairs, cunningly shaped to anchor only those people blessed with pointed buttocks.

"I guess membership in a lonely hearts club isn't something you want talked about out loud in public, Lieutenant." Stern gave an embarrassed giggle. "A confession that you've flunked out in the school of human relationships!"

"The lonely are legend," I quoted happily. "Anyway, I'm a cop, not an analyst, and it's Patty Keller who interests me."

"Of course," he said, nodding eagerly. "I can't tell you very much about her, Lieutenant, I'm afraid. You see, I only met her the one time. The club fixed up the date for us as usual—around three months back, as I remember—and that was the only time I met her."

"The date wasn't successful?"

"I'm afraid not." His head shook sadly, and I wished he'd stop using it for punctuation—another five minutes of it and I'd need a couple of tranquilizers.

"What kind of a girl was she?" I prodded.

"She wasn't very attractive—physically, I mean," he said carefully. "Not that I attach too much importance to looks, you understand. She just didn't know how to make the best of herself and her clothes were all wrong. But they weren't really important—only the external signs of conflict."

I gritted my teeth. "Then how about we get down to the essentials, Mr. Stern? I got my own fantasy of the perfect female and I'm willing to bet money she's no more unreal than yours, so why don't we stay with facts?"

"Yes, sir," he said and swallowed hard. "Of course, the essentials! Well, I'd say she was a maladjusted personality, Lieutenant—I guess that's about the size of it!"

"You mean like she was unhappy—goddam miserable, even?" I grated.

"That's it!" He smiled dubiously, then saw the look on my face and didn't push his facial muscles any more. "She had a miserable home life, she said, then her parents died and she thought she'd be free to do what she always wanted—become an actress. But she wasn't getting any breaks and her money was running out fast." His head twitched again. "It was a depressing evening, Lieutenant, I can tell you!"

"Did she say anything about taking her own life?—maybe hint a little?"

His eyebrows knit together in a troubled line. "Now you mention it, I seem to recall she said she couldn't go on much longer like this—unless something happened soon, she'd have to end it all." He shrugged. "By that time I wasn't listening too good—all I wanted was out— and I figured she meant she'd go back to Pumpkin Creek or wherever it was she came from in the first place."

"She just wasn't your type?"

"That's for sure," he said fervently. "I'm the nervous type myself—kind of shy—I'm looking for an outgiving girl, Lieutenant, someone to boost my ego. One more night with Patty Keller and it could have been me stepping off that ledge!"

I felt a sudden draft on the back of my neck and turned my head to see a big, muscular blond-haired guy come into the office without bothering to knock. He wore a skintight sweatshirt along with a pair of faded jeans that were so tight you could see just about everything he had.

"Hi there, Harv," he said to Stern in a booming voice. "How's the old love life? Still coming on big and strong?" He ignored Stern's murderous glare and grinned at me like we were old friends.

"Old Harvey here is the last of the red-hot lovers," he confided in a loud voice. "Jesus, you should see him in action. There's no stopping him. Don't let the flower in the buttonhole throw you. Beneath that polished exterior beats the heart—should I say heart?—of one of your all-time randy, get-it-off-anywhere, no-fooling-around studs."

"Shut up, Steve!" Stern said venomously. "You aren't even funny! Can't you see the *lieutenant* isn't amused?"

"Lieutenant?" the giant repeated slowly, and for a moment his face fell apart. "You mean—like a cop?"

"Lieutenant Wheeler—from the county sheriff's office!" Stern snapped. "This is Steve Loomas, Lieutenant, a client of mine with a misguided sense of humor."

"Yeah," Loomas said weakly. "That's me—always working for the laughs. I guess I walked in at the wrong time, huh?"

"We were about all through," I told him. "Tell me something—what does a guy like you want with flowers?"

"Huh?" He looked at me like I was just out of Mars, with three heads all saying something different at the same time.

"Mr. Stern said you were a client," I explained patiently. "So—unless he's running a bordello in the back room—you buy flowers from him, right?"

"Oh—sure—flowers!!" Loomas nodded vigorously. "Yeah—all the time."

"So what do you want with them?" I persisted.

"Well—" he gave me a sickly grin. "You know how it is, Lieutenant, a guy likes to keep his pad looking nice."

"Like you never know who's about to drop in for tea?" I suggested sweetly.

His mouth dropped open as he stared at me blankly for a moment, then he made an effort and clamped his jaw tight.

"Sure, sure, Lieutenant, that's about the size of it." He edged toward the door. "Well, I sure am sorry for interrupting you guys. See you later, Harv—see you around, Lieutenant!"

"I wouldn't be surprised," I said honestly.

The door closed with a soft click and without Loomas' bulk, the office expanded back to its former size.

"He's a nice guy but—" Stern tapped his forehead significantly "—an actor—an out-of-work actor, mostly—he doesn't have too much up here!"

"Maybe because he's got so much everywhere else?" I suggested brightly. "Just one more question, Mr. Stern. How do you get along with the Arkrights?"

"The Arkrights?" He looked genuinely bewildered for a moment. "Oh—the Happiness Club Arkrights—just fine, Lieutenant. Why do you ask?"

"They strike me as being a couple of odd-ball characters," I said. "I wondered what their effect is on a client. They just don't seem the type to be running a lonely hearts organization—I can't see them having the sympathetic approach."

"Maybe you're right," he said politely. "I met them the first time after I joined the club, but I don't think I've seen either of them since then. Most of the real work is done by their receptionist, I think."

The look in his eyes said he was remembering Sherry Rand, and I didn't blame him one bit. In fact, I was right in there with him.

"Thanks for your time, Mr. Stern," I told him, and slid my nonpointed buttocks out of the uncomfortable chair.

"Not at all, Lieutenant." He escorted me to the door. "I wish I could help more—a young girl like that killing herself!" His head started wagging again. "A terrible tragedy—terrible!"

I had a steak sandwich in a diner after I left the florist, and got back to the office a little after two in the afternoon. Annabelle Jackson lifted her honey blonde head and looked at me like I was a hot news flash.

"How nice of you to stop by, Lieutenant!" She smiled sweetly. "The Sheriff's been waiting all morning—just hoping you might spare him a few minutes."

"It's one of my charity days," I explained modestly. "You know how it is—today I am dedicated to spreading sweetness and light. If I can bring a little sunshine into the Sheriff's sordid existence by sparing him a couple of

THE STRIPPER

minutes, who am I to deny him so much pleasure for such a little effort on my part?"

She tapped a pencil on the desktop thoughtfully while she considered. "I don't think he sees it quite that way," she said finally. "But why don't you go in and find out for yourself?"

"There's no hurry," I said hastily, and lit a cigarette to prove it. "I just got to thinking—how long is it since we had a date—even a small one?"

"Not long enough!" she said tartly. "I can still remember the unpleasant detail!"

"It was your own fault," I said reasonably. "You needn't have put up so much of a fight. All that yelling."

"I had to yell!" she retorted, her voice rising a few octaves. "Those five amplifiers of yours were all going at full volume—remember?"

"Ah yes, I remember it well," I said dreamily. "So why don't we start over? How about tomorrow night?"

"Not tomorrow night or any night during the next thirty years," she said decisively.

"Well—" I shrugged casually. "When you get real lonely, let me know, and I'll give you an introduction to a lonely hearts club that guarantees to find either the perfect mate or an adequate hotel window high enough above the sidewalk. And they don't even use computers."

An ominous growl behind me made me leap a couple of inches into the air. I looked around and saw the maneating sheriff just about to pounce.

"I hate to disturb you, Lieutenant," Lavers growled nastily. "I know it's in bad taste to mention work while you're around. But would you mind very much stepping inside my office just for a moment—" the veins stood out on his neck as he shrieked the last word at the top of his voice—"now!"

"Yessir!" I skipped past him fast in case he decided to stab me with the hot end of his cigar while I was real close.

He slammed the door shut and while the whole office

was still rocking, waddled around to his chair and plunked down into it wearily. I sat in the nearest visitor's chair with a look of polite attention on my face because when you get right down to it, I prefer being assigned on an indefinite basis to the Sheriff's office as an alternative to being returned to the homicide bureau, where so many guys outrank me, it makes for ulcers.

"That Jefferson report," Lavers said coldly. "I'd like to congratulate you on a masterly thesis, Wheeler. Your exposition of the psychoneurosis of a con man is fascinating."

"Thank you, sir," I said with appropriate modesty. "It was nothing."

"You're damned right it was nothing!" he snarled. "The one thing you didn't bother explaining was why Jefferson's still walking around a free man after he conned that finance company out of twenty thousand dollars!"

"I thought you knew that already, sir," I said respectfully. "We know he did it, but we can't prove it—there's not one single piece of evidence that would stand up in court."

"And you're prepared to let it go at that?"

"What do you suggest, sir?" I still kept it polite. "I should follow him to Mexico and stay right behind him until he passes one of those unmarked, small-denomination bills?"

"The deputy mayor owns some stock in that finance company!!" Lavers grumbled.

"Leave us hope he doesn't own stock in the insurance company that covered the finance company!" I suggested cheerfully.

The Sheriff brooded for a few seconds, then shrugged his massive shoulders. "All right! How about this Keller girl?—or did you just stay in bed this morning?"

I gave him a run-down on what had happened up to now, and the only thing I left out was my coming date with Sherry Rand. Even a cop is entitled to some kind of private life. The Sheriff would accuse me of putting sex

THE STRIPPER

before duty, and as a matter of principle I hate ever admitting he's right.

"The way you tell it, it all adds up to suicide," Lavers said when I'd finished. "That's the way the cousin tells it—plus this Stern character she had a date with. Maybe we should leave it at that?"

"I'd like to kick it around some more," I told him. "I've got the wrong feeling about it, Sheriff. The Arkrights would be more at home running a funeral parlor than a lonely hearts club. Harvey Stern could have cheerfully murdered Loomas when he made that crack about being the last of the red-hot lovers."

"I guess you've been around enough women by now to develop some feminine intuition!" he said sourly. "You know how accurate that is?"

"Don't forget the apomorphine, Sheriff," I reminded him. "How do you explain that?"

"Pure coincidence," he snorted. "I see no connection between a bad oyster and suicide, no matter how you cut it. If you were considering knocking someone off, Wheeler, I ask you—would you give her something to make her throw *up?*" His voice rose to a pitch of frustration.

"If I knew she was going to be perched on a fifteen-story ledge I might," I commented. "Besides, we're not in a month with an *R* in it."

"With that keen sense of humor, you can laugh yourself down to a sergeant in no time at all," he said coldly. Then he folded his paws over his paunch, leaned back, and said indulgently, "All right, Wheeler, just how do you propose further investigating the case, if I may ask?"

"With your permission, sir," I said, ignoring his sarcasm, "I'd like us to solicit the help of Miss Jackson."

"Dammit, Wheeler!" he said hotly. "You leave that girl alone! She's the best secretary I've ever had and I'm not about to take a chance on losing her because—"

I figured it would take a little time and I was right. It took fifteen minutes before he called Annabelle into the office, and another ten to bring her up to date on the situation. My throat was running dry by the time I'd finished, and I could tell right away by the incredulous look on her face that I hadn't made a good job of it.

"You mean," she almost spluttered, "you want me to go and join this—this lonely hearts club?"

"Right on the button, honey chile," I said admiringly. "It's the only lead we've got so far and we need somebody on the inside."

Annabelle took a deep breath and smoothed the clinging sheath dress down over her hips, so that her generously rounded curves jutted prominently like landscaping in paradise.

"Me?" she repeated in a disbelieving voice. "Join a lonely hearts club? Do I look the type who needs to join a lonely hearts club?"

"No," I replied, "but you could, quite easily. "You could wear the wrong kind of clothes for a start, comb your hair the wrong way—wear a pair of glasses with plain lenses maybe. Just let yourself go."

"And then what?" she snarled ferociously.

"You've been in Pine City for six months. You work as a stenographer in City Hall, but not for the Sheriff, of course! You don't know anybody here and you're real lonely. Your job bores you. What you really want is a glamorous career—an actress or a model—something like that. You don't care about a man's looks or his income bracket, only his soul. An intelligent, sensitive and refined gentleman is your ideal."

Annabelle looked at me hopelessly for a moment, then appealed to Lavers.

"Is he out of his mind, Sheriff?" she pleaded.

"That's always been my opinion," Lavers said smugly. "You can relate it to the phases of the moon mostly, I find."

"Then I don't have to do this crazy stunt he's babbling about?"

THE STRIPPER

"It's entirely up to you, my dear," Lavers said easily. "I think it's a pretty irregular suggestion!"

"From Lieutenant Wheeler that's strictly routine!" she said coldly. "Thank you, Sheriff."

"Sure, you don't have to do it," I agreed. "Chances are this kid, Patty Keller, did really kill herself and wasn't murdered at all. It doesn't make any real difference whether we find out for sure or not—except I keep hoping that some other poor kid who's alone and desperate in a big city doesn't wind up the same way all because we didn't pursue—"

"Sheriff?" Annabelle bit her lower lip doubtfully. "Do you honestly think it would help if I did like he says?"

"You've got a lot of courage," he muttered, "asking a man holding political office to be honest! If I must—then the answer's yes, there's a slight chance it could help. But that's no reason for you to do it if you don't want."

"O.K.," Annabelle said dismally. "Then I'll do it!"

"That's what I like about the South," I said admiringly, "they've got courage and integrity!"

"I sure wish you-all had told me that the last time I was in your apartment, Lieutenant," Annabelle said bleakly. "I might have stayed!"

Chapter Four

THE REPULSIVE GRIN OF ADMIRATION ON LOUIS' FACE when he greeted Sherry Rand died a sudden death when he saw me in back of her.

"Back again, Lieutenant?" he said hoarsely.

"Strictly for pleasure, friend," I said amiably. "Maybe you can find us a ringside table?"

"Sure, sure!" He nodded emphatically, "Anything you want, Lieutenant."

He gave us a table that was hard up against the raised dais, took our order for cocktails, then lumbered away. I took another look at Sherry Rand and thought happily of the long intimate hours ahead of us, depending on just how fast I could get her out of the Club Extravaganza and back to my apartment.

"This is fine," she said approvingly. "We should get a real good view from here."

"I've got one already," I said objectively.

She was looking just as sultry, and her hair was just as carelessly brushed as it had been in the Arkright Hap-

THE STRIPPER 169

piness Club—maybe even more so. She was wearing a black dress which clung seductively to her full, lush figure. Her unconfined breasts looked even more spectacular, and I could just make out the faint indentations her nipples made against the material. As she moved ahead of me into the club, I admired the slow swing of her ripe, rounded buttocks. Why we needed to go into a sex club, I didn't know. I had it all right there with me, and I didn't need to pay good money to watch other people doing it. A voyeur, I definitely am not.

An undersized waiter served the drinks while we sat at the table in the semi-darkness facing the stage and watching Estrelita going through her paces with her python, kissing it and sliding it up between her legs, virtually making love to it. Then a guy and a girl got onto the stage, slowly stripped off their clothes as they made lewd faces at each other, overdoing the whole bit with exaggerated suggestiveness, then when they were both naked, coming together on a moldy divan covered with red velvet. The guy—it was either Damien or Roger, I couldn't tell—then started to go through his jerky repertoire of lovemaking positions. The spotlight stayed fixed on them as their bodies slapped together.

"Boring, isn't it?" Sherry whispered. "There are only so many things they can do."

"You never know," I said. "There's always a chance of learning something new."

"I doubt it," she said, looking steadily at the coupled couple on the stage, who by now were looking rather bored with the whole thing. "Not with these two." She sighed wistfully. "Still, I like a man with energy and with staying power. It makes all the difference."

It turned out there was a story of some sort. Another girl came out onto the stage from the wings, and looked in mock surprise at the two of them, the girl now kneeling forward on the divan and the guy taking her from behind, his fingers digging into her buttocks. The second girl was slightly overweight, and after a moment of staring, apparently decided to get into the act, and started peeling off her clothes.

"Now this is getting better," I said quietly to Sherry.

She looked at me doubtfully. "Do you really think so? I think it's all unbelievably sordid."

I shrugged. "To each his own," I said.

Everybody was looking even more bored, and I thought if they did the same thing maybe three or four times a day, they had every reason to be. The second girl had finished stripping, and now completely naked, moved across to the couch to join the other two.

From then on it was all go as they went into their act, the two women making love to each other and to the guy, who was either Roger or Damien, going down on him while he gave each of them head in turn, straddling him, easing down on his indefatigable column while they played with each other's boobs and kissed each other full on the mouth. They creaked through the act, and finally it was over to a polite spattering of applause.

"Do you like to make it with two women, Al?" Sherry asked.

I shrugged. "It makes for added interest, I guess."

"It certainly keeps you busy," she said. "I don't know if I would like to make it with another woman, though. It would all depend on the circumstances, I guess. A spontaneous action. Maybe if I had had enough to drink, or hopped up on the weed. There would have to be a guy, though."

"With staying power."

"Oh sure. What would be the point if it's all over in one minute flat, just when a girl is starting to get worked up?"

The conversation was beginning to have a vaguely erotic effect on me. I recognised a come-on in the tone of her voice and in the sultry way she was looking at me. Maybe she was putting me through some sort of test.

I ordered fresh drinks and the waiter delivered them just in time—a second before the whole room was suddenly plunged into darkness. Five seconds later a single spotlight picked out Deadpan Dolores standing motionless on the stage in a graceful pose with her arms raised above her head. A long flowing black robe covered her completely from neck to ankles. The house lights brightened slowly and the robe became completely transparent, revealing the ripe, firmly fleshed body beneath it. Her nipples looked extremely large and vivid beneath the lights, and between her marblelike thighs her strawberry-blonde pubis came to a small wispy tuft. The silence was so complete you could almost hear a pin drop. It seemed to be electrically charged, as if at any moment, all hell would break loose. And a moment later it did.

Suddenly Dolores burst into action in a volcanic eruption of energy, her torso weaving and gyrating in a fantastic symmetry of motion to a single throbbing drumbeat. Her eyes were half-closed and there was a look of something close to rapture on her downcast face as her body performed the incredible, the unbelievable, the impossible.

I had never seen anything like it before—a dance without the movements of a dancer, a woman caught in the throes of a rising, orgasmic passion, whose pelvis jerked forward, whose legs were parted—she was a woman who was actually making love; her body writhed, and her hands moved slowly down her flanks, drawing in to the parted pink lips of her labia; it was not hard to imagine a guy there with her, filling her, lifting her to the peaks of ecstasy. To the rising beat of the drum, her movements became more frantic, and there was a look on her face of a woman who had completely abandoned herself to animal passion. Then, at the height of her orgasmic fury, she flung herself onto the stage, her body went rigid, twitched a few times, then slumped. The lights slowly faded, and then there was nothing.

The hushed silence continued for some seconds longer, and then suddenly there was a loud and prolonged round of applause. "Jesus," I whispered in awe. "That was really something."

The lights came on, and the stage was empty. "I thought it was cute," Sherry said, an amused glint in her eyes. "It looked so easy. I'm sure I could do it."

"Not here," I pleaded.

"Not here," she said quietly. "Later perhaps. There's plenty of time.". She reached over and laid her hand gently on mine. "I'm glad you brought me here, Al. I really am. Sleazy as it all is, it does make a change. I find it somehow relaxing."

"Yeah,"I said hoarsely. "Real relaxing."

"Hello!" Sherry smiled warmly at a spot a couple of feet over my head.

"We met already!" I said blankly.

"Hello," a voice said right over my head, and I leaped six inches out of my chair.

Dolores moved into my line of vision, wearing a black dress that was open all the way down to the navel, and with crossed straps only just covering the tips of her magnificent breasts. Her wide mouth was curved in a smile as she sat down between us, the waiter having produced a chair from nowhere in no time.

"Did you enjoy the show, Lieutenant?" she asked, her voice dripping with sensuality.

"He couldn't take his eyes off you," Sherry said quickly.

Dolores smiled at her sweetly. "That's nice. Don't you think he looks rather nervous? Or is it just frustration?"

A burst of raucous laughter from a nearby table saved me from trying to think up a snappy answer. Sherry turned her head casually to see who was making the noise, then her face brightened with recognition.

"I know that man from somewhere, I'm sure!" she said determinedly. "Maybe he's a member of the club."

I looked across and saw a familiar carnation, flanked by the two women who had put on the exhibition earlier with Roger or Damien, or whoever. The table in front of them was crowded with bottles and they looked like they were having themselves a ball. "He's having a ball," I commented.

"He always does," Dolores said in an amused voice. "He's a real big spender. Harv, they call him. I don't know the rest of it."

"I guess I must be mistaken," Sherry said drily. "With the company he keeps, I couldn't have met him at our club."

"He's here maybe four nights a week," Dolores said. "The two girls with him are not doing it for love, either, although he thinks it's just his personality, of course, that they're real stuck on him."

Sherry stood up and peered around the dim room. Reconnaissance successful, she said, "Back in a moment. What did they use to say? A girl has to powder her nose."

Left alone with Dolores, I couldn't think of anything to say. All I could do was gape at the smooth inner flanges of her breasts sweeping up from the deep valley that divided them. Then I turned my attention to Harvey's table. About then, two men walked up to it.

The first guy was medium height and a little heavy with it, wearing a dark suit. His bald head gleamed as he leaned forward to speak with Stern, but I lost interest right there when I saw the second guy. Although he was better dressed, it was for sure the same Steve Loomas, muscles and all, I'd met that morning in the florist's shop.

The smaller one is Miles Rovak—the owner," Dolores said when I asked her. "That shows just how much dear old Harv rates. Rovak wouldn't be bothered talking to more than a couple of customers during the whole week!"

"Who's the blond character with him?" I asked casually.

"Steve something—Loomas—he works for Miles," she said. "I had to bat him down hard one time, and since then we don't talk much any more."

"Excuse me a minute, Dolores," I said getting to my feet. "I'm sure Sherry will be back in a minute. Have a drink while you're waiting."

"My!" Dolores batted her eyelids up at me. "You sure are a free spender, Lieutenant! Is it all right if I have the good Scotch?"

I walked across to the most popular table in the whole room and smiled down at the florid-faced guy with the pink carnation in his lapel.

"Hello there, Harv," I said pleasantly. "Looks like you'll make that diploma yet in the school of human relationships!"

Stern looked up at me vaguely for a moment, then his face paled a little. "Good evening, Lieutenant," he said with no enthusiasm at all. "This is a surprise—seeing you here."

The two women looked at me stonily. "You know this man, Harvey?" Rovak asked in a clipped voice.

"This is Lieutenant Wheeler—from the sheriff's office," Stern answered in a strangled voice. "We met this morning."

"It's nice," I said mildly, "meeting people again this way. How are the flowers, Mr. Loomas? Not wilting yet, I hope."

"Huh?" He looked at me blankly.

"All those flowers you bought from Harvey's shop this morning," I reminded him. "Remember?"

"Oh. Yeah." He smiled bravely. "The flowers. No, they're not wilting."

"My name is Miles Rovak," the bald-headed guy said obviously working hard at getting some warmth into his voice. "Nice to have you here, Lieutenant—I'm the owner of the club."

"Thanks," I said. "I liked the floor show fine. I guess I had about the best view in the house!"

"We do our best," he said absently. "You're here on pleasure, not business?"

"Right," I agreed. "I just wanted to say hello to Mr. Stern. Don't let me break up the party."

"Real nice meeting you," Rovak said, then snapped his fingers. "Louis!"

The ugly face of the head waiter appeared right beside him in two seconds flat. "Yeah, boss?" Louis asked anxiously.

"The Lieutenant's check," Rovak said easily. "I want you should tear it up."

"Yeah, boss." Louis had a pained expression on his face.

"That isn't necessary," I said.

"Real nice having you visit, Lieutenant," Rovak said. "I want you should be my guest any time."

"Well, thanks," I said sincerely. "Any time you're in the county jail I hope I can do the same for you!"

"Hey, listen!" Loomas objected loudly, then shut up suddenly as Rovak's elbow knifed into his solar plexus.

"It's a joke," the club owner said in a tired voice. "You know you don't have a brain, Steve—so why knock yourself out trying to use it, huh?"

I went back to my own table and found Sherry but no Dolores.

"What happened to Deadpan Dolores?" I asked.

"She had to get ready for her next number."

I nodded. "I don't know about you," I said, "but I think I've seen enough. What about you?"

"I guess so," she replied. "That sort of thing can get a bit repetitive after a while. So what do you suggest, Al?"

"What about my apartment?" I said vaguely.

"That sounds just fine." She smiled warmly at me, while I gaped back in amazement.

On the way out I noticed that the party at Stern's table had shrunk a little. Rovak and Loomas had gone, so again there was just the florist with a well-worn female on either side of him. Right then I figured him for the star pupil of the lonely hearts club.

We got back to my apartment maybe a half hour later, and I left Sherry in the living room while I went through to the kitchen to get some ice. When I got back I saw she had made herself comfortable on the divan. I left the ice bucket on the table, then slipped a cassette into the stereo. A moment later, the soft milky strains of clarinet oozed out from the speakers into the room.

"Smooth," Sherry said. "This music is relaxing."

I fixed us a couple of drinks and handed her one. She smiled lazily at me.

"Now that you've managed to get me into your apartment, what happens next? It always interests me. I like to watch a man's technique. They vary so much."

"But always with the same end result?"

"More or less. Sometimes the end result can be a bit of an anti-climax after the build-up. Sometimes there's hardly any build-up, and boy, the climax is something else again. Do you think I'm being too frank, Al?" she asked, looking steadily up at me.

I shook my head. "Not at all. Go ahead. I find it refreshing."

"I was thinking about you making it with two women. It could be interesting. Another couple of drinks and it wouldn't matter all that much."

"I don't know who I can rustle up right now," I said. "It mightn't be easy."

She gave an airy wave of her hand. "It was just an idle thought. Maybe one day I'll get around to thinking about it again." She drank a little. "It tastes O.K.," she announced. "No, Al. Just the two of us. It makes for greater coziness. Maybe we can dream up a few fantasies between us, make up for the lack." Her legs were crossed, and I let my eyes follow the shapely curve of her thigh up to one rounded buttock. She smiled dreamily. "Why *did* you ask me for a date tonight?" she asked suddenly. "Did it have anything to do with the Arkright Happiness Club?"

"Only the half of it," I admitted.

"O.K.," she said and sighed gently. "I should have guessed there would be something like that behind it. So you've got some questions to ask me?"

"They'll keep," I told her.

"No. Let's get them over with, so we can concentrate on other things."

"The guy in the club tonight," I said. "The short one with the red face and the carnation, having himself a ball with the hired help. You were right—you had seen him at the Happiness Club. His name is Stern—Harvey Stern."

"I thought his face was familiar," she said comfortably. "But I don't remember anything else about him—if you're about to ask."

"I wasn't," I said. "Stern figures you do most of the real work around the place. Is that right?"

"Just the routine." She shrugged. "The Arkrights pay real well—so I have to earn my keep."

"Did they tell you why I was asking questions about Patty Keller?"

"She killed herself," Sherry said in a somber voice. "It sounded horrible."

"It was," I agreed. "I saw it happen. You remember Patty at all?"

"Vaguely."

"What happens when somebody walks into the Happiness Club, wanting to join up?"

"They see me first. I pass them on to one of the Arkrights, and after the interview's finished, whichever Arkright handled it gives me the details so I can make out the personal file on the new member. Then I cross check all the files and sort out the eligibles for one of the Arkrights to make the decision."

"Decision?" I queried.

"Who will be the new member's first date," Sherry explained patiently. "And that's about it—I handle the accounts, too."

"You remember whether it was Jacob or Sarah Arkright that made the decision on Patty Keller's first date?"

"No." She Shook her head firmly. "Sorry, Al. Next question?"

"No more questions," I said. "Another drink, though."

I took our glasses over to the table and made fresh

drinks. When I had finished, I turned around and saw Sherry standing by the divan, wriggling out of her dress.

"Hey, what are you doing?" I yelped.

She let the dress drop onto the floor, and smiled at me archly. "Taking a short cut. I hope you don't mind. Or do you really want to go through the whole seduction bit, and waste more time?"

She wore a pair of flimsy, almost transparent briefs, and I saw the the deep suntan did have a hundred percent coverage. Her breasts jutted proudly, their dark pink tops swollen with desire. Her hips were rounded, her thighs firm, and the gauzy briefs clung possessively to her mound. Aware of the slow hardening in my groin, I put the drinks back on the table because I didn't want to spill good Scotch all over the carpet.

Sherry slipped her thumbs into the waistband of her briefs, rolled them down over her thighs and stepped delicately out of them. Suddenly, I felt my throat go dry. I gulped. The sight of her standing there in nothing but her all-over tan, with the small triangle of curling pubic hair nestling snugly between her thighs, made my blood surge and my heart beat faster. She was a perfect specimen of womanhood, arousing the raging beast in any man. I gulped again, and began to unbutton my shirt, because if this was going to be a party, I certainly wasn't going to be a party-pooper.

About a minute later, we came together on the divan, holding her tightly, our lips glued together, our tongues darting, and my hands clasping the pliant flesh of her buttocks. My swollen yard throbbed and strained against her as she moved beneath me and parted her legs—and then I was sliding smoothly into her, and a deep, rich, velvety feeling enveloped me. The sensation was smooth and creamy, and as our movements increased against each other, and her legs came up and clamped me in a viselike grip, I thought if I died right now, it wouldn't really matter. I was already in paradise.

"Right now," Sherry murmured in my ear. Let's see how much staying power you've got."

"Don't worry," I murmured right back at her. "I'm staying."

"So hang on in there, Al," she said with a throaty chuckle, her fingers digging relentlessly into my shoulders.

Chapter Five

I WAS BACK AGAIN WITH THAT FAMILY ALBUM PHOTO, circa 1927, and any time now I was going to say, "I love my wife—but, oh, you kid!" then put on my raccoon coat and get the hell out of there.

Sarah Arkright was seated in back of her desk, a look of frozen distaste on her face, while her ever-faithful spouse Jacob stood beside her, his hand on her shoulder. I couldn't make up my mind whether he was giving her physical support, or maybe he'd keel over sideways if he took his hand away.

"This is a most outrageous request, Lieutenant!" Sarah said harshly. "First you take two of our personal files away with you, and now you want to see another dozen or more! I can't possibly allow it."

"I can subpoena them," I said pleasantly. "You wouldn't want to put me to all that trouble would you, Mrs. Arkright?"

"I can't think of one good reason why not," she said

THE STRIPPER

acidly. "You may be a police officer, young man, but your manners are disgusting!"

"Now, now, Sarah!" Jacob smiled at me nervously and once again I figured the guy who'd made his teeth had a lot to answer for.

"Don't pay any mind to what Sarah says, Lieutenant," he went on quickly. "It's just her way—I guess you could say her bark is worse than her bite."

I shuddered at the sudden thought of Sarah about to bite, and reached for a cigarette to steady my nerves; then remembered I couldn't smoke in the office because the foul smell of tobacco was something else they didn't tolerate, along with lieutenants.

"Sure," I said to Arkright. "It's just that I'd like a little more co-operation from your wife. We're trying to nail down just why the Keller girl killed herself—and as she was one of your clients, I'd figure you'd be anxious to help."

"I don't see what searching through all our confidential files will accomplish," Sarah snapped. "A proper investigation is one thing, Lieutenant, while pandering to morbid curiosity is quite another!"

"The last date you organized for Patty Keller was with Harvey Stern," I said. "That makes us interested in Stern, naturally. His personal folder shows he's dated over a dozen girls since he's been a member of your club. We'd like to know a little more about these girls—how they made out with him. That's why I want to see their records."

Sarah primped her hideously red hair absently with one talon-like hand.

"I refuse!" Her brittle voice shook with anger. "I shall see our lawyers about this—this unwarrantable invasion of our privacy!"

"Now, now, Sarah!" Jacob repeated uncomfortably.

"Oh—shut up!" she snarled at him.

Behind the rimless glasses, his eyes swam with mortification. He took his hand away from her shoulder, let the fingers fiddle with the too-small knot of his tie for a few moments, then walked away from her stiffly, with all the bounce gone out of him.

"We have a duplicate of Harvey Stern's file," he said in a rusty voice. "I'll check the names of the girls from it, then get their files for you." He opened the door and stepped outside, closing the door behind him noiselessly.

"Well!" Sarah Arkright gobbled for a moment while that fuzzy look that was always around the edges, spread right across her eyes.

"It might be easier if I check those files in the outer office, Mrs. Arkright," I said politely, and stood up.

"Since my husband sees fit to ignore my opinions, I am powerless to stop you, Lieutenant," she said flatly. The hollows in her cheeks deepened, giving her raddled face an even gaunter look.

"But I shall still see our lawyers—it's quite obvious that only a lawsuit will teach you any appreciation of the rights of respectable people!"

I got to the door, then looked back at her for a moment.

"Mrs. Arkright?" My morbid curiosity got the better of me. "What do you do for kicks?"

"What?" Her face was a dull scarlet.

Jacob Arkright and Sherry Rand were busy searching a row of filing cabinets when I came into the outer office. I lit the cigarette I'd been wanting for the last ten minutes, then walked over and joined them.

"Shouldn't keep you long," Arkright smiled at me. "Oh—this is Miss Rand—but you've probably met already?"

The ashes of a passionate fire burned briefly in Sherry's eyes as she looked at me, then her full lips curved into a faintly mocking smile.

"We've met, Mr. Arkright," she said politely. "As a matter of fact, we found we share a common interest."

"Really?" Jacob looked pleased at the thought that

someone in his organization had made friends with the law. "What's that, Miss Rand?"

"Primitive dances," Sherry said innocently. "Fertility rites. The lieutenant is something of an expert. He says it gives him staying power, and I'd go along with that."

"Fascinating!" Arkright said vaguely. He fished out a new file to add to the already impressive stack Sherry was holding. "There—I think that about does it, Lieutenant!"

"Thanks a lot," I told him. "You mind if I borrow them for a little while?"

"Certainly not." He beamed at me anxiously. "You will return them as soon as possible?"

"For sure," I agreed.

"Good. Now, if you'll excuse me, Lieutenant, I feel I should be getting back to my wife."

"Of course," I said gravely. "I think she's missing your helping hand right now."

He gulped and a wan look spread across his face as he went back to the explosion waiting for him behind the door. After he'd gone Sherry moved in and leaned her delightful weight against me.

"I haven't seen you since breakfast," she murmured. "Did you miss me so bad you just had to come around the office?"

"I hate to disappoint you, honey," I said sadly. "But it's not you. It's that Sarah Arkright I'm crazy for—twenty-three skidoo! We're about to run away together and open a speakeasy in Chi. I got a friend who makes first grade booze in a bathtub out of sour apples and the dregs from Sterno cans. We got it made, Sarah and me!"

"What?—the bathtub booze?" Sherry asked coldly.

Then she backed off smartly, leaving me with my arms full of personal files. I looked down at them hopefully, wondering if there were any kinks and fetishes hidden under those white covers.

"Is that it then?" I asked her.

"What?"

"The folders. Have I got them all?"

"Yes, that's the lot."

There was a sudden burst of sound from the Arkrights' office—her thin voice rising to a crescendo, followed by the sound of a shattering vase.

"Sounds like Jacob's not making out too well in there," I observed. "Who's the boss of the outfit, anyway, him or her?—or are they equal partners?"

"They share about fifty per cent of the club between them," Sherry said casually. "The other fifty per cent is owned by a silent partner. I've never even met him—he never comes into the office at all."

"A partner who's not only silent, but invisible!" I was impressed. "For sure he's not a politician!"

"I don't know what he is." Sherry yawned sensuously. "His name's Rovak."

I gave her the beady-eyed look usually reserved for finance company managers. Then I remembered she'd left our table when Dolores and I had seen him in the Extravaganza last night. "Rovak, huh? And his first names's Miles. I shouldn't be surprised."

"You do know him!" She looked mildly surprised. "What's he like, Al?"

"You're on the level?" I stared at her suspiciously. "His name is Miles Rovak?—for real?—and he owns half this lonely hearts bureau?"

There was another resounding crash from inside the Arkrights' office and once again Sarah's voice was raised in bitter vituperation.

"That's right," Sherry said solemnly. "Why? Is it important?"

"I don't know, honey," I said honestly. "But it could be. I guess I'd better take these files down to the Sheriff's office before Sarah finishes with her husband and comes looking for me!"

"I hope she's not too tough on him," Sherry said. "Jacob's a nice little guy—mostly—and I like everything about him except for those gypsy hands that keep wand-

THE STRIPPER

ering the whole time." She made a face. "You know—*clammy!*"

"Cheez!" I said feelingly. "If I'd been married to Sarah for as long as he has, my hands would be clammy, too—along with my mind!"

"You don't have a mind, Al," she corrected me. "You're just one big bundle of desire, with nerve ends like radar."

"Don't forget the staying power."

"And staying power."

"So did I hear you complaining?"

She shook her head. "No complaints, Al," she said softly. "No complaints at all."

I took the files down to the office and found the Sheriff was out visiting with the mayor at City Hall, which was a break. Sergeant Polnik ambled into the office with a worried look on his face.

"Lieutenant?" His forehead corrugated alarmingly and I gave him my full attention because I always have a nervous feeling that if he ever has three separate thoughts in one day, there'll be a whirring noise inside his head and everything will fall apart.

"What can I do for you, Sergeant?" I asked sympathetically.

"Well, the Sheriff says I'm assigned to help you on this suicide case." He brooded for a moment. "I don't know what we're looking for, Lieutenant, and it worries me." He hesitated for a moment to make sure his meaning came across crystal clear. "I mean, like I'd feel better if you told me to do something, Lieutenant. I've been sitting around waiting since yesterday morning, and now I'm worried the way the Sheriff keeps on looking at me every time he goes by!"

"Polnik," I said sorrowfully, "I've been neglecting you!"

I started in to rack my brains for something I could give him to do, when I had a sudden inspiraton.

"See these?" I pointed to the heap of files on the desk.

"Sure, Lieutenant." His eyes lit up suddenly. "What is it? Porn?"

I shook my head. "These are files from a lonely hearts club. Each one represents a female member of that club, and I want you to question each and every one of them."

Polnik stared at me for a few moments, his jaw hanging slack, then slowly a beatific smile spread across his face.

"One day I knew it would happen," he said simply. "I knew if I waited long enough, I would get my chance. And now, here it is. Beautiful women. Why should *you* get all the breaks, Lieutenant?"

"Why indeed?" I remarked. "Now all these women have one thing in common," I told him. "They all had a date, organized by the lonely hearts club, with the same guy—Harvey Stern. Get them talking about Stern. I figure he could be the boy we're after. Use your technique, Polnik. Get them to open up their little hearts to you."

Polnik was glass-eyed at the thought. "You can trust me, Lieutenant."

He stacked the files into an orderly pile with loving care, then carried them out of the office. I figured he had enough work to keep him busy for the next couple of days, just so long as he took time out to sleep. He has the same trouble I've got—when work means females, he's dedicated.

I called the Club Extravaganza and asked to speak to Mr. Rovak, but he wasn't there. "Who wants him?" the girl at the other end asked.

"That's a good question," I told her and hung up.

The directory gave his home address as out on Ocean Beach, and I figured the ten-mile run down there wouldn't be wasted on a sunny afternoon right after lunch. I made one more call before I left the office, to Captain Johns in the homicide bureau, and asked him would he get somebody to run a check on Rovak, Loomas, and Stern, and see if they had any record. Johns said O.K., it was no trouble, and how was life in the Sheriff's office? I told him it was just fine if you happened to be a sheriff—and how was life in the bureau these days? It was my own fault for asking. By the time he'd finished detailing the major faults of the homicide bureau I could have been halfway to Ocean Beach already.

Chapter Six

THE ROAD SEEMED TO SLIDE STRAIGHT DOWN THE SIDE OF a cliff, and right at the bottom was Rovak's house. It was quite a place—white stucco and palm trees, and a high adobe wall in front to keep out the peasants. But the iron gates across the driveway were wide open, so I guessed Rovak wasn't figuring on a revolution this year.

I drove in and parked behind an aristocratic Mercedes, and got out. The house was flanked by a long concrete walk which led to a diamond-shaped pool. Beyond the pool, the Pacific Ocean sparkled in the afternoon sunlight, and a wooden jetty probed out far enough into deep water to accommodate the massive cabin cruiser secured at its head.

A couple of cane lounging chairs were beside the pool, and one of them was occupied. Even from that distance, I recognized the female form, supine and topless, and walked more briskly toward it. When I got closer, she heard me coming and raised her head a couple of inches

THE STRIPPER

to look at me. A bundle of fur lying across her bare midriff yapped reprovingly at her sudden movement.

"Oh, Jesus," a familiar voice said in dismay. "Somebody must be paying him to haunt us now, Bobo."

I looked appreciatively down at the figure relaxing in the cane chair. "Well, as I live and gasp," I said. "If it isn't Deadpan Dolores."

At the sound of my voice, the pooch whimpered the canine equivalent of "Take to the hills, men!"—then leaped from Dolores' midriff onto the concrete and skulked under the protection of the lounging chair.

She regarded me with an expression of frank distaste on the broad planes of her face. "I don't mind so much at the Club," she said coldly, "because I only work there. But what gives you the right to invade my privacy in my leisure time, Lieutenant?"

All she wore was a tiny pair of turquoise briefs that accentuated the bulge of her pubis. The nipples were taut on her slightly flattened breasts. "What now, Lieutenant?" she demanded. "Can't a girl relax in private, without having you burst in to disturb the peace? The air of simple tranquility?"

I stood there admiring her tan, and the way her boobs gently rose and fell, and I felt myself start to get poetic myself. "A vision of beauty lying beneath the waxing breeze," I said. "Caressed by the sun. Have I by chance, inadvertently, stumbled across paradise. Have I come on a simple mission only to find Serendipity?"

"Screw you, Lieutenant!" she snapped.

"I would like to stay, I really would, but alas, I don't have the time. I'm looking for Miles Rovak."

"He's down there—" Dolores pointed toward the jetty "—on the boat. So do me a favor and fall overboard, will you?"

"I just can't figure out why you don't like me," I said sorrowfully. "It's not my fault I'm a cop. It was either that or work for a living."

"Oh, very funny," she growled. "Such a comedian."

She didn't seem to be encouraging me to hang around, so I thought it was a good time to go see Rovak, and headed toward the jetty. I reached the end of the jetty about thirty seconds later and stepped onto the snow-white deck of the cruiser. A head of blond curls, long overdue for a cut, appeared out of the hatchway a few seconds later, and a look of surprise on Steve Loomas' face as he stared at me.

"Hell!" he croaked finally. "For a moment there, you had me wondering if you was real, Lieutenant!"

"Everybody's saying that," I said uncomfortably. "I'm beginning to get a complex."

He came out on the deck and flexed his muscles in an automatic reflex against the slight breeze coming in off the ocean. He was wearing the same tight, faded jeans, and a striped sweatshirt. Close up, those king-size muscles were impressive, and he flexed them a little more, maybe not so much for my benefit as to make sure they didn't seize up on him suddenly.

"I'm looking for Miles Rovak," I told him. "Dolores said he was out here on board the boat."

"Yeah, he's here," Loomas said, nodding. "I'll get him for you." He stuck his head back down the hatchway and yelled, "Mr. Rovak—Lieutenant Wheeler's up here—wants to see you." Then he smiled at me uncertainly. "We keep on bumping into each other all over, don't we, Lieutenant?"

"Like they say, it's a small world," I agreed.

Just then Rovak arrived on the deck. His bald head was bright pink from a little over-exposure to the sun. He carried with him an unconscious air of authority, and an arrogant strength of will showed in the harsh lines etched deeply into his face.

"You wanted to see me, Lieutenant?" he asked brusquely.

"Some questions," I told him. "About a girl called Patty Keller."

"Patty Keller . . ." He repeated the name a couple of

times, then shook his head. "I don't think I ever heard the name before."

"She's dead," I explained. "Went off a hotel window ledge a couple of days back. We're trying to find out why."

Rovak shook his head slowly. "I can't help you, Lieutenant. I'm sure I never knew the poor kid. What makes you think I can help, anyway?"

"A string of coincidences so long you wouldn't believe them," I said amiably. "The only relative the Keller girl had in town was a cousin who turned out to be a stripper, Dolores, who works in your club. Patty belonged to a lonely hearts club and her last date there was with a florist, Stern. While I'm talking to shy, introverted old Harv, who should breeze in but Loomas here?"

Out of the corner of my eye I saw Loomas looking studiously out to sea.

"Last night I was at your club," I continued, talking to Rovak. "And who do I meet but Harv, having a ball with two of the star performers sitting at his table. This guy needs a lonely hearts club? I asked myself. Somebody tells me he's a regular client at your club, Mr. Rovak. He's got himself a reputation. A big spender, that somebody called him. Anyway, I went over to his table to say hello, and who should be there but Steve Loomas again."

"I don't get the significance," Rovak said curtly.

"Patty Keller's cousin works at your club," I said patiently. "Stern, her lonely hearts date, is a regular client at your club. Loomas, his pal who calls him the last of the red-hot lovers, works for you. And then this morning I hit the biggest coincidence yet. I find out you don't just own the Extravaganza. You also own fifty percent of the Arkright Happiness Club."

"Is there some new law against legitimate investments?" he snapped.

"Not the last time I looked," I admitted. "I'm just curious to know when a coincidence stops being one—I figured you might be able to tell me."

Rovak took a cigar from his shirt pocket, bit off the end and spat it over the side, then rammed it between his teeth in an irritated gesture.

"I don't know from coincidence!" He found a match and lit the cigar, wreathing his face in fragrant smoke for a moment. "What little sense I can make out of your spiel, is that you're investigating the cause of some poor kid's suicide, right? So—for the second and last time—I never even heard of her until you told me her name. And a coincidence is just a goddamned coincidence!"

"Maybe if we come at it a different way, Mr. Rovak?" I suggested politely. "The way it's worked out, you're the hub of the whole thing—coincidentally. That makes things kind of convenient for me because you know everybody concerned. Like Harvey Stern, for example. Tell me about him."

"All I know about Stern you've said already," He grunted. "A fat little guy with a red face who must sell a hell of a lot of flowers if the money he spends in my place is any indication!"

"Can you figure one good reason why a guy who's a big spender at your club would need to be a member of your lonely hearts club at the same time?"

Rovak grunted sourly, then shook his head. "No," he admitted, "I guess I can't at that."

"Now, maybe, you can begin to understand why I'm so fascinated by coincidence," I told him. "Especially where Harvey Stern is involved."

"You figure old Harv was the reason why this kid knocked herself off?" Steve Loomas asked incredulously.

"Don't knock yourself out thinking, Steve," I said kindly. "It must take most of your strength to keep those muscles working now."

"He's got a point," Rovak growled. "Is that what you think?"

"Maybe," I said.

"You seem to be going to a hell of a lot of trouble to establish why this kid killed herself." He looked at me curiously. "Is it that important, Wheeler? I mean, supposing you do prove she did it because of Stern—there's still nothing you can do about it, is there? Maybe it's a shame, but it's no crime to be the reason for somebody killing themselves, is it?"

"Not as long as Patty Keller *did* kill herself," I said softly.

Rovak puffed his cigar for a few moments, his hard eyes boring into mine. "There's some doubt about the matter?" he asked finally.

"There's a lot of doubt about the matter," I agreed with him. "And it keeps getting bigger all the time!"

Loomas had a grayish tinge under his deep suntan. "I read about it in the papers," he said hoarsely. "They said she jumped!"

"I was hanging out the window, trying to talk her into changing her mind," I said. "I was sure she had—she was on her way back inside when she swayed suddenly and fell. She never jumped."

"Well," Loomas said, shrugging his massive shoulders, "even so, Lieutenant, that's not murder—is it?"

"The autopsy showed there was apomorphine in her blood stream," I said, and told him what that could do. "If we discover that someone else gave her that, then we'll have a pretty good idea of whether it was murder or not."

"*Now* who's talking about coincidences!" Loomas yapped in my face. "Who would give anybody something like *that* if they wanted to get rid of them? She probably took it herself for some reason!"

"Maybe," I snarled. "On the other hand, maybe old Harv is a good friend of yours or maybe he owes you money, huh?"

"Don't get me wrong, Lieutenant!" Muscles gulped. "I was only trying to point up the possibilities, that's all."

Rovak tossed the butt of his cigar over the guard rail and smiled apologetically at me.

"I'm glad you told us the significance of your investigation, Lieutenant," he said quietly. "I wish I knew more about this Stern guy, so I could help."

"Thanks," I told him. "You could tell me something—just to satisfy my own curiosity. How come a man like you owns fifty percent of a lonely hearts club?"

He grinned frankly. "I guess it does sound kind of strange at that—after you've had a good look at the Extravaganza! But the answer's real simple, Lieutenant, it's a goddamned good investment. The Arkrights have been running that kind of service most of their lives and they're pretty expert at it by now. A couple of years back they came out here from the East with all the know-how but no capital. Somebody put them in touch with me, and I checked their record—it was impressive. So I put up the capital in return for a half-ownership. They run the whole deal, of course. I've never been inside the office, even."

"Like you said—there's no law against investment in a legitimate enterprise," I acknowledged.

The breeze got stronger, whipping up a sudden gust that made Loomas flex his muscles defensively.

"How's the acting racket these days, Steve?" I asked conversationally.

"Acting?" He blinked at me a couple of times. "How the hell would I know?"

"Isn't that your racket?"

"Somebody's been kidding you, Lieutenant!" He laughed. "Me—an actor! I work for Mr. Rovak, look after his boat—things like that."

"I must have a word with good old Harv," I said gently. "I'm a cop with no sense of humor when I'm working."

"It was him that told you I was an actor?" Loomas shook his head bewilderedly. "He must be losing his mind!"

" 'A mostly out-of-work actor' were the actual words he used, as I remember," I said. "Maybe there's a simple answer—like he's a congenital liar?"

"Maybe it isn't as simple as that," Rovak said sharply.

THE STRIPPER

"I've been thinking—since you told me why you're so interested in that Keller girl's death—that I don't go for that long string of coincidence any more than you do, Lieutenant! The more I hear you talk, the more it sounds like Stern is the guy in back of all these coincidences!"

"You could be right," I nodded. "If I keep on plugging hard enough, I figure sooner or later I'm going to find out for sure."

"Is there anything I can do to help?" he volunteered.

"I don't think so," I said, "but thanks for suggesting it—and thanks for being patient with all my questions."

I stepped back onto the jetty, then headed toward the pool. Dolores was sprawled face down on her lounging chair, the tiny briefs leaving most of her golden buttocks with their thin dividing cleavage almost completely bare. A wad of hair peered up at me from under the chair then vanished quickly, and a moment later I heard a whimpering noise that was definitely neurotic.

"You should buy that pooch of yours some analysis," I said to Dolores' shapely back. "He's developing a fixation about me!"

"Doesn't everybody?" she asked coldly.

I lit a cigarette, taking my time about it, while I admired the view on the lounging chair. Then Dolores rolled over slowly onto her back and glared up at me.

"You have eyes like redhot rivets!" she snapped.

"Is it my fault you happen to be an exotic, ravishingly beautiful woman?" I asked heatedly. "Am I responsible for the long-stemmed loveliness of your legs?—the geometric perfection of the rest of your anatomy?—the hundred-per-cent-plus desirability quotient you have? Blame your mother and father if you must blame somebody, but not me—I'm strictly an innocent bystander!"

"Well!" Her eyes widened with surprise and maybe something else, I couldn't be sure. "I never knew a cop could be that poetic before!"

She sat up on the chair to take a closer look at me.

"Do you really mean that?" she asked. "You're not just having me on?"

"Uh-huh," I grunted.

She was still watching me with an intent look in her eyes. Her bare breasts rose and fell steadily. Her nipples were still swollen. Maybe the sun was slowly doing things to her.

"Kidding aside, Lieutenant, what does appeal to you most about me—if anything?"

"You really want to know?" I said soberly, and when she nodded, said, "Your face."

"You're kidding!"

"The hell I'm kidding," I said abruptly. "The first time I ever saw you was in the picture outside the club. Sure, you got a great figure, but it was your face that attracted me most. It's not beautiful, you understand, but it's got personality and intelligence."

She was staring at me in amazement. "Jesus Christ!" she said in an awestruck voice. "What are you saying? Nobody has ever told me anything like that before."

I shrugged. "Well, there you are. I've said it."

She shook her head from side to side, her eyes filled almost to overflowing for a moment, then she blinked fiercely and turned her head away.

"Christ, you'll have me going on like some starry-eyed college kid in a moment."

"Or like your cousin—Patty?" I suggested.

She looked back at me, the hurt showing on her face. "Did you have to spoil it that way?" she whispered.

"The feeling is—and it's getting stronger by the minute—that she didn't kill herself after all," I said briskly. "Now it looks like she was murdered. I thought you might like to know."

I started walking again, past the chair, toward my car on the driveway.

"Lieutenant!" she called behind me, her voice suddenly frantic. "Wait a minute, Lieutenant. Hey, come back here!"

THE STRIPPER

I kept going until I reached my car, then reversed down the driveway out onto the road and pointed its nose up toward Pine City again.

As I drove, I wondered if I was getting any place at all—or if Patty Keller actually had been murdered. All I had was that string of coincidences I had detailed for Rovak—and maybe they meant nothing. Right then I couldn't see any alternative to the unoriginal squeeze play I had been using all the time. If you don't watch it, it can become a sucker's play. You keep seeing the same people over and over again, asking the same questions. You try to look wise and make vaguely ominous remarks—and all the time you're hoping that somehow, someplace, you'll get some kind of result from somebody. For all you know, the guilty party is two jumps ahead of you the whole time and silently laughing his head off as he watches your fool antics.

It was a cheering thought to keep me company on the way back to the city. Later, I wondered why I'd gotten this strong feeling about the kid's death. Maybe because I was right there when it happened. That sounded like a reasonable answer and I'd have been happy to stay with it, only I knew it wasn't true. The real reason why it had gotten so deep under my skin was because a girl called Patty Keller had died suddenly and unpleasantly—and nobody in the whole wide world gave a goddamn about it. In back of my mind was the uneasy conviction that if it had happened to a guy named Wheeler instead of a girl named Keller, the reaction would have been about the same. So somebody had to worry about the girl and I was elected. Because if I didn't worry for her, who would worry for me?

It was about then I figured if Dolores sent Bobo to a headshrinker for analysis, maybe I should go along, too. We could share our fixations along with a couple of rubber bones on the headshrinker's doormat.

Chapter Seven

"APOMORPHINE?" STERN REPEATED. "I NEVER HEARD OF it before, Lieutenant! Is it something you can buy in a drugstore?"

"Not without a prescription," I said. "But I guess that wouldn't stop anybody if they wanted some bad enough."

The white carnation in his lapel seemed to wilt a little. I didn't blame it at all—the heavy, cloying atmosphere inside the florist's shop, choked with the scent of a hundred different flowers was enough to make even an orchid wilt.

Harvey Stern's pink and white complexion changed color rapidly, like a chameleon, alternating between the two colors but favoring white most of the time.

"Murder!" he said breathlessly. "It sounds so—so fantastic, Lieutenant! A harmless, pathetic girl like Patty! Who would want to kill her?"

"You—maybe?" I growled.

"Me?" His plump body quivered agitatedly. "You're joking, Lieutenant!"

"You both belonged to the same lonely hearts club," I

THE STRIPPER

said evenly. "You were the only date she ever had through that club. The last time I was in here you told me about it. You felt embarrassed belonging to such a club, you said, it was a confession that you'd flunked out in the school of human relationships. You were the nervous type, you told me, you needed somebody to boost your ego."

"I only told you the truth—as I see it at least," he said defensively.

"Then Loomas came into your office and told me you were the last of the red-hot lovers," I went on. "No woman could resist you. Last night I saw you in the Extravaganza, whooping it up with a couple of the performers. You didn't look the nervous type then, Harv. You looked like you were enjoying it just fine—until you saw me, anyway."

"Well—I—" He stuttered helplessly to a standstill.

"Your old buddy, Steve Loomas, just dropped in to buy some flowers," I snarled. "He's an actor—a mostly out-of-work actor. He works for Rovak, the sex club owner, and you knew damned well he did."

"I—I was upset—nervous," Stern babbled incoherently. "I didn't know what I was saying."

"I got your personal file from Jacob Arkright," I pounded him again. "Patty Keller was the last one of more than a dozen dates arranged for you through the Happiness Club. We took the files of every girl who ever had a date with you, Harv, and they're being checked right now. All we need to do is find another suicide—a sudden death, even—and you're in more trouble than you and a brace of good lawyers can handle!"

He covered his face with his hands, his body still shaking violently.

"Lieutenant," he pleaded in a quavering voice, "if that girl was murdered, I swear I didn't do it! I had no reason—no motive—this whole conception is a nightmare!"

"If you're a congenital liar, Harv, this kind of shock treatment could have therapeutic value," I said coldly.

"But I don't think you are. My bet is you lied for good reason. Either you murdered the girl or you're trying to cover for somebody else. I'd think it over real hard because time's running out on you fast. Any minute now it's going to be too late to tell the truth because nobody will believe it—whatever it is!"

I turned away from him and walked out of the shop—not too fast in case he changed his mind right then and wanted to call me back. But he didn't. He just stood there with his hands still covering his face and his body twitching like he had palsy. If it was a severe traumatic reaction maybe it did him some good—but for sure it didn't do me any good at all.

It was around six when I got back to the Sheriff's office, and the breeze had gotten a lot more violent in the last hour, like it would be blowing up a storm before the night was through. I opened the office door to step inside and nearly cannoned into a woman on her way out.

"Sorry," I said, real polite, and stood to one side to let her go through.

She reminded me vaguely of Patty Keller, I thought absently as I glanced at her. The same straggly blonde hair, the face devoid of make-up; her clothes didn't fit so she looked shapeless, whether she really was or not. She gave me a filthy look as she drew level, and I figured that was typical of all the females who could spend ten years on a desert island with a whole detachment of Marines and never get a second look even.

"Good night, Lieutenant!" she hissed at me suddenly. "Or don't you speak to your friends anymore?"

"Huh?" I croaked feebly. "We've met someplace before?"

"Al Wheeler!" Her fist suddenly beat a frantic tattoo against my chest and I figured she must have flipped her lid for sure. "You—you fiend!" The heel of her shoe ground against my shin with excruciating accuracy. "This is all your fault!"

"Lady," I whimpered, "either I got an identical twin I

THE STRIPPER

haven't even met yet—or you have a great big hole in your head! I don't know you from a crowd!"

"That's what makes me so mad!" she hissed, then clobbered me across the side of my face with her purse. "It was all your idea in the first place—I'd be a big help, you said! Join that lonely hearts club and—"

"Lonely hearts club" I peered closely into her face. "It *is* you?" I said feebly. "Annabelle?"

"On my way to my first date, courtesy the Arkright Happiness Club," she snarled. "And you don't even recognize me—that does up my ego real fine. Now I feel confident!"

"Annabelle, honey!" I said hastily. "You're a genius—it's a masterpiece no less! Nobody would recognize the real you—the glamorous, magnificently beautiful southern rose, with those proud generous curves jutting—"

I collected the purse on the other side of my face.

"Where they jut is none of your business, Al Wheeler!" Annabelle said fiercely. "And if I ever find out this is just your idea of a funny gag, I'll—" The purse crunched against the bridge of my nose with eye-watering emphasis. Then she marched off with a determined stride, leaving me to wonder whether Sherman would have ever made it to Savannah if he'd had Annabelle around to contend with.

Sheriff Lavers was sitting in his office, a pile of white file folders stacked on the desk in front of him. He was busy reading one of them and didn't notice me come in. I watched respectfully for a few seconds, then cleared my throat gently.

"Occupation: county sheriff," I murmured. "Desirable companion: young, clean, and nubile, one who knows how to make a man feel twenty years younger.

Lavers lifted his head and looked at me thoughtfully for a while, then shook his head slowly in open admiration. "How did you guess?"

"We all have the same dreams, Sheriff," I said modestly. "Sometimes it frightens me—millions of guys sharing the same dream every night, with the same girl. I bet she's scared to go to sleep nights!"

"If you're one of those millions, I understand her problem," he grunted. "Polnik told me about these—" he gestured toward the stack of folders. "He's still out checking on the women involved. There was a kind of glazed look in his eyes when he left, so I'm not too sure when we can expect him back—if ever!"

"That Polnik—" I sighed gently. "He gets all the breaks around here."

"Oh, sure," Lavers grunted. "He gets the girls from the lonely hearts club, while you're stuck with the performers at the sex club. Maybe we can arrange a swap for you."

"Thank you, sir, but no," I said quickly. "I think a good law enforcement officer should stick with the assignment given him, rough as it may be!"

The Sheriff's eyes rolled toward the ceiling in mute appeal, but for once the luck of the Wheelers held good, and no bolt of lightning descended upon my head.

He tapped the stack of personal files with one finger. "Did you take a good look at these, Wheeler?"

"Not yet, Sheriff."

"A couple of interesting points," he rumbled. "They can keep for the moment. What I want to know first is what progress you've made so far—if any?"

"Progress, sir?" I gave him a summary of the day's events, keeping my voice matter-of-fact like the super-efficient cop I am.

"That reminds me," the Sheriff said when I was all through, "Johns called you back this afternoon. No record on Rovak or Stern, but Loomas did two years in San Quentin for a mugging rap—got out around eighteen months back."

"It's interesting but it doesn't prove anything," I said glumly.

"Let's get back to the personal files for a moment,"

Lavers said. "These represent every date Stern's had through the Arkright Happiness Club?"

"That's right," I said. "But we won't know much about the women concerned until Polnik gets back and tells us something about them—or the ones he's gotten to contact so far, anyway."

The Sheriff had that nasty, smug look on his face he always gets when he's about to pull a fast one.

"We got—" he ran his finger down the spines of the folders as he counted "—fourteen files equaling fourteen females, and the one thing they got in common is they all dated Stern through the lonely hearts bureau—right?"

"Right," I said cautiously.

He shook his head triumphantly. "Only half right, Wheeler. There's another factor, common to nine of them. Those nine have also dated a guy named George Crocker."

"But not Patty Keller," I said. "She only had the one date and that was with Harvey Stern."

Lavers fumbled in his top pocket for a cigar, then changed his mind and took out his pipe and tobacco pouch from the top drawer of his desk instead. I didn't like that—the pipe meant he was getting to feel mellow and that nearly always means he's outsmarted me already.

"Maybe," he suggested as his pipe bowl burrowed into the pouch.

"What do you mean, maybe?" I said coldly. "It's an established fact."

"Only if you're sure you can trust the records," he said, with a damn sight too much logic for my liking. "Only if these files are always kept completely up to date by the Arkrights. Maybe Patty Keller did have a date with this Crocker—after the one she had with Stern—but for some good reason it wasn't noted on her file."

"Could be," I said glumly. "Why don't we take a look at Crocker's file and check if there's a lead in it someplace?"

"I sent a patrol car around there especially to pick it

up," Lavers growled. "I called Arkright and told him my men would be there to collect Crocker's file, and he put on a big act how his wife was going to sue for a piddling little ten million dollars or something—invasion of privacy, some crap like that. I told him it was up to him—either he turned it over voluntarily, or we'd get a court order."

The Sheriff grinned fiendishly. "I also told him if he made me go to the trouble of getting a judge's signature for one little file, I'd make sure a posse of reporters came with me when I arrived to search his premises!"

"You're a real cagey sheriff, Sheriff," I said coldly. "So where is the file on George Crocker now?"

"That's a good question," he growled. "It's disappeared from the filing cabinet."

"Who said?"

"Arkright, for a start. He had hysterics all over the office, so the boys told me. They didn't believe him, naturally, and he told them to go ahead and search the whole office. They made a real job of it but they didn't find any folder with the name of George Crocker on it."

"You figure Arkright's either hidden or destroyed it?"

Lavers shrugged his wide shoulders. "Arkright—his wife—the receptionist—an unknown quantity called X—your guess is as good as mine, Wheeler."

A cloud of dense smoke from his pipe drifted my way, and one sniff confirmed my worst suspicions. "Why don't you try tobacco in that thing sometime?" I said, and nearly choked.

The phone rang and Lavers had a look of vague disappointment on his face as he picked it up. Maybe he'd had a red-hot answer all ready for me.

"County Sheriff," he said, then grunted sourly, "Yeah, he's here."

He passed the phone across to me. I hauled myself out of the chair to get it, then said, "Wheeler," into the mouthpiece.

"Lieutenant, this is Harvey Stern," an agitated voice

THE STRIPPER

announced in my ear. "I've—I've been thinking over what you said earlier. I think maybe you're right!"

"About what?"

"About me telling the truth before it's too late for anyone to believe it," he gabbled. "I'm still in the shop. Do you think you could come out and see me right away? It's difficult to talk over the phone—it's all very involved and—"

"Sure," I told him. "I'll be right out, Harv. You wait there for me."

"I'll most certainly do that, Lieutenant." He sounded almost grateful as he hung up.

I handed the phone back to the Sheriff, and he looked at me inquiringly.

"That was Harvey Stern," I explained. "He's ready to talk—wants me to go out to his shop right away."

"All right," he grunted. "Don't forget to ask him about George Crocker—and you'd better call me when you're through talking to him. I'll be home most likely—even a county sheriff has to eat."

"Looking at you, Sheriff, nobody would ever guess!" I said admiringly, then got out of there fast.

Around thirty minutes later I parked outside the shop and climbed out. The neon sign was lit, announcing brightly to the world that one Harvey Stern, Florist, dwelt within the portals beneath; but the front door was closed and nobody answered the bell. If Harv had changed his mind about talking to me, I figured he sure had picked a lousy time to do it. After I'd hit the bell a half-dozen times, I tried the door and found it wasn't locked. Sometimes there are advantages to being a simple-minded character like me.

Inside the shop, the overpowering mingled scents of a hundred different flowers hit my sinuses with a triumphant tenacity as I closed the door and fumbled for the light switch. A couple of seconds later when I flooded the interior with light, I saw that the shop was empty except for the flowers. I called out Stern's name a couple of times and didn't get any answer, so I walked through toward the office in back with the faint hope he was waiting there for me and he'd suddenly gotten stone deaf at the same time.

I opened the office door, stepped inside, and switched on the light. Stern was there O.K., sitting in back of his desk, but he wasn't waiting for me. He wasn't waiting for anything any more, except Judgment Day maybe. His body was slumped forward across the desk and a trail of blood had seeped from the hole in the side of his head, down one side of his face, to form a dark pool on the desktop.

There was a gun still clutched in his right hand and close to it an envelope with my name written across the front. I picked it up and opened it, extracting the note from inside. Stern's signature was at the bottom; his typing was very neat and his prose was to the point, almost terse:

> *You were right, Lieutenant—it was my fault Patty killed herself. I took her out a few times and I guess I kidded her along a little so she figured we were going to be married. Then she started getting on my nerves so I told her it was all over and we were through. She got hysterical and told me she was pregnant and if I didn't marry her, she'd kill herself. I thought she was pulling the old routine on me, so I told her fine, go ahead and kill yourself, it'll save us both a whole lot of trouble. I never dreamed she was serious about it. I guess I've been half out of my mind ever since. I don't think I can face the truth coming out. This way out is the best for me. This way I don't have to see the look on my friends' faces after they know the truth.*

I dropped the note back onto the desktop beside a tall, slender vase of calla lilies. They seemed kind of appropriate and I wondered if Harv had thought of that before he pulled the trigger—and I had my doubts on both scores.

Chapter Eight

"THE MINISTER, THE DOCTOR, AND THE FLORIST," DOC Murphy said happily. "We're all mostly concerned with births, marriages, and deaths. The happy and unhappy triumvirate!"

"A man blows his brains out, and the doctor gives us philosophy yet!" Sheriff Lavers said disgustedly. "You have a perverted sense of timing, Doctor!"

"You should remember, Sheriff," Murphy said gleefully, "that it's mostly death that gives both of us a living!"

"You don't really believe Stern blew his brains out, Sheriff?" I asked incredulously.

Lavers looked at me coldly for a couple of seconds, then sighed heavily. "Here we go again!" he snarled. "The man who can't tolerate any simple and logical explanation for anything! They must have a word for people like him in psychiatry, Doctor!"

"Sure," Murphy said promptly. "I could have given it to you a long time back—'nuts'!"

"When the two of you are through with the song-and-dance routine," I said patiently, "maybe we can talk a little logic?"

"The man shot himself," Lavers snorted. "That's self-evident! He left a signed note giving his reasons—that's also self-evident. What more do you want?—a repeat confession from beyond the grave on a ouija board?"

Two white-faced guys in white coats loaded the corpse onto a stretcher and wheeled it out of the office on its first stage of the trip to the morgue. I lit a cigarette to take the suffocating onslaught of flower scent out of my nostrils and tried to keep from blowing my stack.

"I think it's all a little too neat," I said mildly. "It all adds up a little too easy—like somebody laid it out real careful."

"This may come as a surprise to you, Wheeler," Lavers said heavily, "but sometimes things really work out that way—real neat!"

"Doc," I appealed to Murphy, "Patty Keller wasn't pregnant, was she?"

"No, sir," Murphy said confidently. "She wasn't."

"It doesn't prove anything," Lavers said quickly. "She probably told Stern that, trying to force him to marry her, and when he wouldn't—when she threatened to kill herself and he said it was a great idea—that was the last straw. She was a lonely girl with nobody to turn to for help, and Stern treating her the way he did was enough to knock her right off balance. What do you think, Doctor?"

Murphy's satanic face sobered down a little as he thought about it for a moment. "It's possible," he conceded finally. "It was pretty terrible—and total—rejection, at that!"

"Anything else, Wheeler?" the Sheriff asked triumphantly.

"How about the apomorphine?"

"How about it?" he said irritably. He turned to Murphy. "Doc, have you considered the possibility that she meant to use it as a cough medicine? Didn't you say it had that use too?"

"Yes—but that's very unlikely. No one would give themselves a big shot of it for that purpose."

"She had no medical training," Lavers snorted. "Look at all the people who take five times the normal dose of something because they think it will do them five times the good! It happens all the time."

"When I came into the shop, it was in darkness," I persisted. "I switched on the lights and walked through to the office. When I got in here, this room was also in darkness."

"So?" Lavers grated.

"So Stern called me and said he was ready to talk and for me to come right out," I said. "Then what happened? He sat at his desk and thought about it—decided he couldn't face the truth getting out and he'd rather die first. So he types a note, explaining all the reasons, seals it in an envelope and addresses it to me. Takes a gun out of the drawer or wherever it was, then switches out the light—goes back and sits down behind his desk and shoots himself? If you were in his place, would you bother about the light?"

"Maybe," Lavers said. "Who knows what a guy will bother about when he's in a frame of mind to kill himself?"

"Oh, brother!" I said feelingly. "Then how about the mysterious George Crocker you discovered in those files? How about the odd coincidence that when you look for his file in the lonely hearts office, it's suddenly disappeared?"

"Could be coincidence," he said stoutly. "Could be there's some scandal attached to Crocker that the Arkright's don't want made public."

"Could be the county sheriff's got rocks in his head," I said disgustedly. "How about *that?*"

"Like I told you before, Wheeler," he grunted, "you just can't take a simple explanation for anything. I sin-

THE STRIPPER

cerely think you should consult the doctor here about seeing a good psychiatrist and having some analysis. It's getting to be a fetish with you—you have to complicate the most uncomplicated issues!"

"If I need a headshrinker, so do you," I said icily. "But at least I don't need a body-shrinker, too!" I stormed out of the office, hearing Murphy's raucous cackle rising to a crescendo in back of me.

It took a couple of hours, a couple of drinks in a midtown bar, and a rare steak in a restaurant way over my income bracket, before I'd cooled off enough to think about the Sheriff without lighting a magnesium flare inside my head. By that time the evening was all shot anyway, and there was nothing left to do but go home to bed.

It was after eleven-thirty when I walked into my apartment and found I had company, an attractive girl, with an intelligent face and strawberry-blonde hair, wearing an orange and green dress you could almost see through—enough, anyway, to reveal the outline of her firm, high breasts.

"Don't you ever come home, Al Wheeler?" she asked softly. "We've been sitting around all evening real lonesome, haven't we, Bobo?"

The mound of fur sprawled in her lap moved economically, and from somewhere inside there came a small, plaintive yapping sound.

"Dolores Keller," I said. "As I live and my dreams come true! How the hell did you get in here?"

She smiled lazily. "I told the janitor I was your cousin, just got into town unexpectedly from Monotonous, Montana, and he let me in. He also said you've got more cousins—"

Bobo raised his head suddenly and gave out with a growl that sounded almost doglike.

"You figure 'cousins' is a dirty word in dog language?" I asked interestedly.

"Like it is in janitor's language?" Dolores smiled

sweetly. "Anyway—you finally made it. Aren't you going to offer me a drink or something?"

"Sure," I said. "Take your choice. Scotch on the rocks, with a dash of soda—the way I like it—or Scotch on the rocks?"

"Don't confuse me with detail," she said. "You make it—I'll drink it."

I got ice cubes and glasses from the kitchen, then made the drinks and took them over to the couch.

"I don't like asking personal questions," I said as I sat down beside her, "but that pooch—is he house-trained?"

"Don't listen to his insults, honey boy!" Dolores crooned apologetically to the bundle of fur. "He can't recognize a gentleman when he sees one!"

She got up and carried Bobo over to the nearest armchair and lowered him into it gently. He whined reproachfully for a full five seconds, then relapsed into sleep again.

"You ever wonder if he got bitten by a tsetse fly sometime?" I queried.

"He can't adjust to night club hours, poor darling," she said as she sat down beside me again.

"Talking of night clubs—how come you're not working at the Extravaganza tonight?"

"Even a stripper gets a night off sometime," she said. "And here I've wasted it sitting around waiting for you."

"If I'd known you were coming, I'd have been home early," I told her. "How come I'm honored so unexpectedly?"

"You rushed off so quickly this afternoon, from Rovak's place. I didn't get a chance to talk to you."

"Talk to me? What about?"

She turned toward me, and the broad planes of her face were set in a suddenly serious mold, while her dark eyes watched me intently.

"The rest of it is something you said about Patty—that she was murdered?"

"That was the firm opinion of the sheriff's office this af-

THE STRIPPER

ternoon," I said gloomily. "But now I'm the only guy who still subscribes to the same theory."

"What happened to change everyone else's mind?" she asked curiously.

I told her about Stern, the note he'd left for me, and how Lavers figured that tied up everything nice and neat. Her face tautened as she listened, and there was a somber look in her eyes when I'd finished.

"I don't believe it—Patty saying she was pregnant and threatening to kill herself if he didn't marry her," she said in a low voice. "She wasn't like that. She didn't have the kind of self-centered determination to play it that way. She was just a naïve kid who'd lived in the sticks all her life until she came to Pine City. He was lying, Al!"

"That's how I figure it, too," I agreed. "The only reason Harv had for writing that note was because somebody had a gun at his head while he wrote it. But I got to prove it—and that's the hard part."

"I'll help you!" she said eagerly.

I looked at her doubtfully. "How come you suddenly got a big change of heart about the country cousin?" I asked. "The first time I saw you, it was one big joke—the lonely hearts club and all. You got a whole barrel-load of laughs out of it."

"I guess I was just trying to keep it that way," she whispered. "I was scared to let it get close enough to hurt me, Al. You can understand that?"

"Maybe," I said. "How do you figure on helping me?"

"I'll do anything you say," she said eagerly, "anything at all!"

"Don't tempt me," I told her. "You could be sorry you made that very generous offer."

"No, seriously, Al," she said. "Tell me what I can do to help."

"Right now, I wouldn't even know," I confessed. "You could tell me about Rovak maybe? Did you know he's got fifty percent of the Arkright Happiness Club?"

Dolores's eyes widened. "No, I didn't," she said flatly. "You think he had anything to do with Patty's death?"

"Not directly," I said truthfully. "But my guess is he knows a lot more than he's telling. There's something phony about that lonely hearts club, and Rovak being a half-owner, he must know what it is."

"I can't see any connection between the two clubs," Dolores said blankly. "I mean, they are so completely different. Can you?"

"I can't see anything and that's the main reason I'm steadily losing my mind," I growled. "You ever hear of a guy called George Crocker?"

"No, not that I recall." She shook her head. "Where does he figure in this?"

"That's something else I don't know," I said. "What do you know about Loomas?"

"No more than I did the first time you asked me. He works for Rovak—looks after his boat—comes into the club a lot." She shrugged gracefully. "That's about all."

"Was he an actor one time, do you know?"

"If he was, I never heard about it," she said. "I don't like him at all, not even one little bit of him. He's a woman-chaser but that only makes him a man. There's something else again, though—underneath all that bronzed muscle is a nasty, vicious streak of violence."

"He did a couple of years in San Quentin for mugging," I said. "You wouldn't figure a guy like that would know a boat from a bathtub. Does Rovak ever use it much?—or is it just tied up to that jetty the whole time, looking real pretty?"

"He uses it O.K.," Dolores said firmly. "He's away for a couple of days at a time about once a month—real deep sea stuff, I think."

"I guess it's no crime for Loomas to be a real sailor," I said sourly. "Maybe I should go back to the Arkrights and start over." I climbed onto my feet wearily. "About here, we need another drink."

Back on the couch with fresh drinks, the line of ques-

THE STRIPPER

tioning didn't look any more promising than before. I sat in silence, thinking but for a savage quirk of fate I could have been born with a kilt, and have spent a short blissful life blending Scotch for home consumption instead of export to the bluidy Yanks.

"What you need is a change of pace, Al Wheeler," Dolores said suddenly. "Think about something else for a while."

"Like what?"

She pretended to think for a moment. "Well, what about sex?" she suggested.

"My, that would be a change of pace," I said, seeing for the first time the hungry look in her eyes. "Does this come under the heading of helping out?"

"Maybe the therapy will be good for you," she said with a foxy smile. "It will help relax your mind. Now come on, Al, don't be nervous. We're two grown-up people and we don't need to beat around the bush. If we both want something—and I'm sure *you* do—why shouldn't we get out there and take it? Life's too short."

She stood up, and before I could do anything more than gulp a couple of times, she had whipped off her dress and tossed it with some disdain onto the couch.

"You don't think I'm being too direct, do you, Al?" she asked. "But you did say some nice things about me up there at Rovak's house. I was touched. You struck a soft spot, Al."

She stood in front of me in a pair of tiny black briefs, which, while I watched, she slowly peeled away from her. I could feel myself hardening, and there was a dryness in my throat. I gulped again, and thought, the hell with it, there were times when surrender was the order of the day. The tips of her breasts were still engorged, and the delta of strawberry-blonde hair at her crotch swirled up the line of her slit, which was open a fraction to reveal the tiny bubble of her clitoris.

"Well, Al?" she crooned. "What are you waiting for? You're not shy, are you?"

I didn't need any more encouragement, and a couple of moments later, my clothes were lying in an untidy, tangled pile on the floor at my feet. My throbbing yard stood rigidly upward in an effort to bridge the gap between us, which Dolores was already doing, moving slowly toward me with a hazy look in her eyes and her full lips curved in a sensuous smile.

She was right. It was perfect therapy, and for a while I couldn't think of anything else as she worked her experienced magic on me. She writhed against me, as our bodies strained in rising passion, our legs and arms entwining as we made fierce battle on the couch, which was barely large enough for the two of us, so that there was always the danger of rolling off it onto the floor. Dolores' lips moved over my body like quicksilver, her tongue circling all my erogenous zones, not leaving a single one out. Her lips and tongue did fantastic things to my heated prick, as her fingers played gentle arpeggios beneath my balls. She gave deep throaty cries like a wild jungle cat, and as she brought herself up over me, straddling me and easing herself down onto my column, which she was holding steady with the loosely circled fingers of one hand, she was actually purring.

My yard was absorbed completely in her moist enclosing sheath, gripped by her gently contracting vaginal muscles as she began to move over me, her pelvis rising and falling, the muscles gripping, and I was squeezing her breasts beneath my cupped hands. Then we were on the floor, with her beneath me, her legs drawn up and clamping my strongly lunging body, her teeth sunk into my lips, drawing blood, and her hands roving wildly over my back. I plunged deeply into her, as far as I could go, and she gave soft moaning cries, yelled obscenities, and pleaded for more.

It went on like that for what seemed ages, until finally, seeing and feeling she had reached her peak, I could hold back no longer, and the force of our spurting tumultuous orgasm made my head spin, and her frantic cries echoed hollowly from a vast distance.

A short while later, as we gradually got our second wind, Dolores smiled at me like a cat that's just had the cream, and ran her fingers lightly through my hair.

"Al," she drawled lazily. "For a start, that wasn't so bad."

"Aren't you tired?" I asked in rising alarm.

"I don't tire easily," and then immediately set out to prove it.

Chapter Nine

MAYBE EVERY FAMILY HAS A PRIVATE AFFLICTION, BUT they don't talk about it outside their own four walls, and the Wheelers are no exception. One member of the family in every third generation inherits the curse of the Wheelers, and in this one it had to be me. It's nothing real serious—just an occasional, sudden stabbing pain in the solar plexus which hits when it's least expected. I got it the next morning the moment I stepped into the outer office of the Arkright Happiness Club. The attacks have grown rarer as I get older and lately I'd figured maybe I'd outgrown it—a guy like me still having twinges of conscience—it's ridiculous.

But the twinge hit me the same moment I saw the welcoming smile on Sherry Rand's face. "Hello, Al," she greeted me pleasantly. "Where were you last night? I figured you might have called me."

For a moment I was tempted to tell her the truth, but then I knew she wouldn't understand, and the whole thing with Dolores had been strictly therapeutic, even though it

THE STRIPPER

had left me a walking wreck. In my experience, women tended not to appreciate such fine distinctions.

"I got involved, honey," I told her, which was nothing but the truth.

"I read about it in the morning papers." She shuddered faintly. "He was that fat little man with a carnation you spoke with at the club the other night, wasn't he?"

"That's right," I said. "Harvey Stern—one of life's little tragedies. Are the Arkrights busy dispensing happiness right now?"

"I'll tell them you're here," Sherry said. She lifted the phone, and a few seconds later told me I could go right on in. "How's the staying power, Al?" she asked me in a more intimate tone, and I could feel the dark circles under my eyes widen.

"Uh," I said noncommittally. "I'll call you, huh?"

"Oh, so that's it," she said coldly. "Had your fun, and now that's the end of it, is it? I'm just another trophy pinned on your living room wall?"

"It's just all this wet weather," I mumbled as I headed toward the Arkrights' office. "It kind of numbs my vitality."

"It hasn't rained in a week!" she snapped.

"But that's only on the West Coast," I croaked, and escaped into the temporary sanctuary of the inner office.

Sarah Arkright was sitting stiffly in back of the desk, and Jacob Arkright was standing slightly behind her, his hand resting gently on her shoulder. Right then I began to wonder if they were real people at all. They could be wax dummies, wired internally with sound tapes, and each morning Sherry would dust them off first thing and they'd be all set for another day.

Jacob wore a different suit—a crumpled brown this time, and a brown tie with white dots on it, with the small tight knot looking more than ever like an angry boil on his high stretched collar. He smiled nervously at me while his rimless glasses glittered with a high-polished benevolence.

"Good morning, Lieutenant," he said rustily. "We read about Harvey Stern—"

"In the morning papers?" I reproved him. "I trust you're not contaminated by the standards of modern journalism?"

Sarah's angular face got a pinched look as she glared at me coldly. She'd changed the shapeless black dress for a shapeless blue dress and it was no improvement. I figured she sat the whole time because if she moved you'd hear the bones grating together, and that would be something nobody would want to hear before lunch, anyway.

"Now that the whole sad story of Patty Keller is finished," she said sharply, "perhaps you'll be good enough to return all the files you have that belong to this office, Lieutenant?"

"Sure," I nodded. "I'll have them sent around today—if the Sheriff hasn't sent them already. I was just wondering—did that George Crocker file turn up yet?"

"No," she said flatly, "it hasn't."

"I can't understand it, Lieutenant." Jacob shook his head bewilderedly. "I can't understand it at all. It's most irregular."

"More to the point," Sarah asked in that brittle voice, "is it of any further importance now?"

"I think so," I said easily. "But then I don't think either Patty Keller or Harvey Stern killed themselves."

Her faded blue eyes got a little more fuzzy around the edges as she stared at me. "Are you out of your mind?" she asked, and it sounded like a genuine question.

"But the papers said—they quoted Sheriff Lavers—" Jacob protested weakly. "I find this most confusing, Lieutenant!"

"You and me both!" I agreed fervently. "But that's my theory and I'm about to prove it. My guess now is that George Crocker's the key to the whole mystery—find him and I've found all the answers. I'd like you to tell me all you remember about him, please."

They looked at each other helplessly, then back at me.

THE STRIPPER

"Was he tall or short? thin or fat?" I said patiently.

"Thin," Jacob said firmly.

"Fat!" Sarah snorted.

"Tall," Jacob said.

"Short!" Sarah snapped.

"Let's try it another way," I pleaded. "Which one of you first interviewed him?"

They glared at each other for a long moment, then announced, "I did!" simultaneously.

"Maybe it was your silent partner who handled George Crocker for the club—Miles Rovak?" I suggested.

"That's absurd, he's never even been inside the office," Sarah said.

"I'd like to believe that, Mrs. Arkright," I said pleasantly, "but somehow I just can't bring myself to have explicit faith in your memory—or your husband's either."

"You have been both rude and objectionable on each occasion you've been inside this office, Lieutenant!" She leaned toward me, her bony fist gently pounding the desktop. "We will not tolerate it any longer. If you wish to speak to either of us again, at any time in the future, we shall insist on having our lawyer present. Good day, Lieutenant!"

"Sarah?" Jacob's voice quavered a little. "I don't think—"

"Exactly!" she snarled. "And you never have in the thirty-five years we've been married!"

The phone rang and she snatched the instrument up from the desk. "What is it?" She listened for a few seconds and the hollows in her cheeks were shaded a pallid blue color. "The stupid fool!" she said softly. "Why didn't he—? Never mind! Yes, I think you are right, it's the only thing you can do—increase the consignment by one. I'm busy right now so I'll have to call you back later."

She hung up and raised her tufted eyebrows a fraction. "Are you still here, Lieutenant?"

"One more question and I'm gone," I said. "Are you

frightened of Rovak? Is that why your memory suddenly fails when I ask questions about George Crocker?"

She smiled thinly. "Your rudeness is equaled by your imagination, Lieutenant. That is ridiculous!"

I retraced my steps into the outer office. Sherry had her head bent over some papers and she didn't look up as I went past. It was a bleak, unfriendly world and if I hadn't been so goddamned tired, maybe I would have done something about it.

From the Arkright Happiness Club, I drove to the Lavers Lair for Lovelorn Lieutenants, but he wasn't in his office, and neither was Annabelle Jackson. I sat in a chair and smoked a couple of cigarettes; then a living monolithic slab shuffled in, a look of intense gloom set deep on its crudely chiseled face.

"A lousy morning, huh, Lieutenant?" Sergeant Polnik said dolefully. "All that work wasted. Damn inconsiderate of that guy knocking himself off and leaving a note like that. It kind of takes the sting out of the investigation."

"O.K., Sergeant," I said. "What did you find out? Tell me all about it. Don't miss a thing. No detail is too trivial."

A slow smile spread across his repulsive face. "Well, the first female on the list is a Gladys Vlotnik, and she lives out on Casey Street, but when I get there—"

I had no place else to go and nothing to do but listen to him, and that was just as well, because Polnik was the conscientious type cop. If he walked down a street just once, he could tell you the exact color of the curtains in all the windows—and insisted on telling.

He'd drawn a blank on the first four names from the list—none of them were living at the same addresses any more. They'd all moved, leaving no forwarding addresses. The fifth had been a middle-aged schoolteacher who'd had hysterics at the first mention of the Arkright Happiness Club and the name of Harvey Stern, then had driven Polnik out of her apartment with the sharp end of an umbrella.

"I figured she was a little—you know, Lieutenant?" Polnik tapped the side of his head significantly. "Anyway, the next one is real cute. Friendly like. Name's Lola Lundy. She's a dancer in one of the clubs, and she looked like she just got out of bed. All she was wearing was a slip, and she didn't care what I could see under it, Christ, you could see everything she had, just about. Big ones—" he made cupping motions with his hands about a foot out from his barrel chest—"you know?"

"Did she tell you anything interesting about the lonely hearts club?" I asked, breaking across his happy memories.

"Yeah, a whole lot," he said feelingly. "It was around three in the afternoon when I got there, but she hadn't had breakfast yet, what with her working such late hours and all. So she opened a bottle of Canadian Club and—"

"For breakfast?"

"She said it helped keep up her strength," he said defensively. "Then she invited me to join her, and after that we got to talking, and before I knew it the bottle was empty, it was dark outside and she was still talking." The light faded regretfully from his eyes. "Christ, that woman could talk."

"What did she say!" I grated.

"Say? Oh, yeah—the Arkright Happiness Club? Well, she'd just gotten into town—this was six months back—and she was all alone and she wanted some guys to take her out and show her a good time. So she joined up with the club."

"Maybe she had her back teeth filled at the dentist's, too?" I snarled. "I want to know about Harvey Stern and that's all—you understand, Sergeant?"

Polnik blinked rapidly. "Stern? Yeah. She didn't like him at all. Said he was slimy. Couldn't keep his hands to himself. Wandering hands he had, she said. He kept wanting to find out if she had any money in the bank the whole time, so after the second date she had with him, she told him to screw."

"And that's all about Stern?"

"That's all about Stern," he agreed placidly.

"Maybe we can save ourselves a little time here," I said slowly. "Did any of the others say anything more about Stern than Lola did?"

"No, Lieutenant. A couple more said about the same. He seemed like he was more interested in any money they might have than he was in them."

"Well, thanks, anyway." I bared my teeth at him, and hoped it would pass for a smile, but the way he reared back said it didn't.

"There was one woman who's dead now," he volunteered hopefully. "She got married—some guy she met through the club, the old bat who owned the apartments told me—and she was killed in an auto accident in New Mexico three weeks later."

"What was her name?"

"I got it right here, Lieutenant." He thumbed laboriously through his notebook until he found the right entry. "Yeah—Joan Penton."

"Was that her married name?"

"I guess not—the old bat never did find out the name of the little fat guy she married."

"Little fat guy?" I prodded him. "Did the old bat say anything else about him?"

"She didn't like the look of him at all." Polnik shook his head sadly. "Dressed too neat for an honest man, she said, with that carnation in his buttonhole and all."

"None of the others either married or dead?"

"Not the ones I talked to. But I guess the first four I never got to see could be either married, or dead, or both, huh?"

"I guess they could, at that," I said. "Thanks, Sergeant. Nobody mentioned a guy called Crocker—George Crocker—by any chance?"

"Crocker? Oh, sure—Lola talked about him all the time. She figured she was crazy for the guy until one night he tried to talk her into going for a weekend cruise on his

THE STRIPPER 225

boat, and then got real nasty when she refused. The way she tells it, he tossed her into his car and said she was going anyway, but he had to stop for a red light about a mile out of town and she dived out the car and ran. She never saw him again after that, she said, and didn't want to, either. Is this Crocker important, Lieutenant?"

"The way I figure it, he is," I said. "What else did you get on him from Lola?"

"Nothing much," he admitted. "She was too busy drinking all the time and telling me to keep my big hands—anyway, she didn't talk much about Crocker after telling me how he turned nasty in the car that last time."

"She must have said something more than that!" I growled desperately. "What was this Crocker, he had a boat for weekend cruising? A millionaire yachtsman?—a fisherman?—what?"

"That's right!" Polnik slapped his forehead, and I watched expectantly to see his hand splinter, but it didn't. "He was a great big handsome hunk of man, she said, and he was an actor."

"Thanks, Sergeant," I said gratefully. "You've been a big help!"

"I have?" His forehead corrugated alarmingly as he tried to figure out why. "Cheez! I'm sure glad all that time wasn't wasted, Lieutenant."

"Sure," I said. "Have you seen Miss Jackson this morning?"

"No," he said, shaking his head. "The Sheriff figured she was just late getting in. He had to leave by nine-thirty and get over to City Hall for a special meeting or something."

I reached for the phone and dialed the number of Annabelle's apartment, then listened to the phone ring for a couple of minutes without anyone answering. A sudden painful twinge in my solar plexus reminded me Annabelle had gone out on her first date organized by the lonely hearts club the night before—courtesy, Al Wheeler.

"Drop over to her apartment and see if she's sick or

something," I told Polnik, and gave him the address. "If she's not home, check with the janitor or anybody around and find out if anyone's seen her this morning."

"Sure," he said and started to get out of his chair when the phone rang. I lifted it and said, "Sheriff's office," into the mouthpiece.

"I'd like to talk with Miss Annabelle Jackson, please?" a crisp feminine voice said.

"She's not in today," I told the voice.

"Oh?" She hesitated for a moment. "Then connect me with Lieutenant Wheeler, please!"

"This is Wheeler speaking."

"I'm Jenny Carter," the voice said heatedly, "Annabelle's roommate—and I'd like to know just what you've done with her, Lieutenant!"

"I haven't done a thing with her, Jenny," I said, "and I never knew she had a roommate."

"Since a couple of months back." She chuckled briefly. "That's after your time, I think, Lieutenant."

"I guess that's right," I said. Annabelle doesn't seem to trust me any more for some peculiar reason."

"For five distinctly sound reasons," she said briskly. "She told me them—one by one. But seriously, I'm worried about her—she didn't come home at all last night. What have you done with her, Lieutenant?"

"I haven't done anything with her, Jenny!" I protested. "Believe me—I was about to send a sergeant out to the apartment to check if she was there or not."

"But she was out working for you last night!" she said accusingly. "She told me something about it—some crazy idea of yours that she should join this lonely hearts club. She went out on her first blind date from the club last night and she never came back. And now you say you don't even know what's happened to her?"

"Take it easy," I told her. "We'll find out all right. There's probably some logical explanation—"

"—Like she's been murdered!" Jenny Carter screamed hysterically.

THE STRIPPER

"Like she met some wonderful guy and they went to Reno and got married," I yelled. "You stop worrying. We'll call you just as soon as we've got a line on Annabelle." Then I hung up on her quickly before I got some more hysterics.

Polnik looked at me inquiringly. "Was that about Miss Jackson, Lieutenant?"

"Her roommate," I said shortly. "Annabelle hasn't been home all night. There's no need for you to go out to the apartment now, but there's something else you can do for me."

"You name it, Lieutenant," he said dutifully.

"Go around to the Arkright Happiness Club right away," I told him. "Tell them your name is Jackson, and you're Annabelle's older brother. Last night she went out on her first date from the club and she hasn't been home since, and unless they find out what's happened to her right away, you're going to the police."

"Me—a cop—go to the police?" Polnik said feebly.

"You aren't supposed to be a cop!" I snarled. "You're just her older brother—you can be a telegraph linesman if you want!"

"Cheez! You figure I could be a railroad engineer?" he asked hopefully.

"Why not?" I said hopelessly.

"Thanks, Lieutenant!" Polnik's chest swelled with pride. "That's what I always wanted to be when I was a kid. If only Mom could see me now!"

Chapter Ten

POLNIK GOT BACK TO THE OFFICE AROUND THREE IN THE afternoon, with a look of misery on his face.

"It was no good, Lieutenant," he said apologetically. "I did like you said and the receptionist—Cheez! what a dragon that one is!—took me right in to the Arkrights. I gave them the spiel and banged the desk a couple of times to make it look good, but they swore I must have the wrong happiness club, they didn't know from any Annabelle Jackson. We argued for maybe a half hour with me saying I knew for sure this was the right club, and them saying I had to be wrong. They offered to let me search their files and I did—but there was nothing there with Miss Jackson's name on it." He shrugged his gorilla shoulders. "So then I didn't know what the hell to do so I came back here." He looked at me with sublime faith. "I figured you'd tell me what to do next."

"I wish I knew," I said bitterly. "You did all you could down there—it's no fault of yours, Sergeant. Pleading no knowledge of Annabelle was the obvious out for them."

THE STRIPPER

"Does the Sheriff know yet?" he asked.

"He hasn't been back," I said. "I guess that meeting's going to take all day."

"He's over in City Hall," Polnik said eagerly. "You want me to go over there right now and tell him, Lieutenant?"

"No!" I said sharply. I remembered how Lavers had reacted to my idea of getting Annabelle to join the lonely hearts club in the first place. Now that he was convinced the case was sewn up tight by Stern's confession, his reaction to the news of Annabelle's disappearance would be violent. I didn't see how he could help, anyway, and I had enough problems without adding the County Sheriff to them.

"So what do we do now, Lieutenant?" Polnik's rasping voice broke my train of thought. "You was just kidding when you said you didn't know, huh?"

I wondered fleetingly if a jury would bring in justifiable homicide if I shot him where he stood. "I'm thinking, Sergeant," I muttered hoarsely. "Even for a Wheeler, it takes a little time."

The phone rang and I grabbed it.

"Lieutenant Wheeler?" a husky feminine voice asked.

"That's me," I snarled, and thought if this was Jenny Carter I'd find out where she was, then go around there and throttle her with my bare hands.

"Al!" The voice was so faint I could only just hear it. "This is Dolores."

"Hi," I said bleakly. "I can hardly hear you."

"I'm calling from the Extravaganza," she said. "I can't speak any louder in case somebody hears me. Al, you remember our talk last night?" She gurgled throatily. "We *did* talk for a while, remember? And I asked how I could help?"

"Sure, I remember," I said.

"Well, I don't know if this means anything or not, but I heard Rovak talking with Loomas—and they're definitely taking out the boat tonight and they expect to be gone for a couple of days. Rovak said something about being sure to have the consignment ready for loading by ten tonight. Is it important, Al?"

"I think so," I said. "Very important."

"This is rehearsal day down here," she said. "That's why I'm at the club all afternoon. But I could get away around five and meet you. I know Rovak's house pretty well, Al. If you want, I think I could smuggle you in so you can see what goes on."

"I'd like that very much, Dolores," I said sincerely. "Where will I meet you?"

"There's a bar two blocks south of the Extravaganza called the Bird of Paradise. I'll be there at five, or a little after."

"O.K.," I said. "And thanks a million, honey."

"See you in the Bird of Paradise," she said, and hung up.

I put the phone down and looked at Polnik. "I just got a lead, I think," I told him. "It's going to take a while to follow through. Meantime I want you to run a check on the woman who married Harvey Stern and then got killed in an auto accident. What was her name?"

"Joan Penton?"

"If it was Stern, it's likely he didn't use his real name, and they probably got married in Nevada," I said. "Sweat on it, Sergeant—this may be the first concrete piece of evidence we can get. I want to know where they were married, and under what name—the details of the auto accident—and whether the girl left any money and who got it—and was she insured and if so, who collected that?"

"O.K., Lieutenant," Polnik said and nodded ponderously. "I'll get onto it right now."

"I'll be gone I don't know how long," I said. "When the Sheriff gets back you'd better tell him what's happened."

"What will I say when he asked where the—where you are, Lieutenant?"

"Tell him I went out," I said. "But if he doesn't hear from me by midnight to contact the Coast Guard and have them look for a forty-foot cabin cruiser, registered under the name of Miles Rovak."

The Sergeant scribbled frantically in his notebook, then looked at me blankly. "What if they find this boat and you ain't on it, Lieutenant?"

"Don't say things like that!" I shuddered. "Every time I get to feeling a dedicated cop, somebody always has to louse it up for me real good! If I'm not on board that boat, it's likely I'll be gone for around three weeks—then the chances are I'll get washed up on a beach someplace."

"Just so long as you're coming back, Lieutenant," Polnik said heartily. "I wouldn't like to feel you was leaving us for good."

I parked a little way down from the Bird of Paradise, in the first available space, then walked back to the bar. Inside it was one of those dimly lit, elegant bars that cater to the boss-secretary and different husband-different wife combinations. I felt like a blind man until my eyes got used to the gloom, then I threaded my way around some empty tables to a corner booth. A waiter who looked like he was working his way through the morgue so he could sleep nights in the graveyard without the other vampires sneering at him, took my order, then padded silently away—on cloven hooves, maybe.

I lit a cigarette and checked my watch. It was five after five, but Dolores had said she might be a little late. The waiter served my drink and then I saw her come into the bar, so I told him to bring a couple more of the same.

The waiter's eyebrows shot up and he gave me a look that penetrated right to my cirrhosis of the liver. It was a damn shame I was jackknifed behind the table. It kept him from taking my full measure—for the brass-handled box.

"Make them double," I said. "I'm feeling a little faint."

Just then Dolores arrived at the table, and the waiter

turned his penetrating look on her. She was wearing an apricot-colored dress that emphasized every curve she had, and topped off with about six inches of deep cleavage. The waiter double-checked the size of her boobs, re-echoed my order, and made his way unsteadily back to the bar.

"It's nice to see you again," Dolores murmured, squeezing into the seat opposite. "I cleaned up your apartment for you after you'd gone this morning. It needed a woman's touch."

I nodded appreciatively. "That I like. The woman's touch."

The waiter served the drinks, putting one glass in front of Dolores, then hesitating for a moment when he saw the untouched first drink still in front of me. He looked back and forth between us, and then just back and forth between Dolores till I wondered if he was considering her cleavage as a likely place to deposit the Scotch. Finally he placed the glass about an eighth of an inch in front of her as a kind of oblation, then went away.

"Tell me more about this boat ride that's scheduled for tonight," I asked Dolores when the waiter was well out of earshot.

"I don't know much more than I told you over the phone, Al," she said. "I was passing Rovak's office—the door wasn't all the way shut and I heard their voices, so I stopped to listen. Like I told you, Rovak told Loomas to have the boat ready to leave tonight and be sure to have the consignment loaded by ten—and they'd be gone a couple of days. 'The usual run,' he said. Whatever that is."

"Anything else?"

"Let me think." She tapped one finger against her cheek absently. "Yes, there was something else. Rovak said this would be the last consignment they'd be running for a while, until things cooled down again."

"How do you figure on smuggling me into the house?"

"At the end of rehearsal I pretended to faint," she said.

THE STRIPPER 233

"Then I said I felt sick, and Rovak told me to go home and not bother about coming back to the club, so I won't be missed. If I arrive at his house tonight, tell him I figured the sea air would do me good and I knew he wouldn't mind me staying the night, I don't see how he can argue about it, do you?"

"I guess not," I agreed. "But he'll argue for sure if he sees me right beside you."

"I thought about that," Dolores said confidently. "If we take my car, you can keep out of sight on the floor of the back seat when I drive in. I'll park on his driveway and get out fast, so nobody will come close to the car. You wait in there until I get a chance to come back and take you into the house. How about that?"

"I don't have any better ideas," I said.

"Are you having Rovak's place staked out?" she asked.

"I'd look awful stupid if I did and Rovak's consignment turned out to be fishing bait!" I shuddered at the thought. "This is strictly a one-man—and a one-woman—operation, honey. I'm trying to find some proof that Rovak's mixed up in a racket which somehow involved your cousin Patty. And what we're about to do is strictly illegal for anybody, but goes double for a cop! Nobody knows anything about this—not even the Sheriff—except you and me."

Dolores tasted her drink, her eyes bubbling with excitement.

"This could be quite exciting," she said enthusiastically.

I grunted. "Do you have a time schedule worked out?"

"Sure. I figure we don't want to get out there too early. For one thing we want to be sure Rovak's already there—and he might get suspicious about my sudden recovery, too. I thought after we've had a couple of drinks here we could eat, then leave around eight. That would get us there around eight-thirty, in plenty of time before the boat leaves."

"That makes sense," I agreed.

We followed Dolores' timetable very closely—a couple

more drinks in the bar, then a steak in a restaurant around the corner. It was near enough to eight o'clock when we got into her car and started out.

A half-hour later we came over the crest of the road that seemed to drop almost perpendicularly down the side of a cliff to where Rovak's house nestled right at the bottom. Dolores braked the car to a stop on the crest, then turned and smiled at me nervously.

"Now I get butterflies," she said throatily. "You think maybe now is the time for you to disappear into the back seat, Al? We'll be there in a couple of minutes."

"Sure," I said. "But we made good time and there's no real hurry, so why don't we talk for a few minutes first? Cigarette?"

"Thanks." She switched off the motor, then slid a cigarette out of the pack I offered her. I lit it, and one for myself, then leaned back against the upholstery. I put my free arm around her shoulders, letting my fingers brush gently against the taut curve of her left breast. She sighed gently and snuggled closer to me.

"It's a beautiful night," I said. "But no moon—I guess maybe that's why Rovak picked it."

"So he's got less chance of being seen?" Dolores murmured against my shoulder. "That doesn't sound like his boat trip is very legal does it?"

"I was wondering," I said lazily, "just how Miles has it figured—the iron gates left open so you can drive right in and park well down on the driveway close to the house. Rovak and Loomas waiting in the shadows on either side, so when you stop the car they each open one of the back doors and ram a gun into my face. After that I join Annabelle Jackson as extra loading for the consignment, and the boat takes off on schedule. Then sometime in the early hours of the morning they dump us into the ocean, and the operation's a complete success."

Her body stiffened suddenly. "Al—what are you talking about? Have you gone out of your mind?"

"It was a nice try, honey," I said. "You wait around

THE STRIPPER

my apartment last night until I get home with a double-barreled excuse—one, you've had a change of heart and now you're grieving for your cousin Patty real bad and you want to help justice—and two, you're just crazy about Wheeler, anyway. What you really wanted to know was had I swallowed Stern's fake suicide and the note he'd written tidying up everything so nicely."

"You can't mean that, Al?" she said in a choked voice. "After all I've done to—"

"I don't know how Annabelle suddenly got to be a problem," I went on, "but she obviously did. And you had one other problem, too—that was me. So the smart thing was to take care of both at the same time. That meant getting me onto the boat with no fuss—and no county sheriff hot on my trail. When you heard my sergeant had been around to the lonely hearts club, making like he's Annabelle's brother and not getting anyplace, you gave him time to report back to me. Then you called at the psychological moment and gave me a lead which would bring me right out to Rovak's boat of my own free will."

"I don't know how you can even think such things, Al Wheeler!" she said in a muffled voice. "It's all lies—dreadful lies!"

"I told you once, Dolores, my sweet, that it was your intelligence that appealed to me most about you," I reminded her. "You should have remembered that, then maybe you would have played it a little smarter than you did. A stake-out around Rovak's house? It was clumsy, sweetheart. It wasn't subtle at all. You must really think I'm stupid."

"I need a cigarette," she said in an indistinct voice, picking up her bag from the seat behind her.

She had the gun halfway out before I clamped my hand over her fingers and squeezed until she whimpered with pain and relaxed her grip so that the gun slipped back into her bag.

"Nice try," I said respectfully.

"Fuck you, Wheeler!" she snarled. "Take your hands off me!"

I took my arm from around her shoulders, lifted her bag and the car keys in one hand, and opened the car door on her side with the other. "Out!" I ordered, and gave her a shove of encouragement.

She turned and looked at me contemptuously when we were both standing beside the car.

"What now?" she sneered. "We wait for reinforcements?"

"Take off your shoes," I told her. She hesitated for a moment, then did as she was told. "Now the dress," I said.

"Wait a minute!" she exclaimed angrily. "I'm not—"

"Come on, sweetheart," I said casually. "You want me to rip it off? Come to think of it, it might be more fun that way. Yeah, bring out the macho in me, sweaty armpits and a breathless manner. Wheeler the rapist. Business with pleasure."

Slowly Dolores removed the dress, and that left her in only her briefs. Her nipples looked very dark in the moonlight. She shivered suddenly in the slight breeze that came in off the ocean as I tossed her dress and shoes into the back of the car.

"Here's your big chance," I said as I got back into the car, "to run barefoot in the breeze, over turf and glen. To be free, untrammeled and all the rest of it."

"You bastard!" she said from between clenched teeth. "You fucking —"

I let the car roll down the hill slowly in second, while I eased the thirty-eight out of its belt holster and put it on the seat beside me. As the car neared the bottom of the hill, I flicked the headlight beams on high, and their brilliant light showed that the iron gates across the driveway were wide open. I drove slowly into the driveway and saw the Mercedes parked about thirty feet ahead. If Rovak and Loomas were where I figured they had to be—one on either side of the driveway—the headlights would blind them enough so they couldn't distinguish who was driving the car. So I was safe until I stopped and that gave me a whole three or four seconds. Just enough time to ease the car door open a little, and pick up the thirty-eight.

I braked the car to a stop a few feet in back of the Mercedes, then flung the door wide open and jumped out as I heard the sudden flurry of footsteps on either side of the car. Both the back doors were wrenched open and I heard Rovak's harsh voice growl, "O.K., cop! Come out nice and easy or—"

By that time I'd straightened up and could see the massive bulk of Steve Loomas, hunched forward as he leaned into the back of the car.

"Hey, boss!" he yelped frantically. "There's nobody here!"

"You're so right, George!" I said as I rammed the barrel of the thirty-eight against the side of his head. "Tell Rovak to drop his gun or I'll splatter your brains over the upholstery!"

"Boss!" Loomas stuttered wildly. "Don't—"

The sudden explosion of Rovak's gun was shatteringly loud inside the confines of the car. I'd taken the obvious precaution of standing right in back of Loomas, and Rovak had no way of getting at me except through that massive-muscled body, but that wasn't about to deter him. He fired three shots from his side of the car, and Loomas' whole body quivered as each slug slammed into his chest. Then he toppled forward slowly into the back seat, and as his bulk fell away from me, Rovak's silhouetted head suddenly appeared in my line of vision. I guess he saw me at the same time because he fired another shot, making the mistake of not elevating his gun quickly enough, so the slug took Loomas neatly between the eyes—but you can only kill a man once and Loomas was already dead before that slug hit.

I lifted the thirty-eight carefully and squeezed the trigger twice. Rovak screamed thinly and spun around, then disappeared out of my line of sight. I heard the clatter as his gun dropped on the driveway, and raced around the back of the car toward him.

When I got there he was down on his hands and knees, and there was a steady splashing sound as an ever-widening pool appeared on the concrete beneath his bowed head. His gun lay a few feet away, and I kicked it into the bushes lining the driveway, then put my hand on his shoulder.

"Rovak?" I said. "Where are you hit?"

He pulled his shoulder away from my hand violently, then suddenly his arms splayed sideways and he pitched forward onto his face and lay still. I knelt down and turned him over gently; he was already dead, and there was nothing recognizable left of his face below the forehead.

I got to my feet and raced toward the front door of the house and found it was slightly open when I got there. I slammed it wide open with my foot and yelled, "Outside, you guys, and fast! Rovak's got trouble!" Then I flattened myself against the wall beside the open door and waited.

Heavy footsteps clumped down the hallway, and a moment later a hairy, muscle-bound gorilla lumbered out of the doorway and past me, heading toward the car. I caught up with him in a couple of paces and slammed the gun barrel down across the back of his head. He got tired of running all at once and collapsed to the ground. I got back beside the open door again and waited another thirty seconds but nobody else came out.

A closer inspection revealed the unconscious gorilla was my old buddy, Louis, the maître d' of the Extravaganza, and it got to be like old home week. He didn't look like he was going to wake up for a long time, so I left him while I searched inside. The whole place was deserted, and it made me feel better, being sure there had only been the three of them in the house. When I got back to the driveway again, Louis was grunting painfully as he

THE STRIPPER

struggled up into a sitting position. I nudged his left ear with the thirty-eight and he stopped grunting right away.

"Rovak and Loomas are dead," I said conversationally. "I'd as soon have you dead, too, because it would be neater that way. So do an old buddy a favor and try something, huh, so I'll have an excuse?"

He squinted up at me, his head wobbling nervously on the short, squat neck, his eyes pleading.

"Don't kill me, Lieutenant!" he quavered. "I'll do anything you say—anything!"

"Get up on your feet and we'll go take a look at the boat," I said. "The consignment's already loaded, right?"

"I don't know what you're talking about," he mumbled as he staggered to his feet.

"That does it!" I said happily.

"Wait!" he screamed. "Sure, sure—you're right! The consignment's already loaded just like you said, Lieutenant!"

"So let's go unload it," I prodded his spine with the gun to emphasize the point.

We walked down the jetty, then climbed on board the cruiser's immaculate white deck.

"Where are they?" I asked.

"Down below—locked in the cabin," Louis mumbled.

"You got a key?"

"Yeah—right here." He pulled a key chain out of his pocket and handed it to me.

"That's good, Louis," I said approvingly. "You keep going this way and you could live another whole ten minutes yet!"

I made him go first down the ladder that led to the cabin, and followed behind, but not too close. When we got there I gave him back the key, let him unlock the door and lead the way inside. The consignment had been loaded all right. Directly opposite us, with their backs pressed hard against the bulkhead, were three cowering girls—and the one in the middle was Annabelle Jackson.

She saw the gun in my hand and made a rapid recovery.

"Well," she sniffed, "if it isn't Al Wheeler! You sure took your time about getting here."

"I would've made it a lot sooner," I said apologetically, "but your roommate was so upset the way you just disappeared, I had to comfort her."

"Jenny?" Annabelle said suspiciously.

"There we were," I said nostalgically, "sitting in your apartment with me busy comforting Jenny—and Jenny busy being comforted. The hours just flew!"

"Jenny?" she snarled.

"Tell me something," I asked. "How come they picked you for a phony so fast?"

"A little elementary psychology, Lieutenant," she said coldly, "which you apparently overlooked. Every girl tries to make the best of her looks—so if one girl deliberately tries to make the worst of them, she obviously must have a good reason. After they grabbed me, they checked at City Hall and found out who I worked for. So then that dreadful man—Rovak—said I could be useful two ways."

"You'd fetch a good price as part of this consignment," I said, "and he could use you as bait for me."

Annabelle looked annoyed. "How did you know?"

"Elementary psychology," I said easily. "Just one more question before we go back to the house and call up the posse. Who did you see when you registered with the lonely hearts club? The receptionist—Sherry Rand?"

"No," Annabelle shook her head. "She was out to lunch when I got there—so Mrs. Arkright interviewed me, then organized the first date with that muscle-bound beast, George Crocker!"

"Alias Steve Loomas," I said brightly, "and speak softly of the dead."

"You killed him?" Her eyes widened as she stared at me in horror.

"What's the fun in being a hero if you can't leave a few

THE STRIPPER

dead villains lying around?" I said reasonably. "I'm glad Sherry Rand isn't involved in this."

"Another of your conquests—hero?" she asked icily.

"Only one on this case," I smiled sweetly at her. "Being so busy with Jenny didn't leave me much time."

Chapter Eleven

IT HAD GOTTEN TO BE A REAL LATE NIGHT WHAT WITH the explanations to the County Sheriff and the sheer bliss of watching the changing expressions on his face while he listened. He almost took the two corpses in his stride after that, but they never really worried me because I knew ballistics would prove Rovak had killed Loomas and not me. The best of it was watching Lavers' face when he stopped at the top of the hill on the way back to town and picked up Dolores, who was huddled on the side of the road, shivering violently, and who, in only her briefs, had climbed defiantly into the car, the look on her face daring anyone to make a smart-ass comment about why she was sitting on the side of the road without any clothes on.

So, even if I was tired, it was still a bright and sunny morning after the long night when I stepped once again into the office of the Arkright Happiness Club. Sherry Rand's face was stony when she looked up and saw me.

"Lieutenant Wheeler," she said icily, "you know, I was

stupid enough to think you might really call me last night—that shows just how naïve I can get, doesn't it?"

"I was busy, honey," I said regretfully. "Real busy!"

"Funny thing," she said through a yawn. "I didn't read about it in the morning papers."

"But you will," I said cheerfully. "Are the Arkrights at home?"

"Sure," she said. "I'll tell them you're here."

"This time you don't need to bother, Sherry honey," I told her. "I'll announce myself."

I opened the door of the private office and stepped inside. Sarah Arkright was sitting in back of her desk as ever, but Jacob had pulled a switch on me. He was perched beside her—in a smaller chair naturally—and they looked like they were going over the monthly accounts.

Sarah's eyes widened for a moment when she first saw me, then the fuzziness spread quickly from the outer edges across her pupils, leaving two opaque masks to hide her thoughts.

"This is beyond all tolerance!" she snapped. "Don't you even have the decency to wait until you're invited into a private office before you walk in, Lieutenant!"

"I must say," Jacob put in his squeaky two bits, "this is hardly a civilized attitude, Lieutenant!"

"You might as well get used to uncivilized attitudes," I said easily. "Where you're going, you'll run up against them all the time."

I pulled a chair away from the wall and sat down facing them, then lit a cigarette.

"Put that disgusting thing out immediately!" Sarah's gaunt cheeks flamed a violent red. "How dare you! How dare—"

"The consignment never got away last night," I said conversationally. "Rovak killed Loomas—and I killed Rovak. Louis and Dolores Keller are under arrest and they spent most of the night talking their heads off in the D.A.'s office downtown. You mind if I smoke?"

Jacob's skin turned a dirty gray color as he stared at me. His mouth dropped open so wide that the dime-store teeth that had given him such faithful service these last thirty or so years suddenly gave up trying, and the top plate collapsed onto the bottom with an uneasy clacking sound.

Sarah stiffened her back into an even more upright position in her chair, if that were possible. Her bony fingers intertwined, then locked solid with a brittle sound.

We shall consult our lawyer—of course!" she said firmly, then looked at her husband for approval for the first time in her life; but he didn't even notice—he was too busy with one hand shielding his mouth, making frantic gobbling noises as he tried to juggle that top plate back into position again.

"A nice racket you had going here for a while," I said, "making it all ways—even legitimately. Miles Rovak had a hot connection with the Latin American bordello trade, and they were always willing to pay big money for girls who were young and preferably blonde. With Loomas, or George Crocker—whatever name you prefer—dazzling the girls with his muscles and finally persuading them to come cruising on his boat, that side of the deal was sewn up real fine."

"Not a word," Sarah said in a cracked voice. "Not a word until we consult with our lawyer!"

"Sure," I said and nodded politely. "Then you had Stern working the older clients—the middle-aged spinsters who were getting even more lonely and more foolish. If he couldn't con them out of their hard-earned money any other way, he'd even marry them. Of course afterwards he'd take some insurance on their lives, and if they were fortunate enough to sustain a fatal accident on their honeymoon—well, that's life, kids, ain't it?

"We got the detail on Joan Penton—the late Joan Penton, I should say. It wasn't really so tough for Stern that Rovak forced him to write that note to me, then killed him. If he hadn't, he wouldn't have had much of a future

THE STRIPPER

anyway, once he was found out. What do you say, Mrs. Arkright?"

Sarah licked her lips which were white around the edges and said nothing; Jacob still struggled with his teeth and moaned softly to himself the whole time—but not about the teeth, I guessed.

"Dolores told us all about Patty—her country cousin from the sticks who got under her feet the whole time," I went on amiably. "How the fool kid would stick her nose into other people's business. How she was stagestruck and wanted to be a great actress. How she sneaked up close to a door that wasn't properly closed one night when she was staying in Dolores' apartment, and overheard a confidential conversation between Dolores and Rovak concerning the Latin American trade."

I shook my head admiringly. "That Patty! Whatever else you can say about her, you have to admit she was single-minded. She offered a trade—her silence in return for the organization making her into a big star! I guess you have to be just out of the sticks to offer that kind of deal!"

My cigarette had burned down to a stub and there wasn't an ash tray in the room, so I walked across to the desk and dropped the butt into the vase of withered carnations. It made a faint, squelching hiss as it hit the water and it sounded an adequate requiem for good old Harv—the guy who always had a carnation in his buttonhole.

"When she was standing out on that hotel ledge, I talked with her through the window," I said. "She didn't look like she was going to jump at all. The only thing that interested her was the time—she kept on asking what time it was every few minutes. When it got around to three o'clock, she said she'd come back in. She started toward me, then the nausea hit her and she lost her balance and fell. The autopsy revealed the shot of apomorphine—you know that?"

"Not a word without consulting our . . ." Sarah's voice shook so much she couldn't finish the sentence.

"When Dolores told us about Patty's deal—that she'd keep quiet about your white slave trade as long as you made her a big star—" I shrugged "then it hit me. She was just a naïve country kid who didn't know from nothing. It would be easy—real easy—to con her into thinking a fake suicide attempt would land her on the front pages of all the newspapers and launch her into a successful acting career. Once she was convinced that all she had to do was stand on a narrow ledge for a certain length of time and then climb back into the window again, it would be just as easy to convince her she ought to have an injection before she went out there—to steady her nerves."

"My guess is," I went on, "that you told her it would take, say, a good solid half hour on that ledge to make a real impression on the public—it didn't matter much what precise length of time you advised as long as it allowed more than enough time for the injection to take effect. But when she got out there, five minutes seemed like about five years to her, and when she saw the crowd that had collected, she figured she could cut short the time and come back in sooner. I was there and saw her make that decision—but she made it about ten seconds too late."

I put my hands on the edge of the desk and leaned on them.

"Which one of you sold the idea to Patty Keller?" I asked softly. "Which one was it who pushed the needle into her arm and deliberately gave her the apomorphine, knowing that the violent reaction was bound to send her over the edge?"

Jacob dropped his head, showing the gleaming whiteness of his skull, with the heavy hair tonic plastering the last remnants of his hair tight against it.

"It was wrong," he mumbled, and tears trickled down his cheeks in a token of remorse that was too late by one hell of a large margin. "Wrong! I never really did agree to getting rid of that child in that way, Sarah, you know it!"

THE STRIPPER

"Oh—stop sniveling!" Sarah said contemptuously. The bones in her hands cracked as she unlocked the fingers. "Yes, Lieutenant, everything you've said is true. It was my idea to persuade that stupid girl to get out onto the ledge—and it was I who gave her that injection!"

"You sound like you're proud of it," I said wonderingly.

"You don't understand!" she said fiercely. "You're like the rest of them, hidebound with a stupid, sentimental morality that divorces human beings from any real contact with one another. In every city throughout the whole world, there are millions of desperate, pathetic people, cut off completely from any real contact with any other human. The lonely, Lieutenant—"

"—are legend!" I finished it for her. "I should have known that wasn't one of Dolores' original phrases!"

"That was why we started out Happiness Club in the first place," she said proudly. "To help the lonely, the lost and afraid little people of the earth! What could a stupid little moron like Patty Keller hope for in her life?— nothing! I did her a kindness—a great and wonderful kindness. She went from the ecstasy of seeing her dreams start to come true—as she thought—into almost instant and peaceful oblivion.

"The girls who took our cruise, Lieutenant? All of them were lonely and afraid—why else would they come to us in the first place? None of them would find a decent husband—there are not enough men to go around, let alone decent men! We sent them where they would enjoy contact with more men than they'd ever dreamed of in their wildest moments. We sent them where they could work for their pleasure and enjoy the most intimate of human contacts incessantly until—" Her voice had been rising steadily as she spoke, until it finally broke into a high-pitched scream.

"Sarah!" Jacob gripped her arm imploringly, with a vigor that was a far cry from the family photo album, circa 1927. "Sarah, dear—please, don't do that!"

She stared down with incredulous horror at his hand for a moment, as if she had never seen it before. Then she thrust it violently away from her.

"Don't you dare touch me!" she screamed at him. "You filthy, vile creature! Don't you dare touch me! In the thirty years of our married life, I've never allowed you to touch me! So don't you dare think that—"

Her eyes dulled suddenly and she slumped back into the chair, just as Lavers and a uniformed cop came charging into the room.

"What the hell goes on in here, Wheeler?" the Sheriff asked quickly. "We could hear her screaming—"

"She's only fainted," I said. "She confessed to the Keller girl's murder. She sold her the idea that standing out on a ledge, pretending to be about to throw herself over, would make a wonderful publicity story for an aspiring young actress—and she gave her the shot of apomorphine. But I don't think we'll ever get a conviction, Sheriff." I turned to Polnik, "Call an ambulance," I told him, "And tell them they'll probably need a restrainer along, too."

"Poor Sarah—the excitement's been too much for her!" Jacob cackled suddenly. "Maybe I'm the strong one, after all!"

I walked out of the office and closed the door behind me. I took time out to light a cigarette before I went over to Sherry's desk.

"Hi there," I said, grinning warmly at her. "Tonight is definitely and irrevocably a free night for Wheeler. Dare I say it—the old staying power has stayed. So if you'd like to come over to my apartment—"

"Screw, Wheeler!" she said, and she didn't even bother to look at me while she said it.

So around ten that night, I was sitting in my lonely apartment, listening to lonely music from my stereo, while I drank a lonely drink. The world was bleak and had shrunk into four lonely walls, and I couldn't make up my

THE STRIPPER 249

mind whether to go out and get drunk or stay home and get drunk. Then the buzzer sounded.

I opened the door cautiously, and there was a pocket-sized Venus with soft black hair that curled lovingly around her shoulders, who looked up at me with a brilliant smile on her pretty face.

"Lieutenant Wheeler?" she asked in a soft, melodious voice.

"That's me," I said, still cautious. I had never seen her before in my life.

"I'm Jenny Carter," she said calmly, and took a deep breath that swelled out her cashmere sweater in the most interesting way. "Annabelle won't believe me anyway when I tell her—so I figured I might just as well come over here, and see what happens. I can try, can't I? We don't have anything to lose."

I opened the door wider. "Come in," I said.

More Hilarious Humor from SIGNET

- ☐ AGATHA CRUMM by Bill Hoest. (W9422—$1.50)
- ☐ THE LOCKHORNS—"IS THIS THE STEAK OR THE CHARCOAL?" by Bill Hoest. (Y8475—$1.25)
- ☐ THE LOCKHORNS #6—"OF COURSE I LOVE YOU—WHAT DO I KNOW?" by Bill Hoest. (E9984—$1.75)
- ☐ THE LOCKHORNS #2—"LORETTA, THE MEATLOAF IS MOVING" by Bill Hoest. (Y8167—$1.25)
- ☐ THE LOCKHORNS #5—"I SEE YOU BURNED THE COLD CUTS AGAIN" by Bill Hoest. (W9711—$1.50)
- ☐ THIS BOOK IS FOR THE BIRDS by Tom Wilson. (Y9080—$1.25)
- ☐ IT'S HARD TO BE HIP OVER THIRTY by Judith Viorst. (Y4124—$1.25)
- ☐ PEOPLE AND OTHER AGGRAVATIONS by Judith Viorst. (Y5016—$1.25)
- ☐ MIXED NUTS by E.C. McKenzie. (Y8091—$1.25)
- ☐ SALTED PEANUTS by E.C. McKenzie. (Y9547—$1.25)
- ☐ MORE BUMPER SNICKERS by Bill Hoest. (W8762—$1.50)

Buy them at your local bookstore or use this convenient coupon for ordering.

THE NEW AMERICAN LIBRARY, INC.,
P.O. Box 999, Bergenfield, New Jersey 07621

Please send me the books I have checked above. I am enclosing $_____ (please add $1.00 to this order to cover postage and handling). Send check or money order—no cash or C.O.D.'s. Prices and numbers are subject to change without notice.

Name_____

Address_____

City _____ State _____ Zip Code _____

Allow 4-6 weeks for delivery.
This offer is subject to withdrawal without notice.